THE GRIM REAPER'S Lawyer

Copyright © 2022 by Mea Monique
Cover designer: Jiyen Chen
Editor: Falcon Faerie Fiction
Proofreader: Bancy

Title: The Grim Reaper's Lawyer; Life After Death
Name: Monique, Mea (author)
Description: First edition
Identifiers: ISBN 9798987146309 (Print)

www.meamonique.com

A Playlist to Die For

DEAD MAN WALKING – BRENT FAIYEZ

HARD TIMES – PARAMORE

HOW DEEP – TAI VERDES

BLESSINGS – RILEYY LANEZ

DIE FOR YOU – THE WEEKND

LIFE GOES ON – BTS

FROM EDEN – HOZIER

GODSPEED – FRANK OCEAN

REAPER – SIA

SOLD – LANA LUBANY

ALL THE STARS – KENDRICK LAMAR AND SZA

DYING 4 YOUR LOVE – SNOH AALEGRA

HEAVEN – PINK SWEAT$

LOCKED OUT OF HEAVEN – BRUNO MARS

YOU OWE ME – NAS FEAT. GINUWINE

DEATH OF A BACHELOR – PANIC! AT THE DISCO

GOOD AS HELL – LIZZO

I'LL KILL YOU – SUMMER WALKER FEAT. JHENÉ AIKO

SAVE YOU – RUM.GOLD

ANGEL BABY – TROYE SIVAN

KARMA – TAYLOR SWIFT

MIMOSAS – LATENIGHTJIGGY

REDEMPTION – ALAYISHA

YOU MUST SCAN THE CODE THROUGH THE SPOTIFY APP

THE GRIM REAPER'S *Lawyer*

MEA MONIQUE

For those who feel that you must
Water yourself down for others
Let them choke

CONTENT WARNING

This book contains explicit language, descriptive sexual content, reference to a criminal case about sexual assault, and death.

While the application of the laws (Reaper's Code of Conduct) in this book reflects some similarities to our judicial system, it is in no way a true reflection; therefore, it should not be taken literally. Any discussion of law in this book is not legal advice nor should be used in the court of law.

Digest the information at your own discretion.

REAPER'S CODE OF CONDUCT

RULE ONE
NEVER MIX UP HUMAN SOULS.

RULE TWO
ALWAYS COLLECT SOULS ON TIME.

RULE THREE
NEVER SAVE A HUMAN LIFE WHO WAS
DESIGNATED TO DIE.

RULE FOUR
NEVER DIRECTLY OR INDIRECTLY HARM
ANOTHER REAPER OR INTERFERE WITH THEIR
DUTIES WITHOUT WRITTEN PERMISSION
FROM THE DIRECTOR.

RULE FIVE
NEVER INTERFERE WITH HUMAN AFFAIRS IN
A WAY THAT WOULD DRASTICALLY ALTER
THE COURSE OF THEIR LIVES.

WELCOME. . .
TO **LIFE AFTER DEATH**

1

WHERE'S JESUS?

MY CLIENT MURDERING me was not how I expected my day to go. But I *really* did not expect to be sitting in front of the Grim Reaper. In a moment like this, I should be full of concerns, but my mind begins to flood with thoughts that I have no control over.

First of all, where are they going to take my body? I know it will go to a morgue, but which one? I don't have a specific reason for why I want to know. I'm just curious.

Who is going to plan my funeral? Am I going to have a funeral? I only had one friend—the old Jamaican lady who lived next to me. She cooked me food and informed me that I looked tired every time she saw me. I didn't mind it though, her food was the truth.

I wonder if someone is going to tow my car. Wouldn't it be weird to drive a dead person's car? My car and I have been through so much and I didn't even get a proper goodbye.

Finally, I wonder why the afterlife looks like an office. I expected, at the very least, fluffy clouds and a golden palace of some sort. Disappointed is an understatement for how unimpressed I am feeling right now.

"You know," I say as I look around the room, then to the Grim Reaper sitting across the desk wearing an all black suit, "I expected a lot more from the afterlife."

His eyes narrow. "And what did you expect?"

Maybe I shouldn't offend the Grim Reaper. But then again, I'm dead. What's the worst that can happen?

I should probably be way more upset about dying. However, it was for the best. I'm now free from the shackles of my mundane life. I woke up, went to a job I hated, came home, and did it all over again the next day.

Every. Single. Day.

I shrug one shoulder. "I don't know. Jesus, maybe? Mimosas? Wine? A garden? *Food*?" I place an emphasis on food because I can just imagine how divine heavenly food must taste. Especially, considering I don't have to worry about what I eat anymore. Like I said—I'm dead. Eating a bunch of fried food won't give me a heart attack.

I should be relaxing by Jesus with a mimosa in one hand and a cheesecake in the other. Instead, I'm in a gloomy office consisting of all black furniture. Black desk and chair, black couch with black throw pillows, and a black rug. The only thing that is not black are the walls, but they are a dark gray. That's not any better. He could really use a window and color to liven up the place a little bit. I'm thinking he should have gone with some pastel neutral colors like beige, white, or green.

Oh yes!

Green. That would really brighten up the place, since—

"Well, sorry to disappoint, but you're in Eden," he

explains, interrupting my train of thought about his office décor.

I'm in a place called Eden, but there's no Jesus. How does that even make any sense? This is not how any religion described the afterlife. Even the atheists got it wrong. I expected my physical form to be ghost-like. Shouldn't I have angel wings? A halo? Instead, I have a physical body and am wearing the same suit I had on when I died. Correction: when I was *murdered*.

"What exactly is Eden? Because it seems different than the Eden I've heard of," I ask, gardens with fruit trees coming to mind.

He sighs. "Eden handles all afterlife affairs. It is made up of Grim Reapers who manage human lifespans, collect souls, and determine soul placement after death. There are seven departments: Heaven, Hell, Soul Directory, Reaper's Resources, Collection, IT and—most recently formed— Reaper's Court. I work for the Collection department. One of our responsibilities is to collect souls."

Not only is life depressing, but the afterlife is no better. I thought I was supposed to be in an eternal paradise, or at least something close to that, but here I find myself in a place that handles 'all afterlife affairs'. Is existence just an endless cycle of working for the man?

"That sounds great and all, but why am I here? You just said you all determine soul placement...so can you, you know, *place me?*"

He grins and clasps his hands on his desk. "Not yet. I brought you here because I need you to do something for me."

My face scrunches in confusion at his statement. "I'm dead. What could I possibly do for you?"

I have always been concerned about the stigma surrounding Grim Reapers. Most books described them as mysterious, black cloak wearing, entities that prey on mortal souls. But what if their favorite color is yellow? What if they enjoy a warm apple pie from McDonald's rather than feasting on human souls? What if they smile all the time?

I'm glad the stories are false. The Grim Reaper sitting in front of me has a captivating smile. But, I mean, *everything* about him is captivating. His dark black hair is neatly fixed with a few strands laying across his forehead and his features reflect Asian heritage. He is wearing an all-black suit with silver accessories including a lapel chain, rings, and an expensive watch. As physically attractive as he is, the way he carries himself is more so. He has a controlled, but relaxing air about him.

I wouldn't mind helping him. In exchange, I may be able to get some extra stuff for Heaven. Maybe he will let me share it with Michael Jackson, because I have a *lot* of questions for him. I also want to show him the dance moves I learned from the Michael Jackson Experience game. That's assuming he went to Heaven, of course, but a girl can hope.

He leans back in his chair and crosses his arms. "I'm glad you asked." His grin widens. "I need you to be my lawyer."

Except that. I will *not* be doing that.

2

DAMN IT, MR. REYNOLDS

ONE DAY Before I Die

I should've gone to medical school.

No.

I *should've* gotten a master's degree in an easy field. Nope. That does not seem basic enough. I should've just graduated from law school and became a trophy housewife. Not the type that does actual work around the house, but the type that only worries about making it to their Pilates class on time and stresses about what new drink they will be trying from the Starbucks menu. I just want a job that does not make me want to jab my pen into my own eye at least once a day, or that does not involve dealing with other people's messed-up lives. *Ever.*

"Defense, are you going to cross?" The judge arches her eyebrows in curiosity of what I am going to do next. *Girl,* I wish I knew too.

I rise from my chair. "No, your honor. Defense will not cross at this time."

Why?

Because there is not a *single* thing that I can ask the witness to work our way out of the giant crap-hole this case is now in. The prosecution just called a surprise witness to the stand. Which, in simple terms, means I just got screwed and not in a fun way.

Of course, I objected to it. But the judge allowed it after the prosecution argued their reasons for why they had not previously listed that person as a witness. I mentally rolled my eyes the whole time the prosecutor spoke.

I sit down in my chair, cursing vividly in my head. The prosecutor presented a video of my client, Mr. Reynolds, jokingly admitting to the crime he's being charged with to a witness. They called the witness on the stand to confirm the authenticity of it. I didn't even know this video existed. Who kills someone, then gossips about it? Has he never watched a single crime show?

Like ever?

My whole case was based on misidentification. Until this point, the prosecution presented evidence and testimony that shows it's likely my client did it, but left reasonable doubt. I was going to lay my claws into that uncertainty to show they did not satisfy their burden of proof. But now there is a video of my client admitting to it. Mr. Reynolds, so kindly, even went into *specific details* about that night. In other words, my client is screwed, and we haven't even presented our case yet.

At this point, the chances of my client being found not guilty are slim to none. But I get paid by the hour, so it makes no difference to me. Especially, since I know the sick bastard is *actually* guilty.

I feel a tug at my sleeve and suck in a deep breath. My patience is running thin. I turn towards my client and fake a smile as I remove his hand from my suit jacket. Mentally, I'm reminding myself to burn this jacket later.

The judge nods and looks at the prosecution. "Will the State be bringing forth any more witnesses?"

I look to my right and see the prosecutor stand up. "The State rests its case, your honor." As he sits down, he turns to look at me and winks. I grip my pen tightly and narrow my eyes at him, thinking of how I would really like to kill that egotistical, poor excuse for a human, who just happens to be my ex-boyfriend—Richard. I detest the name Richard now. Every time I hear it, I shiver in disgust. Not saying there are no decent men with the name Richard. Just that I haven't met one.

I still can't believe I wasted nine months with him. We met when I was working for the State Attorney's office, and this is the first time I've seen him since I left two years ago. I had been blessed enough to go up against other prosecutors until now, but this case has not been a great one for me from the start.

Richard was a hot shot lawyer who dressed well and was *oh so* fine. He had that whole Michael B. Jordan look going for him and walked in a way that just captivated you.

Richard knew he was good looking too, which I thought added to his overall appeal; that easy confidence. We started dating a couple of months after I started at the State Attorney's office, but I had fallen for him instantly. My infatuation with him was quick and consuming, but it had ended just as quickly as it started.

Lo and behold, his self-confidence made him think he could cheat. He thought I wouldn't leave him, that he was 'perfect' and 'any woman should be grateful' to have him. Those were his *exact* words. He still believes, in his delusional mind, that I secretly want to get back together with him. Jesus himself would have to come down and tell me to get back with him, and even then, I would first ask Jesus what he was smoking up there.

Knowing Richard, he set up his case this way to end on a bang so that it remains fresh on the jury's mind. He always tended to play dirty when we worked together, but now I am on the receiving end of it.

I discreetly look to the left to get a feel of the jury's response to that video. One glance at them, and I know it's a wrap. Their faces are twisted in disgust, all directed at my client.

"Okay. We will resume this case tomorrow at 8 a.m." The judge gathers up her paperwork and coffee mug as she addresses the courtroom.

The bailiff stands and announces, "All rise for the Honorable Judge Davis."

Everyone in the courtroom rises and watches as the judge makes her exit, using the convenient door placed behind her bench. Her robe follows her like a cape in the wind.

Once the door closes, my client turns to me with wide, wild eyes. *Ah, shit.* Here we go, again. He grabs my shoulders and shakes me. *Hard.*

"*What are you going to do?*" he exclaims. Still shaking me, he goes on an unhinged rant. "I can't go to jail. *I can't!* I won't survive. What are you going to do? Huh? I pay you three-hundred dollars an hour for you to *work*. That video is fake! It isn't me. I didn't say that. Please do something. I can't go to jail. I will not—"

I interrupt his rant. "Mr. Reynolds! First, I kindly ask for you to let me go." He instantly releases me and mutters an apology. I sigh and turn away from him, rolling my eyes once I'm not directly facing him. He has been a pain in my ass since he was assigned to me by my boss.

"Second, we are still in the courtroom. We are going to continue with our original plan with some slight modifications. Sounds good?" He hesitantly nods and idly walks out of the courtroom. He is out on bail, so he has the privilege of going home to his million-dollar home. He should enjoy this time at home while he can, as he does not have many options and the plea deal is off the table, per his request.

He owns an aviation consulting firm and makes *a lot* of money. He has no close family and has never been married. He does have five women of varying ages that take care of him; however, he refuses to commit to any of them. I do hope those women have another form of income, because they will be losing him as a source soon.

Unfortunately for them, he strangled his employee over money she stole from him, and then let himself get filmed bragging about it. So stupid when you think about it because he had so many alternatives to murder. Like, maybe a conversation with her? Or reporting her to the authorities? But after having dealt with him, I know rational thoughts are probably too much of a sophisticated task for him.

As I am walking out of the courtroom, Richard appears beside me. He reminds me of an annoying fly that buzzes in

your ear, the one you can never act in time to swat it. Those
flies love to stay all up in your house and food, as if they pay
your bills.

I ignore him as I walk towards the elevator, even taking
out my phone to check the emails I got during trial. I
mentally make a to-do list of preparations for this case
tomorrow. I speed up my walking, so Richard is now falling
behind me like an annoying child looking for attention.

"Joyce. I was wondering if you—"

"No."

I glance at him from the corner of my eye and see he
appears to be shocked. I shake my head and think, *there goes
that ridiculous ego.* Why did God give him those smoking hot
good looks but the shittiest personality?

"You didn't even let me—"

"I don't *care.*"

I should be more stressed about this case, but I didn't
even want to take it in the first place. My boss consistently
assigns me cases with the worst type of people. He knows I'm
good at my job, in fact, this may be the first case in a long
time that I lose. Not that it's my fault my client let himself get
caught on film.

Damn. There goes my streak. What makes it even worse is
that I will be losing to this idiot. *How embarrassing.*

"Joyce, I know you are still hurt, but let me—"

I abruptly stop walking, and Richard bumps into me. I
turn around then lean into him until we are almost nose to
nose. His eyes widen, and he takes a step back, looking at me
as though I've lost my mind. Little does he know, I'm pretty
sure I lost it a long time ago. Usually, I just ignore him, but

I've had enough of him trailing me and trying to act like we have anything more to talk about.

Hurt?

Is this man insane? I don't even think about him anymore. But with him bothering me like this, I start thinking back to that time. Not to the break-up, but the case I was prosecuting when it all went to shit. I lost more than just that case, and I was depressed and needed support; instead of comfort, I found him in bed with another woman. I left both him and the State Attorney's office after that. I couldn't even work for a while afterwards because I could barely get out of bed.

When I finally needed money again, I tried to get a new job, but a lot of lawyers wouldn't hire me at their firm. Which sucked because I wouldn't go back to being a prosecutor. I ended up settling for working for my current boss—Craig Warner. I am grateful to have an income, but the longer I work for him, the more I have murderous daydreams. I can see why no one else wants to work for him. I was just a sucker in need of a job and fell right into his lap.

Not literally, of course.

I tilt my head, smiling widely at him. "Richard, Richard, *Richard.* Why do I always have to repeat myself to you? Hm?"

"I just wanted a chance to—"

It's like it goes through one ear and out the other. "You should *really* refrain from bothering me. Consider this a complimentary warning while I'm still being nice. If you try talking to me again and it's not about work, my patience will run out. Understand?"

"Well, I really think—"

Still smiling, I take another threatening step towards him. "Do you understand?"

He hesitates, then finally answers, "Yes." It's good that he hesitated. I'm not a violent person by any means, but I do know how to fight because of the environment I grew up in. He knows I can throw a mean right hook. He was on the other end of it when I caught him cheating with my former *best friend*. There's a special place in Hell for them both.

I nod, then turn to press the button to the elevator. It opens five seconds later. I stroll inside, turn around and click the first floor.

I wave at him as the elevator door closes and say, "Perfect. See you tomorrow."

When the door finally shuts, I let out a deep breath and lean against the elevator wall. Today has just been one annoyance after another. Between my hair not cooperating with me this morning, dealing with my annoying client, and the surprise witness that blew up my case—my day couldn't get any worse.

Twenty seconds later, I walk out the elevator. When I step outside, I head directly to my car, Caroline. No specific reason for the name, I just thought it was pretty. I've had her for over ten years. It will be one of my hardest goodbyes when I have to buy a new vehicle.

When I reach my car, I notice a scratch on the driver's side door. I lean down to take a closer look and see a dent too. I stare at the mark for five seconds. Then ten. A minute goes by before I finally look up to the sky and let out an ear-piercing scream.

When I'm done, I shake my head, open my door, and throw my purse in the passenger seat. I drop myself in the driver's seat and start the car. Still trying to calm myself down, I pull out of the parking lot.

It's just a car.

I can fix it. It is not that serious. But my frustration is just a buildup of all the inconveniences I've been dealing with. If this had happened on a different day when I was not already overwhelmed, I would've just laughed. But now I have yet another unnecessary issue to add on my growing list of bullshit.

As I am driving, I consider what I should eat for dinner. I have left over pineapple pizza in the fridge, or I could order from the Jamaican restaurant down the street. I could go for some of their oxtail, but they upped their prices to twenty-two dollars for a small plate.

A small plate.

That is madness. Principle alone prevents me from ordering the meal even though I am craving it. I can buy *two meals* for twenty-two dollars.

I park in the driveway of my house and climb out of my car, grabbing my purse as I get out. I reach my front door when my adorably feisty, older next-door neighbor—Ms. Jean—limps unsteadily towards me. Her usual salt and pepper afro is gone, replaced with long braids. She is dressed in her church clothes, which means she had Bible study at her house. I love when all the older ladies get together. It's my prime time to get validation on how beautiful and smart I am, how they wish all their grandchildren could go to school and be like me.

I take pride in that.

"Joyce!" she yells. I meet her half-way to shorten her distance to me. I know better than to try to help her. She is the most stubborn person I know.

I smile gently at her. "Hi, Ms. Jean."

"Child, you look tired. Did you lose a little weight?" she says with a thick Jamaican accent. One thing a Caribbean woman is going to do is make sure you are aware that you aren't looking your best. She makes up for it by shoving a Styrofoam food container at me that I did not notice before. "I made you some food. Eat all of it."

I open it slowly, knowing whatever she gave me is going to be delicious. Inside is the oxtail I was just craving. My knees almost collapse from under me at the sight of it. "You are an absolute angel."

She grins widely, her big brown eyes twinkling. With how beautiful she is now, I know she was a catch in her younger days. "You're welcome, child. Before you go, I need your help."

"Anything you want. Except murder, of course." I lift the food container to my nose and take a deep inhale of its aroma. I lick the corner of my lips, trying to keep myself from drooling. "Actually, I'm good with murder if you keep cooking food like this for me," I tease.

She giggles. "My landlord is telling me I have to move out in thirty days." While I own my house, she moved in last year and has been renting. She sold her previous home when her husband died, and put a huge chunk of the money away in a trust for her grandchildren.

I tilt my head. "Did he give you a reason why?"

She contemplates my question for a moment then shakes her head. "He didn't say. He just said it was within his rights."

"But you didn't do anything wrong? Like paying rent late, or violating the terms in your lease?"

She shakes her head again. "Absolutely not. I have been perfect."

I hold out my empty hand. "Alright. Call him and give me the phone, please. I'll handle it for you."

She does as I say. The landlord picks up after the third ring. "Hello, Jean."

"You are speaking to her lawyer, Joyce Parker."

"What does she need a lawyer for? All I told her is to get out. I have the right to say that."

"Actually, you don't. Pursuant to state law, a landlord can only evict a tenant for (a) violating the terms of their lease or (b) not upholding their responsibilities under the landlord-tenant law."

"But I—"

"I'm not done, *sir*. Ms. Jean has neither violated the terms of her lease, nor has she been late on rent. Therefore, what is your reasoning for telling her she had thirty days to leave? Her lease has six more months."

"She *has* violated the terms of the lease!" Now, he's just making up things.

"Do you have any proof?" I question. I know he does not have proof. If he did, we wouldn't be having this conversation. We would be going to court.

"I-I do. Somewhere around here," he stammers.

I roll my eyes and smile at Ms. Jean, who is observing me closely. "Sure, you do. But let me spell this out for you. You either forget about trying to evict her, or I'll take you to court. You'll not only have to pay your own attorney fees, but also mine as well as the court fees. Choose your battle. I've been looking for something fun to do."

There's a long pause. "I won't be evicting her. But I—"

"Sounds good. If you bother her with this again, you'll have to deal with me in court." I flip the phone shut—it is

very old, but surprisingly functional—and hand it back
to her.

"You should be all good. I must warn you that he is within
his rights to not renew your lease at the end of the term," I
warn her.

She waves her hand dismissively. "I will move out at the
end of my lease. He is a pain in my ass." She places a hand on
my shoulder. "You are truly a blessing, child. I'll cook you
another meal tomorrow as a thank-you."

I grin. "You don't have to...but I would love some curry
chicken."

She lets out a soft laugh, her eyes crinkling in the corner.
"Of course. I will see you tomorrow. God bless you!" I think
all his blessings are missing me, because my life has been
anything but a blessing. But that's an issue I'll discuss with
my therapist. If I ever get one.

"Have a good night, Ms. Jean," I say. I watch as she slowly
makes her way back into her house. I don't move until she is
safely inside. When her door closes, I walk into my house.

As I close my door, my three orange cats run up to greet
me—Hope, August, and Cookie. I bend down to give each of
them a head rub, and watch as they scurry away, fighting
each other playfully as they go. I am a firm believer that three
cats do not make me a cat lady. I would need a minimum of
five.

I do a quick glance around my home to make sure my cats
did not destroy anything.

My home is something I have pride in. The outside is
modern and well-maintained. However, the inside is bright
and colorful. I have a purple couch and an orange sofa chair
with walls that are painted with geometric line designs,

which I did myself. Around the room are curated collections of random knick knacks, adding to the vibrant aesthetic of my home. My favorite thing is the large painting I bought from a local artist. It is a beautiful painting of a black woman painted in various colors, but she is surrounded by nothingness. I could stare at it all day if I had the time.

Once I've made sure everything is still intact, I walk into the kitchen. Dropping my tote purse and food container on the counter, I grab a bottle of wine and a glass. As I pour, my mind drifts.

What am I doing with my life? I hate being a lawyer. Every day I walk into work makes me feel like I'm slowly draining myself. This job is not worth my youth. I'm only thirty years old and there is still so much I haven't done. I need to go out more if I am ever going to meet a decent enough man to settle down with. I've come to terms with there only being decent men. All the *good* men must have died out or are hiding from me.

Just my luck.

I down the rest of my wine and exhale a deep breath, the comfort of home and alcohol helping me feel like I can finally breathe for the first time today. I grab my food, inhaling it within five minutes.

I spend the next couple of hours preparing for court tomorrow. Exhaustion finally takes over my body and I decide to call it quits. I head into my bedroom, stripping my clothes as I walk towards my bed. I collapse onto it, immediately falling asleep.

3

IF WE GO DOWN, WE GO DOWN TOGETHER

.

THE DAY I Die

Jolting awake at the sound of my alarm, I automatically click the snooze button and close my eyes again. Just a couple more minutes.

Nine more minutes, to be exact. That's all I need.

Unfortunately, the peace I requested does not last long. My phone begins to ring. I groan in annoyance and pick it up. The name of my asshole boss lights the screen and I let out an aggravated sigh. Goddamn it, Craig. Can't I have a peaceful morning? Is that too much to ask for? Like, it's six in the morning. I don't have to be at work until nine!

I clear my throat and answer the phone. "Hello?"

"I need you in the office by seven. We have a potential client I want you to talk to."

No. No. No. *No.* If this client is meeting outside of normal office times, that means he probably has a lot of money that my boss wants to get his hands on. Which probably means that this client has done something that I want nothing to do with. I'm not saying everyone with money is guilty, I'm just saying that there's a higher probability.

I beg for the millionth time since I started at the firm, "Can I please stick with white-collar crimes? I do not want to—"

"You work for me. That means you do not have a choice. *Here*. By seven," he demands, then hangs up. I grab my pillow, placing it over my face, screaming as loud as I can. Once I'm satisfied, I remove it and glare at my ceiling.

"He's such a dick," I say to my cats lying at the end of my bed. They just meow in support. I decide at this moment that I am quitting. I am. I hate my job. I hate being a lawyer.

Screw it!

I only have this life. I can't mope around waiting for things to change. I have to do it myself. I'm quitting and opening a liquor store to be closer to my passion—*day drinking*. Before I do that, I'll travel the world since I'll finally have the time. I need to leave this country at least once before I croak.

I throw my covers off and jump out of bed, excited about my newfound purpose. I skip into the bathroom and turn on my speaker as loud as I can. I hop into the shower, humming, singing, and dancing while scrubbing my body. After the same song plays for the fifth time, I finally get out and prepare for the day.

I decide on a pastel blue suit and nude heels. It makes a statement. Bright colors in a courthouse as a lawyer is usually a big no, but I no longer care, so why not leave the legal field with a bang?

I fluff up my curls one last time, then walk into the

kitchen and grab all the ingredients I need to make a delicious mimosa. It is the best way to start a day. I am finally escaping the hell my boss trapped me in. I will name today 'Joyce Freedom Day'. I down my mimosa in three gulps.

Excitedly grabbing my purse and keys, I head to the office one last time. I ignore the dent in my car and jump in the driver's side. On my way, I rehearse my speech. I also practice all my sassy comebacks. You never know what you'll need.

When I arrive, I strut into the small building. I pass by the sign that reads 'Warner Trial Group'. The firm is small, with less than twenty attorneys and it's about to get smaller. When I walk in, the door slams shut behind me, the sound ricocheting off the walls. The receptionist, Jenny, looks up from the computer with a sneer. Despite realizing it's me, her annoyance doesn't falter. Her blonde hair is tied tightly into a bun, not a single hair out of place; uptight, just like her.

"It's seven in the morning. Can you try not being so incredibly loud?" she whines, probably not wanting to be here either.

"Can you try not being a bitch, Jenny?" I retort, without breaking my stride. I hear her gasp as I walk past her and grin to myself. I've been wanting to say that since the first day I got here.

Everyone at the office has always faked being nice to me. They knew what happened at the State Attorney's office.

Everyone in the state knew.

This office is cramped and not a lot of us work here. It's impossible not to hear other people's conversations. When I first joined this firm, the whispers and stares I would get every day bothered me so much that I locked myself away in my personal office all the time.

After the first year, the whispers died down, but I could never connect with anyone here. I only remained here because no one else would hire me. There are just too many lawyers for such a small community, and opportunities are limited. I contemplated moving out of the state, but I am only barred here. I would have to take another exam to be able to practice elsewhere and I refuse to go through another standardized test.

Not in this lifetime, at least.

I approach the conference room and push the door open. The room is occupied by a large, wooden, oval table with two men sitting by it, laughing at whatever Craig just said. They look up at the sound of my arrival.

The potential client is an older gentleman with graying hair, in a well-tailored suit. His watch looks like it cost more than my car.

I turn to look at my dick of a boss. He resembles what people conjure in their minds when they think of a lawyer. Greedy, distrustful, and a know-it-all who knows nothing.

"Joyce, thank you for finally joining us. I know you have a busy day ahead of you with our other client," my boss says, gesturing to a seat. I don't move from the entrance. He begins introducing the client. "This is—"

"I don't care who he is and what shit he did," I reply, cutting him off.

Oh, how he hates when someone cuts him off. Despite this, he does it all the time. His eyebrows jump up to his nonexistent hairline and his face turns a vibrant red. Before he has his usual meltdown, I retrieve my letter of resignation that I wrote in my car on a McDonald's napkin on my way here. I walk to the oval conference table and slam it in front of him.

He picks it up and reads it aloud. "Mr. Fuckface, I quit. Don't argue with me. Argue with your momma for creating such a vile, money-grubbing man."

Rising from his chair, Craig throws the napkin at me. We all watch as it flutters a short distance and lands gently on the table in front of him.

How embarrassing for him.

"Today will be my final day. I will be going to court to finish off Mr. Reynold's case. But I no longer work for you," I inform him. I would stop representing Mr. Reynold's right now, but it would require me to get permission from the judge. She is unlikely to grant it since we are in the middle of trial and I do not have a sufficient reason as to why I can't represent him.

Well, besides the fact that I think he is the scum of the earth.

He stabs a finger towards me. "I took you in when nobody else would!" he yells.

"That does not mean I have to tolerate your blatant disregard for me. You know what happened to me. Everyone knows! I have told you plenty of times that I wanted to stick to white collar crimes." I throw my hands up. "I mean *shit*. I even told you I would take over the Wills and Estate department when the other attorney retired. But you ignored me and kept assigning me violent people who —ten times out of ten—did the fucking crime they are being accused of."

"It's what you were amazing at! I was nurturing your talents, trying to help you."

I roll my eyes. "Did you hear a word I just said? *I didn't want to do it!*"

The client stands, clearly looking uncomfortable. "I will just leave—"

My boss slams his fist on the table, yelling, "You ungrateful bitch. You are not quitting!"

"Oh, really?" I tilt my head and grin. "Well, watch as I strut right the fuck out of here."

He wiggles a finger at me, the vein in his neck still throbbing as if it will burst. "You'll be back, Joyce Parker. Nowhere else will hire you, and when you do return, you'll have to beg me," he seethes. "On your knees."

I chuckle humorlessly as I turn and walk out of the conference room, not bothering to entertain him further. I can hear his shoes pound against the wood floor in anger as he follows me.

"You'll be back!" he yells again. I would rather lick the ground that someone just pissed on than come back here. That is how much I hate being a lawyer, especially for him.

When I reach the entrance, I turn to face him. I do a dramatic bow and stand upright.

"I wish you the best!" I yell, but then I add, "*in Hell!*"

I let out an evil laugh, turn and stride out the door, my middle finger and fat ass waving goodbye to him.

"Members of the jury, I understand you have a verdict." The judge gestures for the bailiff to collect the envelope containing the verdict from the jury foreman. The bailiff takes the envelope and hands it to the judge. The judge opens the envelope, slides the documents out and reviews it. He then hands it to the clerk. This is what I hate about court. All of the unnecessary formalities. Like, just get on with it.

The clerk puts on the glasses that are hanging around her neck. She pulls the paper out and announces the verdict that I fully expected. I can feel everyone hold their breath as they await the fate of my client. The fate that I already know.

Both sides have wrapped up their cases. Now, it's the grand finale.

"On the count of first-degree murder, the jury finds Thomas Reynolds...guilty." Shock radiates off my client, even though I told him this was a likely outcome. He just refused to believe it. Before the trial began, the prosecution offered a plea deal, but my client refused it on the grounds that he was innocent. What a liar.

I sigh and nod my head, fully expecting that. You win some, and you lose some. I tried my best. *I did.* But he dug his own grave. And that poor woman's, apparently.

I don't feel bad about losing this case for my client. It is easier to lose a case when you know that the person is guilty. It's a different feeling when you lose knowing your client is absolutely innocent. Those cases hurt. It sticks with you. It makes you not able to eat for days. Question why you ever became a lawyer.

But there is a different type of loss as a lawyer that is hard to come back from. The type of loss that happens because you failed the victim. That's the loss I think about with every breath I take. Wishing I could go back, wishing I did things differently. But now is not the time to fall into that hole.

I can hear some people clapping and crying. Today, I presented my case, then we did closing argument. It took me less than a day, since my client all but handed them everything they needed to wrap this case up tightly with a bow.

My client snaps out of his daze and grabs my arm roughly. He yanks me closer to him and yells in my face.

"You stupid bitch! *This is all your fault!* I paid you all that money to prove I'm innocent!"

Being a lawyer consists of everyone being angry with you. *All the time.*

Your boss. Your client. Your client's significant other. Potential clients. Opposing party. Opposing party's significant other. Opposing counsel. The judge. The clerk. Security guards. Random people in the grocery store who ask you for legal advice and get mad when you say, "It depends." It really does depend on *your* specific set of facts for fucks sake. The only beings not angry with me are my cats. But they are one more late meal from shunning me forever.

The bailiffs rush over to get him off me. He tries to run away from them, but they cut him off. One of the bailiffs trying to detain him is a rookie that seems flustered at the situation. I spoke to the rookie earlier today while we waited for court to start. He was considering law school in the future, so I gave him some advice. In other words, I told him that if he enjoyed his sanity, he would consider *any* other career path.

I hear the bailiffs shouting. I turn to look at them and see that Mr. Reynolds has managed to take the rookie's gun from his holster.

"If I'm going down, you're coming with me, Joyce!" he yells as he points the gun at me with shaky hands. Damn. 'Joyce Freedom Day' was doing so well. Now this murderous imbecile has to ruin everything.

The atmosphere in the room changes. Everyone stands still. The bailiffs surround him, but no one moves an inch, worried he might pull his finger on the trigger. I raise my hands in the air. Despite my heart beating rapidly in my chest, I calmly say, "Damn it, Mr. Reynolds. Just hand them the—"

A loud *pop* echoes through the room. Before I can process the sound, I feel a burning sensation in my chest. An overwhelming pain consumes me to where I can no longer hold myself up. I fall to my knees, trying to move my hand towards the pain, but I'm too weak. I look to Mr. Reynolds to see him staring at me in shock. He finally drops the gun.

I open my mouth to say something, anything, but no words come out. I can only gasp. Realization hits me at what just occurred.

He actually fucking shot me.

My vision starts to fade. The darkness at the corner of my eyes begins to close in. I collapse to the floor, feeling nothing but darkness wrapping around me. Hands touch me, the room is noisy with activity, but I stare at the ceiling with unseeing eyes as the darkness finally closes in. The noisy chaos fades away. Finally, an overwhelming sense of peace washes over me. I take what I believe to be my last breath.

Hm. I don't feel dead.

I blink my eyes open. I stare up at the same ceiling I thought I was going to look at for the last time.

For goodness sake, I can't even die properly.

Feeling in control over my body again, I groan at the lingering, aching pain. I rub my chest as I stand up, muttering a couple of curse words. I glance around the room and it's still complete chaos. Everyone is panicking. Some people are running out the door. Others are crying. More cops run in, and my client is tackled to the ground. I start talking to try to calm everyone down, but no one pays me any attention. I look towards Richard, and he seems frozen in place, looking in my direction.

"Everyone, it's okay. I'm good. It seems like it was a flesh wound. You see? I'm fine," I assure them. Not a single person looks at me, or seems to hear me over the noise. I repeat myself again. But again, no one answers me. Richard snaps out of whatever shock he is in and runs towards me with wide eyes.

I wave my hand dismissively. "Relax, no need to be dramatic. I'm right here." But when it seems as though he is about to run full force into me, he runs right through me.

Right.

Through.

Me.

Richard drops to the floor and starts screaming, "*Help! I need some help over here!*"

I look down at him and see myself—light brown eyes open, staring at nothingness. No way. This can't be real. I glance down at my hands. I am solid. Not ghost-like. I look at Richard again and see him place his hands on my chest, applying pressure on the wound.

Damn.

My outfit looks fantastic on me. Obviously, it looked better without the pool of blood. My suit shapes my body well, showing off those curves that do not end. It really highlights my smooth brown skin. If I'm going to do an awful job, my outfit can't be awful too. Gratefully, my dark brown curls cooperated with me today. It's like they knew that I didn't need the extra stress in my life.

An officer runs in and drops beside Richard. He takes two fingers, pressing it against my neck. The officer hangs his head down for a brief second then lifts it up and announces to the room, "There's no pulse."

Wow, I wonder who's going to represent my client now, because it won't be me. For obvious reasons.

Richard begins to argue with the officer when I hear someone call my name from behind me. I turn around and there's a tall man wearing an all-black suit. Correction: a *scrumptious* tall man wearing an all-black suit.

"Joyce Parker. Thirty-year-old African American female. Time of death is 4 p.m. Sorry to inform you, but you are dead. You must come with me."

Sorry to inform you.

He said that as if he was telling me that he got my pizza order wrong.

My mouth opens in shock. I ask, "Are you an angel?" Because I didn't know they made 'em like that. I would've died sooner if that's the case.

He rolls his eyes and replies, "I'm a Grim Reaper, ma'am, and you need to come with me."

"And if I don't want to?" I question seriously, wondering if I can just jump back into my body. They do it in movies all the time.

He raises an eyebrow. "What about this situation suggests that you have a choice?"

He makes a solid point.

Despite that, I pretend as if I am walking towards him, then I turn and run for my life.

In every literal sense.

I am *just* about to reach the doors of the courtroom when he appears right in front of it. I crash into his solid, but surprisingly soft chest. He grabs my arms tightly and gives me a look of disappointment. As a response, I lean back in his arms, giving him a smile and wink.

He ignores me.

One minute we are in the courtroom where I died, and the next, we are in an office.

And that's how I met the most aggravating man that I have ever had the displeasure of dealing with in my afterlife.

4

OVER MY (ALREADY) DEAD BODY

I SHAKE my head in confusion, then narrow my eyes at the Grim Reaper sitting in front of me. I couldn't have possibly heard him correctly. Dying must have killed off some of my brain cells.

I squint my eyes. "I'm sorry. I think I heard you wrong. Can you repeat what you just said?"

"I need you to be my lawyer."

"*Oh.*" The fact that he would even joke about this, knowing I was just murdered by my last client, shows he does not respect me.

I cross my arms and sit back in my chair. My intelligence remains intact. *He* may have lost his though, or this must be some type of sick joke.

Why would the Grim Reaper need a lawyer? That doesn't even make any sense. He's the Grim Reaper for crying out loud. What legal matters could he possibly have to deal with? Did a soul sue him for intentional infliction of emotional distress? Because if that's true, I would like to file a complaint against him as well.

The more I think about it, the more I become sure that this is definitely a joke.

Not a funny one.

He looks at me curiously. "'Oh'? Are you not going to ask why?"

I shrug my shoulders. "Mr. Reaper, I'm not asking why, because I don't have the patience to entertain your jokes. Can you just send me over to whoever oversees soul placement? I'm ready for Heaven. Request some wings for me while you're at it." I lean back in my chair, internally smiling at the thought of eternal peace.

I let out a yawn. It's surprising how exhausted I still feel even with being dead. I can still feel the slight ache of being shot. I need a massage and a mimosa, *ASAP*.

He blinks at me, then his lip twitches as if he is trying to hold back his amusement. Again, I don't see what's funny right now.

"I'm confused. What makes you think you are going to Heaven?" he asks, his eyes full of mirth.

I chuckle and cross my legs. I play with a fleck of lint resting on the arm of the chair. The chair is immensely comfortable. At first glance it doesn't seem like it would be, but I enjoy the velvety look and feel to it. He's better at picking out furniture than he is at making jokes.

I reply, "What do you mean, what makes me think I am going to Heaven? If not Heaven, then where the hell am I going?"

He leans forward and tauntingly replies, "Hell, Ms. Parker. You're going to *Hell*."

My mouth gapes open, and I shake my head in disbelief.

After all that I've done in life. After all I've been through. I
want peace.

No.

I *deserve* peace. Not Hell. No way. *No.* He's wrong. One
hundred percent and completely incorrect. I'm astonished at
how he could make such an error.

"You're wrong. You got the wrong person. Go double
check your paperwork. My name is Joyce Parker. That's
spelt J—"

He raises his hand and cuts me off. "I got the right person.
You are Joyce Anne Parker. You are thirty-years old. You grew
up in foster care. You have three cats, which by the way, is
three too many. You—"

"That proves nothing!" I interject with a shout. "There are
over seven billion people in the world. It is possible that you
got the wrong Joyce. So double check. *Now!*" At this point, I
am breathing heavily. Why am I out of breath? I'm dead. The
afterlife really does suck. He does not have sufficient
evidence to say that I am going to Hell. What have I done to
deserve this?

I gasp loudly at a realization. My cats! Who is going to
take care of my *babies*? This day just keeps getting worse.

He stares at me for five seconds then yanks open his
drawer. He retrieves a folder and places it down in front of
me. He sarcastically says, "Take a look, *Joyce.*"

I pick up the folder and notice my name at the top of the
document. There is a picture of myself below my name. I
internally groan. They really could've got a picture of me on a
better day. My curls are super frizzy in this picture, and I look
haggard. I probably pulled an all-nighter for one of my cases.
The document has my place of work, where I lived, some

random facts about me and a summary of my last days of life. I'm assuming this is what they use to keep track of the souls they need to collect.

"Collection reapers are provided with enough information about the souls they collect to ensure it is them. So, you tell me, is that not you?" he asks. I look up at him and squint my eyes. The more I interact with him, the less cute he gets. Men, both dead and alive, are so annoying.

Okay, it's time for plan B.

I bow my head down and let my shoulders shake. Tears start coming out my eyes and I look up at him. I slowly take in a haggard breath. Oh yeah, I am definitely getting to Heaven. My acting skills have always been top tier.

Shakingly, I hiccup every other word, "Please Mr. Reaper, I don't belong in Hell. You've got to help me out. *Please.*" I put my hands in front of me in a prayer position.

He leans forward and rests his elbows on the desk, placing his chin on his clasped hands. He sighs.

Yes! I got him right where I want him.

These cute brown eyes and big pouty lips can fool even the devil.

Shocking me, he responds, "Out of all the choices you could've made to try to get out of going to Hell, you choose fake crying? I expected better from you."

"Can't blame a girl for trying." *So much for plan B.* I roll my eyes and wipe my face. "Why am I being assigned to Hell?" I ask. If I'm going down—literally—I deserve to know why.

"We assign people to Heaven or Hell based on good karma and bad karma. Everything you do goes towards this. This also includes *intent*. If you have bad intentions, then it's still technically bad karma, regardless of the outcome of your actions. Good karma can be anything from helping a neighbor in need to giving to charity. Bad karma includes any actions that will hurt people like stealing, lying, or assault. When you die, the Soul Directory department tallies up all your karma from birth and makes a decision. You used to be set for Heaven, but then your bad karma started to outweigh your good karma. May have been all those criminals you represented."

I aggressively stand up, making my chair screech back a couple of inches.

"This is absolutely...this is fucking...ridiculous!"

I guess the saying 'all lawyers go to Hell' is immensely accurate. But, I was just doing my job. Even though I knew they were guilty, I am literally not allowed to say a peep due to attorney-client privilege. Why am I being punished for a standard I did not create?

"Now, are you finally going to ask why I need you to be my lawyer?"

I slowly sit back down in my chair. I could care less why he needs me to be his lawyer because I don't want to be his lawyer. How is it fair that I died and I *still* have to work? That doesn't even make any sense. What makes even less sense, is why *me?* I am sure lawyers die all the time. I mean, there must be some other lawyer who died right at this very moment.

"No, because I don't want to. I just died because of my job. That's enough trauma for a lifetime, and for the afterlife. Also, my boss was forcing me to take on cases I did not want to. So, I could care less why a Grim Reaper needs a lawyer. Because I. Am. *Done.*"

"You understand if you do not accept the role as my lawyer, you're going to Hell."

"Yes."

"So, are you going to be my lawyer?" he asks again.

I smile as I cross my legs. I place my finger on my chin, tapping it as if I'm contemplating the idea. After three seconds, I drop my smile and respond to him.

"No."

I sit back comfortably in my chair, in an unladylike way. I close my eyes. Hell can't be that bad, right? A little fire ain't never hurt nobody.

I hear a bang on the desk, and my eyes pop open, startled by the sound. I look at him, seeing his fist on the table, and him glaring daggers at me. I wonder if he was a model in his former life. He's got the serious model face thing going for him.

He points at me. "Let me repeat myself because I don't think you understand the gravity of your situation. You're either going to be my lawyer, or you're going to Hell *forever*. What do you choose?"

Understand the gravity of my situation. Who does he think he is? Sounds like something you get told when you are arrested. I do feel like I'm being sent to jail though, without even a trial to argue my case. Who makes the rules around here?

I understand that he needs a lawyer, but why is he so upset? He probably doesn't have to wait long for another lawyer to die in time to represent him. It really doesn't have to be me, and I prefer it not be.

I reply with zero hesitation, "The latter."

He looks taken aback for a moment and says, "I think you meant the former?"

"I know English pretty well, Mr. Reaper. I meant what I said. The *latter.*"

"All those degrees, and you're still making stupid decisions." He shakes his head. "What could possibly be a justifiable reason for choosing eternal damnation?"

I don't know what he did for him to need a lawyer, but it must be something big. Because why the hell else would a Grim Reaper need legal representation? I would rather not put myself in whatever mess he is in. Plus, like I said, I *just* died from being a lawyer. Then, I find out that I'm going to Hell for being a lawyer. My body in the living world is probably still warm. Between that and my trauma from years ago, *I am done.* Therefore, I choose Hell.

Stupid? Probably.

But it's my choice.

Finally.

To make things interesting, I perk up in my chair as if I'm excited to explain to him why I am refusing. "Where shall I begin, hm? I've got three reasons."

I raise one finger in the air. "First, with *every* fiber of my being I hate being a lawyer."

I raise another finger. "Two, I *just* died because a client was angry when he was found guilty of a crime that *he* actually committed. Why he thought *killing* me would change anything, that's beyond me. Maybe you can tell me later."

I settle back into my chair once I make my points. I don't think it's so hard to understand why I said no. Yeah, I can't die again, but who knows what can happen.

I used to enjoy being a lawyer. I once had so much love

for it. But just like life always does, it takes and takes. I lost all the things I loved. First, my childhood. Then, my relationship with Richard and my best friend. It didn't stop there, though. It crushed my passions, too, one by one. I was never the most optimistic of people, but at least I had something I cared about. For my life's finale, it allowed a no-good piece of shit to take away my life. It will *not* take my freedom to choose how I will spend my afterlife.

Even if it's in Hell.

I turn my attention back to the man in front of me. He lifts one of his perfectly shaped brows and points out, "You said three reasons, that was two."

"Oh, you're right." I deliberately left off the third so he would have to play my game. I lift up the third finger and add, "Three, in the little time I've come to know you, I realize that *I don't like you.*" I smile prettily at him. I mean it, too. Since I've met him, he's been nothing but an annoyance.

Weirdly enough, he smiles back at me. I see it has finally clicked for him. *Good.* Over my already-dead body will I be his lawyer.

"Wrong answer," he gently says, a glint of humor in his eyes.

What happens next makes me despise him even more. They were right when they said the devil comes in a pretty package.

He stands and walks around his desk until he is right beside me. I tilt my head back to look at him. He leans down until his face is merely two inches away.

"I'll give you one last chance. Hell or me?" he warns softly. My heart is beating faster at his proximity. His dark brown eyes never lose contact with mine as he waits for my answer. I lean forward, leaving only an inch between us. From this distance, I can smell him. He smells expensive, like he belongs in a Dior ad with Johnny Depp.

"Hell," I reply with a stubborn smirk.

He shakes his head slowly and grabs my hand. The world flickers away. One second, we are in his office, and the next we are in the courtroom I just died in. I'm sitting in the chair next to the defendant, and the judge is requesting the verdict. I look around and see the Grim Reaper in the corner of the room, next to the jury box.

The corner of his mouth lifts and he winks. He mouths, '*Enjoy Hell*'.

Then, he disappears.

Shit.

5
STUCK BETWEEN A ROCK AND A HARD CASE

IN HINDSIGHT, I really need to think things through more. Hell is not a fun place. I have been here for what I think is a month and I can't do this anymore. I tried to stand my ground for as long as I could, but if I'm here another day, I'll go insane.

Whoever claimed Hell is a pit of fire is a lying liar and I hope *they* are suffering in Hell for their deceitful sins. Hell is so much worse. My version was created to personally torment me.

That rat bastard.

I know it is kind of ridiculous that I chose Hell, but I really thought my days of working were over. The idea of being the Grim Reaper's lawyer may not seem horrendous, but it would be awful for me. I was so close to quitting and moving on to do something that would mean something to me. That would make me find my passion in life, like the legal field used to do. Every day I went to work to represent these criminals, I felt like my soul was dying. To do the same job for God knows how long would be like holding myself underwater, and guess what? Everyone who is held under water long enough ends up drowning.

The Grim Reaper placed me in an excruciating Hell. I'm living out the day I died, repeatedly. I wake up, get dressed, eat my breakfast with my mimosa, and go to the office. Once I'm there, I curse out my boss, then I head over to the courthouse. I present my last witness and rest my case. We both give our closing arguments and the trial ends with the jury finding Mr. Reynolds guilty of murder.

This happens, over and over again.

Every.

Single.

Day.

I can't even change what I ate, what I wore, or where I went. It's like I'm on autopilot, but fully aware of what's going on. So basically, my Hell is being a lawyer and dying because I'm a lawyer. He probably finds this comical.

Ha ha ha! Mr. Reaper. You are so funny. Please quit your day job and become a full-time comedian.

After ten days, my stubbornness left, and I have been pleading to him ever since. I don't even know if he can hear me. I am assuming not, because he has yet to retrieve me. So, I think this is it. This is the rest of my afterlife, and all I can think about now is how much I *despise* him.

Just as I start to come to terms with my fate, everyone in the courthouse freezes. We had just gotten to the spicy part where my client had the gun raised at me. I look around and realize I have control over my body.

Hallelujah!

I feel someone touch my shoulder, then a strange sensation around my body. When I blink, I find myself once again in front of the man of the hour—or should I say *month*—in his office.

Immediately, I hiss, "You asshole." He moves to sit on the chair by his desk and gestures for me to do the same. I sit down and glare at him.

"Welcome back, Ms. Parker. It's always a pleasure to see you. How was your vacation?" He smirks as he sits back comfortably in his chair with his arms crossed, and adds, "Would you like to extend it?"

I can't stand to look at him, so I jump up from the chair and pace around the room attempting to convince myself that I'm here. *I'm okay. The time loop is over.*

I shudder at the thought of going back. Is this what everyone in Hell goes through? A torture especially designed for them? I need therapy after that experience. So much therapy. I wonder if they provide those services here. I hope it's a part of the benefits package.

I draw in a deep breath and whirl around to face him.

"You've made your point. But did you have to leave me there for *a month?*" I yell that last word because I'm beyond angry. I was ready to agree to his terms ten days in.

Mr. Reaper deliberately takes a sip of his coffee. How nice that he is enjoying a beverage when I'm five seconds away from a complete mental collapse. He places the cup back on the desk and looks at his simple silver watch.

He finally speaks, "You were there for five minutes. It felt like a month because time goes slower there."

My jaw drops open and I sit there stunned, letting what he said soak in. I blink. I blink again. Then, I completely lose it.

"*Five damn minutes?*" I shriek. I walk over to his desk, lean over to get only inches away from him and point my finger in his face. "Thirty seconds would've been more than enough, but you chose to leave me there for five minutes, knowing the time difference!"

He sighs in annoyance. "Sit back in your chair and stop talking, or I'm sending you back. This time, it'll be for an hour. In case you aren't good at math, that would make it a *year* for you."

I instantly close my mouth and sit down, folding my hands in my lap. I learned the hard way that he means what he says. I may be stubborn, but I'm not all the way stupid.

"Ah, look how obedient you are now. All it took was a trip to Hell." He smirks at me. "Now, let me tell you why I need a lawyer. The Reaper's Court, which is our version of the human's judicial branch, filed a charge against me for breaking some rules that I didn't mean to break. This charge is serious and can lead to a severe punishment for me if I lose. That's where you come in. You need to make sure I do not lose."

He opens a black folder on his desk and pulls out some papers. "While you were away on vacation, I drafted a simple contract. This contract is non-negotiable. It basically says that you will represent me in Reaper's Court."

He lays out the contract in front of me with a black ink pen. Without any hesitation, I pick up the pen, flip to the end of the contract and scrawl my name on the line above my printed name. I place the pen back on his desk and make eye contact with him.

"Kind of feels like I sold my soul," I say.

He tilts his head, concern washing over his face. "Maybe

you did. But now I'm questioning if you're a good lawyer. You didn't even *read* the contract."

My eyebrows tug together. Is he serious right now? Last time I said no, he gave me a non-refundable first-class ticket to Hell.

"You *just* sent me to Hell for saying no. I'm stubborn, but I am in no way stupid. Plus, you said it's non-negotiable, so why does it matter if I read it or not?" I don't agree to be his lawyer, he sends me to Hell. I agree to be his lawyer, he questions my competence.

He points to a highlighted section. "Read this first section, at least." I look at where he pointed and begin to read aloud.

"Joyce Parker, professionally known as a Lawyer, (hereinafter "Party B") agrees to represent Aiden Kim, professionally known as a Grim Reaper, (hereinafter "Party A") in all disputes brought forth against him by Eden." Okay, so far that's expected. Also, his name fits him. Easily rolls off the tongue. *Aiden Kim*. Now, that's a name. Not freaking *Richard*.

I continue reading. "This Agreement shall become effective upon signatures by the Parties and remain in effect for three months or the successful completion of trial—" Hold the damn front door. Three months? This could go on for three months?

I look up from the contract. "You mean to tell me, I must be your attorney for three months or until the trial is finished? Why that long? Also, is that Hell Standard Time or Eastern Standard Time?" I have to ask about the time because, as I've recently learned, it makes all the difference.

He chuckles. "It's normal time, Ms. Parker. It is three months because I do not know how long this could take. Our court is backed up on cases since it's new. So, you will help me with my case, but you are free to help other people too. But continue reading. You didn't get to the good part."

I narrow my eyes at him because what does he mean 'the good part'. I look down at the contract and continue where I left off.

"...remain in effect until three months from the effective date. Party B herein agrees to Party A's right to terminate contract if Party B loses Party A's case. In the event the contract is terminated by Party A for the reason previously stated, Party B will go straight to Hell—"

I stop reading and lean back in my chair. I maintain eye contact with him.

One second goes by.

Two seconds.

Then three.

He looks at me curiously. "I'm surprised you are silent. You usually have—"

I cut him off when I choke out an unrecognizable noise. Laughter follows and my stomach begins to cramp. Tears are coming out my eyes. This man is merciless. It's my own fault at this point. My mistake began with me going to law school in the first place. I could even argue it began when I was born, but I didn't really have a choice in that, did I? If I lose the case, I go back to my Hell time loop. Forever. *How fun.*

After about two minutes of hysterical laughing, I wipe the tears from my face. Still smiling, I hold my hand out in front of me for him to shake. "When do I begin?"

Reluctantly, he shakes my hand. "Tomorrow."

"How does this work? Do I get paid? Is money even a thing here?" I question eagerly.

He sighs in annoyance. "Do you always talk this much?"

I shrug one shoulder. "I'm a lawyer. We love to hear ourselves talk."

He gives me a look. "No, you don't get paid. You're dead. What do you need a paycheck for? Your paycheck is being able to go to Heaven."

"Do you get paid?"

He squints his eyes at me. "Not exactly. All reapers have cards with unlimited funds to use."

"Can you quit being a reaper at any point?"

"No. Everyone who becomes a reaper is required to do fifty years."

Interesting. "So, it's essentially slavery?"

He glares at me. "No. It is not slavery. Without us, Eden wouldn't function."

I arch a brow. "You don't get paid and are forced to work, but that's not slavery? Some would say your rationale of 'Eden wouldn't function without reapers' is similar to those who argued 'the country won't run without slaves'." I shrug. "But if you like it...well then you like it."

He whispers to himself. Well, not really to himself, since I can hear him. "Honest to God, if it was up to me, you'd go to Hell."

I gasp.

Not at his comment of sending me to Hell, but the other word he said.

God.

It makes me realize the most important question to exist. Something I've waited my whole life for.

I lean in and squint my eyes. Inhaling a deep breath, I finally ask what every human to ever live has wanted to know.

"Is God real?"

With zero hesitation, he replies, "No."

I deflate in my chair. *Damn.* The religious people on Earth are going to lose their minds once they get here. Despite having the answer to one of the most controversial questions to exist, I still have a lot of questions about the universe.

I perk up once again. "Are there aliens or are humans the only species—"

"For the love of God, *please stop.*"

6

FIRST DAY AT WORK (AGAIN)

IT IS my first day of work in the afterlife. I am following behind Aiden as we walk through the lobby to get to his office. He walks at a fast pace, which is aggravating considering he is way taller than I am. My legs can only take me so far.

He explained yesterday that during my time at Eden, we will share office space. He further explained it is more 'efficient' that way. I am not too excited about that since his office is all black and dull. I doubt I can thrive in that environment.

As we walk, I am turning my head around like a child at an amusement park.

Eden is *huge*.

I didn't get a chance to explore yesterday because I was so exhausted from my interactions with Aiden and, of course, my experience in Hell. I am unsure of where the building starts and where it ends. I also don't think there's an outside, which makes sense because we aren't on Earth. At least, I don't think we're on Earth. You know what...I don't fully understand the logistics of everything yet.

But I do know everyone lives and works here. I figured this out yesterday when Aiden and I left his office so he could show me where I would be staying. We took an elevator up to one of the residency floors—there's a lot of them—and he showed me to my apartment. He told me if I needed anything that he was next door.

I must say, Eden is beautiful. It has a modern feel with white walls, cream furniture, marble floors and gold decor. There are also so many reapers here. I immediately take notice of the fact that the reapers wear different colored suits. I'm assuming it's because different colors represent different departments. Later, I will need to look up what each suit color means. I also notice some people scanning into their department's office with their wrist. When I take a closer look, I see tattoos of numbers on their wrists.

"How is it possible that everything and everyone is in this one building? Do you ever have too many reapers?" I ask Aiden's back.

Without missing a step or looking back at me, he replies, "How is anything possible?"

"Why is it called Eden?"

"Why is your name Joyce?" he fires back, obviously not wanting to entertain my questions.

"Because I didn't have a choice," I joke, letting out a chuckle. "Why is—" He suddenly stops, causing me to bump into his back. I back up a couple of steps as he turns around to face me.

He glares down at me and says in an aggravated tone, "I have yet to have coffee. Your questions can wait until I have taken my first sip. So could you—I don't know—*stop talking*?" He stresses the last two words.

"Wait, there's coff—" His glare intensifies, and I snap my mouth shut. For now.

We stop by the fully stocked kitchen to make coffee. Afterwards, we walk into his office with our drinks in hand. Well, I have coffee in one hand and a mimosa in the other.

So far, this job has *great* perks. Way better than when I was alive. Aiden tried to take the mimosa away from me, claiming that I can't work while intoxicated. I politely informed him that one mimosa will not do anything to me. It takes a minimum of five for me to feel something. Plus, there's no lawyer association here that will charge me with an ethical violation and, last time I checked, Eden did not have a handbook for lawyers. Therefore, who's going to check me?

Walking into the office, I immediately notice the room looks a little smaller. On the opposite side of the room, there is a black desk and chair that was not there before. I walk over to it. Resting on the desk is a black and gold nameplate that reads, "*Joyce Parker, Esq.*" I run my fingers against it.

Nice.

Aiden points to my side of the room as he walks up to his desk and says, "That is where you will work for the next three months, or less. Hopefully, less. It should be stocked with supplies, my case file, and the rules and procedures for Eden and the Reaper's Court. Please familiarize yourself with everything."

He pauses, then continues, "You also have a phone that can be used anywhere in Eden and in the Living World. There are restrictions, though. Like social media. You are blocked from posting on any platform. For the obvious reason, being that you are dead. You'll find there are specific apps created for Eden that will help you navigate around and answer questions you may have. I programmed my number in it."

I open my mouth to ask another question, but he beats me to it.

"Before you ask, I do not know how we have phones, or how they work. You would need to consult with the IT department."

I snap my mouth shut and nod. I'll table that thought for later. I head towards my desk and sit in the chair. It's quite comfy. I place my drinks on coasters, then examine the contents on the desk. There are files on my desk, neatly labeled and organized. The modern, sleek phone has a purple case and a note attached to it with my login credentials. There's only one thing missing.

I raise my hand to get his attention. He looks up and sighs. "Yes?"

I pinch my fingers together. "Can I please request a little bit of color in the room?"

"No."

"But I—"

He pinches the bridge of his nose and cuts me off. "Absolutely not. Your suit is colorful enough."

He says that as if wearing colors is a sin. It's stylish. I am wearing a pastel pink suit with white heels and gold jewelry. In other words, I look fantastic.

My apartment came fully furnished and stocked with all the clothes I could ever need. It was designed exactly how I would like it to be. When I asked him how it was possible, he said one of the departments, also known as Reaper's Resources, provided my apartment and everything in it. If I needed anything else for my apartment, I could call them.

Eden provides the basic food and necessities you could need. But for specific items, reapers have to go to the Living World. Since I cannot teleport, Aiden will have to take me. I can already predict that this will be aggravating.

While I am wearing a fabulous suit, Aiden, of course, is yet again wearing a plain black suit with silver jewelry. It looks exactly like his outfit yesterday. I wonder if he showered. Do reapers have to shower? I guess they do, since reapers have to eat and drink. Apparently, they have to do this to remain human-like to ensure they do not become too cold and unfeeling in the job.

Thinking about it, that's probably the same reason why they can still get injured. They won't die, of course, but it will hurt a lot until it heals. Fortunately for reapers, they have accelerated healing.

Aiden continues talking, breaking my train of thought, "This is my office that you happen to share with me for a short period of time. It will remain exactly how it looks. Got it?"

I sigh deeply and concede. Obviously, trying to negotiate with him will get me nowhere.

"I guess," I begrudgingly reply. He rolls his eyes and starts looking through papers. I glance down at my desk and get to work. I begin by writing some questions I have for Aiden. I need to get his perspective of the events and then make sure we are on the same page for his first court appearance.

In Reaper's Court, this first appearance is where we will hear the exact charges being presented against Aiden and the potential punishment if he is found guilty. Which I refuse to allow happen again. I cannot take the consequences of losing this case.

The hardest part of this is the fact that while Reaper's Court is similar to the United States judicial system, it is still a relatively new concept here. There are no precedents, which means I am going into this with one hand tied behind my back.

After I get the facts from Aiden, I will use them to give me a starting point for investigating. I look up to Aiden and see he is typing on his desktop. I wave at him, and he looks up at me with an eyebrow arched.

"Can you tell me what happened?"

"It's in the file I gave you," he replies.

"I understand that, but I need you to just walk me through it."

It's important for him to tell me what happened, from when he woke up, to when he closed his eyes that day. I have to make a timeline of the events in order to properly investigate. From there, I will build a defense case. But, of course, he has to be difficult. Which doesn't make any sense, since he asked *me* to be *his* lawyer.

"Fine," he replies as he drags his hand over his face. "I got an email with—"

I cut him off. "Start from when you woke up that morning."

He gives me an annoyed look. "I woke up like I do every morning and got dressed for work. I stopped by the lounge to get coffee and a bagel. Then, I went to Director Taevian's office for our department's weekly meeting. Once the meeting finished, I was talking with Joey about some of the difficult collections we've had. As we were walking towards our office, Joey logged onto his email using my phone to ask IT to send him a new phone. When I got to my office, I got an email with a list of death assignments and collections."

"Who's Joey, exactly?"

"He is another reaper in the Collection department. I'm his supervisor, but we are close friends. He is taking over my supervisory role until my trial is over."

"Explain the structure of the department. Like who reports to who?" I'm still trying to figure out the big picture of how Eden runs. It seems so intricate.

He explains, "Each department has a director. But, the directors can't handle everything, so they have supervisors. The Collection department has about thirty supervisors with over a hundred reapers to manage. Each supervisor has a region of the world they manage with their reapers."

I write that down in my notebook. "So, Director Taevian is the big honcho for this department."

An irritable breath escapes his lips. "Yes." I can tell he is tired of retelling this story, but I'm his lawyer, so he has to suck it up.

"Let's move on. What happened after you got the email?" I ask.

"I reviewed it, then I completed the first death assignment."

"What is a death assignment?"

"In our department, we receive an updated list of recent choices made by people. With these choices, we type them into our system, which gives us a predicted time of death for them. People aren't born with a death date; it is determined by the flow of events in their life. Every choice they make and every choice someone else makes can affect a person's death. When all the choices and events solidify, we get notification of it. We type it into that person's soul profile and then it's finalized. We then go to collect the soul when the time comes."

"That is so interesting." I guess that's why some people say they can feel when something bad is going to happen. I tap my pen on the desk. "Let me ask you an off-topic question. What was the choice that solidified my death?"

His eyes soften. This is the first time I've seen him look at me with anything besides annoyance. "It was when your boss assigned you the case."

I think about this for a second. If my boss hadn't forced me to take that case, maybe I would have lived a longer life. Or if I had tried just a little harder on that case. But I really did the best I could, given all the evidence against him. If I had not messed up when I was a prosecutor, I wouldn't even have been a defense attorney. All the bad things in my life always come back to that one crucial case I lost. That one person. If I had just—

"Sitting there, mulling over your choices and other people's choices will not make a difference. You could have very well died the next day because someone decided to drink and drive. You could have tripped and hit your head. Anything is possible." His voice is gentle.

I nod in agreement with him, but I'm not actually listening. He wouldn't understand why I can't let it go.

"So, it's kind of like free will versus fate," I theorize.

He nods. "Yes. Fate only exists in one instance—soul ties. By tying your soul, both people will be fated to be together for the rest of eternity. Therefore, their collective karma is weighed. Free will allows humans the power to shape their own lives. Even tying your soul is an act of free will. We aren't allowed to intervene with humans, as it is against the rules and could lead to harsh punishments."

"But you intervened in mine, when you decided to not send me to Hell permanently."

"That was a special circumstance. I received permission to get an attorney to represent me. The only restriction I had was that they couldn't have been someone that I knew. I preferred a non-reaper because of the office politics involved. I asked if you could receive an award for helping me, and they agreed that you could go to Heaven due to your karma. Your bad karma was not that weighty. A little less bad karma and you may have chosen to become a reaper."

"Ah, okay. That makes sense." Damn, how cool would it have been to be a reaper? "Let's continue. Who was your assignment?"

"It was Amanda Cole—she is a twin. I received her profile from the Soul Directory department. I inputted her information into the collection system, and her predicted death was the next day. I submitted the death time and date. The next day I went to collect her soul."

"If you did it correctly and you confirmed it, why are there charges against you?"

He shakes his head and sighs deeply. "Because when I got back to my office, Director Taevian burst into my office. He told me I made a mistake and assigned the wrong death to the wrong sister. I told him I assigned the correct sister. But he showed me his phone. His screen showed Amanda with no death assigned, and her sister Alex was dead."

I tilt my head and stand up. I think best when I pace around a little bit. "How is that possible?"

"I don't know. As I said before, I made *sure* it was Amanda.

I have never made a mistake before. Especially one as serious as this. I take my job extremely seriously." He runs his hand through his hair in frustration.

"Did you drink that day?"

Aiden glares at me. "I just told you that I take my job seriously. I do not drink on the job, ever. Unlike you." Clients always get touchy when you ask what they deem to be offensive questions. I am unbothered.

I roll my eyes and hold my hands up, "I *must* ask these types of questions, Mr. Kim. Also, a mimosa gets my brain juices going in the morning." I tap my head as I smile at him, then ask, "Did you drink the night before?"

He glances at my mouth for a split second. "Uh, yes." He clears his throat. "But, not a lot. I wasn't hungover or anything. I had a drink or two with Joey, Taevian, and some other reapers."

That is important, because prosecution is going to bring up every and any reason for why he failed in his duties. I need to talk to everyone he was drinking with that night.

Still walking around, I ask him another question, "Were you in a rush in any way, that day? Like, were you behind on work? Have any plans?"

"I was not in a rush. I was behind on work, but most reapers are. On average, one-hundred and twenty people die per minute. Which means that one-hundred and seventy-eight thousand people die each day. That means that I am very busy, every minute of every hour of *every day*." He runs his hand through his hair. "...and no, I did not have any plans after work, except for meeting up with some friends for dinner."

If he keeps running his hand through his hair, he will start balding. That is, of course, if reapers can even go bald.

"I'm not accusing you of anything. This just covers basic things the prosecuting attorney will consider." I take some notes, then continue, "So, to summarize. You did your job and had confirmation at that moment that it was done correctly, but when you got back it showed that you assigned the wrong sister the death. What do you think happened?"

"I don't know. I tried to find proof that Amanda Cole was the one that was sent to me. But there is only proof that I was sent Alex. I don't know if I imagined things or what."

"Couldn't the system just have glitched?" He shakes his head, "Never has the system glitched. Ever. The system has worked flawlessly. To be sure, I even investigated it myself. The IT department did not report any issues with the system. I just...made a mistake. I don't know exactly how, but that's the only explanation."

"Hm." I don't believe in anything being so perfect that there is no room for error. That's not me being pessimistic, it's just the reality. I know everyone here is dead, but they were once human. There must be something missing here, and I am going to find out exactly what it is.

I place my pen down. "Okay. That's all the questions I have for you. For now, at least."

He nods then looks back to his computer. I grab my purse and head towards the door.

"Where are you going?" he asks.

"To talk to some reapers that aren't you," I reply as I walk out the door. Lawyers have to investigate and confirm what their client is saying. Why? Because every client lies. It's another hard fact. Some do it intentionally, and others do it unconsciously. It's human nature to fib the truth, and I am guessing reapers are no different.

After exiting the office, I head for the elevators and press the call button while I peruse the posted directory. Each department is located on its own floor, and as I run my finger down the numbers, I linger on the Soul Directory department. I am curious to see who works there and how it all works. Stepping into the elevator, I click the button for my destination.

Level Four.

When the elevator arrives, I step out into a waiting room with souls of all races sporting diverse kinds of outfits. I glance around until my eyes land on a soul. It is a man wearing cuffs with a teardrop tattoo on his face. He must feel me staring and makes eye contact.

"What are you looking at, bitch?" he spews. My eyebrows jump up. Not in shock, but in curiosity of whether he knows he's probably going to Hell and cursing at me is not helping his case.

I point to the teardrop tattoo on his face and joke, "I guess I don't have to wonder what they got you in here for." He jumps towards me but cannot move out of his chair. It's as if he is superglued to it. I smile at this realization and stick my tongue out at him. *Enjoy Hell, loser.*

Turning my attention away from him, I glance around the room until my eyes land on the receptionist. She is typing away at her computer. I thought I was stylish, but she has me beat.

She's wearing an emerald, green suit, which I've found is required by her department. But it's the way she has made it her own that captivates me. Her hair is a midnight black, and the loose curls hang down the length of her back. She is wearing delicate gold hoops in her ears and dainty gold rings on her fingers. Her make-up is so flawless you would think it was her natural skin. The only thing giving away that she is wearing make-up at all is her green and gold eyeshadow. *No. It isn't eyeshadow. It is art. She is art.*

Is this love at first sight?

She finally glances up at me and smiles. "What can I do for you?" Her voice is what I think silk would sound like. Her eyes are a magnificent light brown. Almost golden.

I smile back. "Hi, I'm Joyce Parker. I am—"

"Yes! I've heard of you! You are Aiden's lawyer. I'm Yirah," she says excitedly. "I was going to pop by later to say 'hi.' But since you are here, I can go on my lunch break so we can chat." She clicks something on her computer and grabs her pearl-colored purse. She walks around her desk, right next to me.

Looping her arm through mine, she asks, "What do you feel like eating? I'll teleport us there." Oh, how I wish I could teleport. I would take a trip around the world before I went to Heaven.

I think for a moment then snap my fingers. "I could go for some soul food."

She grins. "I know a fantastic soul food restaurant in a small town in North Carolina."

I nod my head in excitement and she tightens her hold on me. In a blink, we are behind a brick building. I can already smell the aroma, causing my mouth to water. She leads us around the building into a hole-in-the-wall restaurant.

It's one of those places that makes you feel like you are visiting family. Tile floors. Dim lights. Buzzing fountain drinks machine. Square tables with the essential condiments, such as ketchup and hot sauce. Erykah Badu playing in the background. It is comforting and familiar.

The staff greets us as we enter and shows us to our seats. Yirah and I scan through the menu, my stomach rumbling with anticipation. A gorgeous dark-skinned woman with long braids and curled ends walks up to us.

"Thank you for coming in. What can I get for you two ladies?" she asks with a deep southern accent.

I nod to Yirah for her to go first. Yirah hums a little, then tells the waitress, "I'll have the catfish with collard greens and macaroni and cheese." The waitress takes note then asks me for my meal choice.

"I'll have the smothered fried pork chops with collard greens and macaroni and cheese." I place my menu on top of Yirah's for the waitress to grab.

"I'll have that right out for y'all. Would you like something to drink? We have fountain drinks."

Yirah shakes her head. "I'll just take water with lemon, please. Thank you."

"I would like a Coke, please. Thank you," I say. The waitress nods, then walks away to the kitchen. We watch as she leaves. Once she is out of ear shot, Yirah turns to me.

"Okay. I need all the details. What is Aiden like? No one is really close to him. The only people he really hangs out with are Joey and Director Jackson." She places her elbows on the table and clasps her hands, placing her chin on them. Her undivided attention is on me.

I unintentionally roll my eyes at his name. "He has a stick so far up his ass, it's a surprise he doesn't cough up wood."

She throws her head back and bursts into laughter. "I'm

not surprised by that. He's hot, though. Most women at Eden think so."

"But is a man being hot enough to counteract his stiff personality? I have an ex-boyfriend who was off the scale hot —not hotter than Aiden, though—and he was a total dick who cheated on me."

We both pause as the waitress brings our drinks. When she walks away again, Yirah replies, "Honestly, Aiden seems cordial with everyone. I never heard anyone say he was an asshole until you." She smirks. "Maybe he just doesn't like you." Which makes zero sense considering I've known him all of one day.

"All I've done is exist! I haven't done anything to him. He has disliked me from *day one*. I swear he is like a sour patch kid. You know those candies that alternate between sour and sweet? Sometimes he is okay, but other times he makes me want to push him off a building." I really can't take the hot and cold. I just want to do my job and then dip. All I ask is for him to be semi-decent while I'm here.

"Maybe he thinks you're fine as hell and acts like that to keep your attention," she suggests with a smirk.

I am pleased with the compliment from her, but I roll my eyes. "Puh-*lease*. I know I'm hot, but he is not acting this way because of that. I've never believed in the 'he bullies you because he likes you' crap."

"Well, we will figure it out before you have to leave."

I wave my hand dismissively. "My job is to help him with his case. I could care less about whether he likes me or not. If he feels strongly about it, well, he can always kiss my ass." As I finish talking, the waitress walks over with both hands filled with our food. My stomach rumbles in anticipation. Thank goodness there's no one else in this restaurant. Nothing is worse than thinking your food is coming, then watching them walk past you to another table. I am not above stealing food. If Aiden was here, he would point out that my mindset may be what got me in my current predicament of almost going to Hell.

She places the food down and smiles. "Enjoy, ladies." She walks away, leaving us to this masterpiece. We both take a bite of our food and groan in unison. I've never had a better pork chop. The rich onion gravy smothered on top does not overpower the taste of the pork. Whoever cooked it knew to not leave it on the stove too long to prevent it from drying out. The macaroni and cheese?

My god.

The cheese is thick, silky, and creamy. It just melts into your mouth. I have to remind myself to breathe as I eat.

"Dare I say it's better than sex," I say with a mouthful.

Yirah, with her eyes closed, nods her head in agreement. "It hits the exact spot every time too."

"It seems as though reapers eat out a lot. Why not just eat and drink at Eden?"

"Girl. Can you imagine if we all just stayed in one place all the time? That would be no fun. Of course, we can eat at Eden, but we can also pop up in a random country and enjoy their delicacies. Plus, the only people who leave Eden for work are the reapers in the Collection department."

I nod my head in understanding. Yeah, I can't imagine staying at Eden all the time. I leave my apartment, go into an elevator and boom...I'm at work.

After another delicious bite of my food, I finally get down to business. I pull out my notepad and pen from my purse. I

place it on the table and take another h₁
asking her questions.

"I'm looking into Aiden's case, and I have
for you about your department."

Yirah nods and motions her hands in a 'con.   ...re,
her mouth too full to respond at the moment.

"What is the Soul Directory department?" I ask.

She swallows then pats her mouth with a napkin, before
answering, "The Soul Directory department is where souls
find out their placement. We work directly with the Collection department. Our department has access to a soul's
whole life, including all their choices. Our system automatically compares lives to see how one person's choice could
affect another's. We send that information to the Collection
department who uses it to confirm the time of death of a
soul. I work as the receptionist, so most of the time I just
call the number of the soul, and direct them to the
assigning reaper who will tell them where they will be
going."

I nod, jotting down some of what she said. I continue my
questioning. "Does any reaper have access to that information?" I take another huge bite of my food while she answers.

She shakes her head. "No. Only reapers who work in the
Soul Directory department have access to that information."

"Is it complicated to get into the system?"

She tilts her head in thought. "Yes, and no. Each department has their designated tattoo to match where they work.
We use those tattoos to get into our systems. Only someone
with a number four can get into the Soul Directory."

I tap my pen on the table. "So, it's hard. But not
impossible."

ه narrows her eyes at my words. "Do you think omeone could have set Aiden up?"

I bite my lower lip. "I am not at liberty to discuss Aiden's case outside of the information I need from you. But I am just considering every possible scenario."

She shrugs. "I understand."

I close my notepad and place my pen on top of it. "That's all the questions I have for you."

She claps her hands. "Perfect. Now tell me all about the ex-boyfriend you mentioned earlier."

I laugh and complain to her about how much of an asshole he was. We spend the rest of lunch in a meandering conversation. Once we finish our food, we lean back and pat our stomachs.

I pause my tummy rub and lean closer to her. I gesture for her to get closer. She leans in with wide eyes, curious to what information I am about to reveal.

I cup my hands around my mouth and whisper, "Can I be placed in Heaven with Tupac? I would love to just sit and have a conversation with him. I grew up on his music. Also, have you seen his smile?"

She stares at me for a moment, then bursts into laughter, covering her mouth with her hand. I stare at her. Excuse me, that was a serious question. Heaven can't just be me, alone. That would get old fast. I'm trying to throw a party.

I lean back and cross my arms. "I'm being serious, Yirah." She wipes at the tear that fell from her eye, and sits back in her chair while trying to catch her breath.

She grins. "Sorry darling. Tupac would not want to be with you."

I gasp. "What, why? I'm amazing."

She shrugs. "He prefers his alone time, and I have a strong feeling you would not know how to remain quiet." I narrow my eyes on her. Then I deflate in my chair. She's right. I would not know how to shut up. Can you blame me? It's *Tupac.*

"What about Prince?"

She shakes her head. "No."

"Bob Marley?"

"No."

"Paul Walker? I was in shambles when he died."

She sighs. "No."

"Elvis Presley?"

"No—wait, why Elvis?"

I chuckle. "I have some questions about how he died."

"I mean...I can't confirm nor deny whether he is even in Heaven," Yirah admits. "It's confidential."

I lean forward with wide eyes. "That answer within itself is an admission."

Yirah feverishly shakes her head. "No. It is not."

I nod with excitement at my newfound knowledge. "It totally is."

She points a finger at me. "You better not tell anyone about this."

I gesture to my heart and make an imaginary 'X' over it. "I cross my heart and hope to die."

"You realize that doesn't mean much, right? Considering you're dead."

"Then, I swear on my father's life."

"You don't know your father," she states as a matter of fact.

Dumbfounded at her knowledge of my life, I squint my

eyes, and point an accusing finger at her. "How do you know that?"

"Joyce, I work at the Soul Directory department. I know almost everything about you."

That definitely slipped my mind. I snap my fingers and nod my head in agreement. "You're absolutely right."

Yirah frowns. "Aiden is doomed."

7
TRUST ME, I'M A LAWYER

AIDEN WALKS into the office and straight to his desk. Yirah dropped me off two hours ago and went back to her department. I was about to go through some more documents to prepare before Aiden's arraignment, but it was just to give myself busy work. I'm already as prepared as I can be. I decide to kill time by having a conversation with Aiden.

"Did you know Elvis is in Hell?" I excitedly inform him.

Aiden looks at me with a blank stare. "I did not ask."

"Now you know."

He raises an eyebrow. "I won't say thank you."

I cross my arms and let out a huff. "I don't know anyone here and I like to talk. I would appreciate it if you could try to hold a decent conversation."

He holds my stare. "I don't want to have a conversation. I'm busy working, which is what you should be doing. My arraignment is in an hour."

I raise an eyebrow. "How are you so busy when you are literally suspended from collecting souls? You're on desk duty. That's hardly intense labor."

He glares at me, and I smile back. Men usually hate it when you smile at their glares. He glances at my lips so quickly that I would've thought I imagined it. Maybe I did. Do I have something in my teeth?

An irritable breath escapes his lips, but he gives in. "*Fine. I'll listen to you talk about random nonsense. But I will not promise I will respond.*"

My smile widens. "Works for me. Lawyers love to hear themselves talk, anyways."

"So, you've said. Trust me. I have first-hand experience of that knowledge," he replies. He grabs the stack of papers on his desk and pulls them closer. His face relaxes as he transfers information from the paperwork into the system. I watch as he slightly bites his lower lip while he types. I begin to imagine how soft his lips probably are. Whether he licks his lips after he eats you—

I shake my head, breaking me out of the daydream about Aiden Kim's mouth.

Damn it, Joyce. You need to get laid ASAP.

I'm his lawyer. I shouldn't be thinking of my client this way.

Remember Joyce. He sent you to Hell and forced you to be his lawyer.

Needing something to distract myself with, I clear my throat. "How did you die? And how old were you?"

He stops typing and turns to look at me, one of his eyebrows arched. "I got hit by a car. Died instantly. I was twenty-five."

"*Wow.* Did it hurt?" I always wondered if it hurts when you die instantly. Well, I suppose I may have died instantly? I don't remember feeling pain for long. I only had a slight ache for a little bit after Aiden brought me to Eden.

"No. It felt like getting hit by a cloud," he answers, completely deadpan.

"Really?" I ask, not realizing how idiotic I sound.

"No, Ms. Parker. I just don't remember if I felt pain or not. It happened so fast."

"Oh, well. I'm sorry that happened to you. Especially at twenty-five. You were very young. How long ago was that?" I question.

"Five years ago."

"Oh! We are the same age!" I tell him, although he already knew that.

"I stopped aging five years ago," he informs me.

"But you've existed for thirty years," I point out.

He rolls his eyes and mutters, "You always have to get the last word in, huh."

"No, I don't," I reply, proving his point. He shakes his head and looks at his computer. I glance at my watch. Seeing it is time to head over to Reaper's Court, I stand up and grab some of the files I may need for reference.

"It's time to head over," I remind Aiden. He nods, stands, then buttons his suit jacket. Whoever is responsible for making the reapers for the Collection department wear an all-black suit deserves an award because *damn*.

I am nervously organizing the papers on the table while thinking over Aiden's case. If I lose, he will be sending me to

Hell. My own afterlife depends on this case, and I barely know what I'm doing.

I glance around the courtroom, taking in my surroundings. The room has plenty of space for people to watch the trial. The set-up is very similar to a courtroom in the Living World except that there is no jury box and instead of a justice scale, there is a scythe carved on the Judge's bench. All the tables and furniture are mahogany with gold accents. The table we are sitting at has a beautiful gold frame going around the rectangular table. It is a stunning courtroom. The nicest I've ever seen.

In the Living World—specifically, the United States—a courtroom consists of a judge, a bailiff, and a clerk. In Reaper's Court, it seems as though the set up is similar.

I turn to my left to see opposing counsel, Chris Dalton. Yet again, another hot reaper. I chatted briefly with him when we walked in, but that has been the extent of our communications with each other so far. He is one of the five reapers who have joined Reaper's Court as lawyers. He is the first Reaper's Court attorney to get a case this serious. He and I will be setting a standard for how future cases are dealt with.

I begin tapping my feet when I run out of things to look at. Aiden gives the table two taps. I look up to see a look of exasperation on his face.

"What are you doing?" he asks.

"Thinking of how if I get a chance to be reincarnated, I'd like to be a rock."

He runs his hand down his face, his hand stopping his mouth, covering it. I can see humor dancing in his eyes. He doesn't have to hide that he thinks I'm funny. I know I am.

"I hate to break it to you, but I don't think you can get

reincarnated as a rock," he says, crushing my dreams with one sentence.

Slightly disappointed, I say, "Existing just keeps getting worserer."

"Not sure that's a word." *Duh.* It's not a word. But remixing a word allows for more emphasis on the situation. He really needs to live a little.

I scoff. "I didn't know they were hiring."

"Who?" he asks, confused at the turn of the conversation.

I give him a look. "The grammar police."

He chuckles. "I would help you get hired, but I'm sure you won't even get an interview."

"Oh, since you're so much smarter than me, then you can represent yourself." I stand, teasingly grabbing my folders as if I'm leaving. We both know I'm not going anywhere.

"I didn't realize you enjoyed Hell that much that you are willing to go back."

I drop back in my seat and cross my arms. "You know I am still on edge from last time."

He chuckles. "I'm on edge from being with you all the time."

"Excuse you, I'm an angel to be around," I inform him. "I'm going to Heaven and everything."

Aiden smirks. "You know the devil was once—"

"Please rise for the honorable Judge Hobbs," a reaper announces, who I can only assume is the Eden's version of a bailiff. Judge Hobbs walks in using the door directly behind his bench. The first thing I notice about him is his bald head. It isn't a bad thing, it suits him very well, especially with the full beard.

"Please take your seats," the judge says after sitting

down. He informs us, "I am Judge Hobbs. During my last life, I was a Hawaiian native. I moved to New York to pursue a law degree. After working as an attorney for ten years, I became a judge in criminal court. I originally worked for the Reaper's Resources department, but put in a transfer when I learned that Reaper's Court was being created." He pauses, looking over all of us to ensure we are listening.

Feeling satisfied, he nods and continues, "As the presiding judge of this case, I will be serving as the finder of law, as well as the finder of fact. In simpler terms, there is no jury to determine your facts. You just have to convince me. Is that understood, counsel?"

"Yes, Judge," Chris, and I answer at the same time. I don't completely know why the Judge gave us his whole life story, but I can only assume it is simply because he's a lawyer. We tend to talk a lot.

The judge continues, "Before we move forward, let me take care of some housekeeping. This is the first major trial since Reaper's Court was established not too long ago. Therefore, this will be a learning curve for us all. We are not dealing with the Living World laws. We are referring to the Reaper's Code of Conduct, also known as the RCC. Keep in mind that this is not as straightforward as the Living World judicial system, where it's either criminal or civil. The RCC contains elements of both, and therefore you should argue your case however you deem necessary. When approaching the RCC, the attorney representing Eden has the burden to prove the charges they bring forth. The defendant's attorney retains all rights to either argue against the claim or argue for a defense. You will receive an email with the conduct allowed in court and procedures that should be followed. Any questions?"

Neither me nor Chris says anything. The judge nods. "Very well. Attorney of Eden, what charges are you bringing forth?"

"We are charging Aiden Kim with violations of Rule One, Two and Three," Chris informs the Judge.

Well, shit.

Why stop at three rules? Just throw in the whole damn book at this point. I rack my brain for a way to argue against his charges, but technically, all three make sense. I flip through my stack of papers until I find the page with the RCC. I quickly skim over the notes I took next to each rule.

RULE ONE
Never mix up human souls.
RULE TWO
Always collect souls on time.
RULE THREE
Never save a human life who was designated to die.
RULE FOUR
Never directly or indirectly harm another reaper or interfere with their duties without written permission from their designated supervisor.
RULE FIVE
Never interfere with human affairs in a way that would drastically alter the course of their lives.

By supposedly mixing up the two souls, Aiden reaped someone who wasn't supposed to die, and broke Rule One. Thus, he did not collect the correct souls on time, breaking the second rule. By collecting the wrong soul, he unintentionally saved a human life that was supposed to be collected, breaking Rule Three.

"What punishment are you requesting?" Judge Hobbs asks.

"We are asking for Mr. Aiden Kim to be stripped from his role as a reaper permanently, and be sentenced to one hundred years in Hell with no possibility of being reincarnated until his sentence is completed," Chris states.

My eyes widen from pure shock. In the living world, this would be like asking for a life sentence with no chance of parole. I expected the possibility of him requesting some time in Hell, but stripping Aiden of his role completely? This is way worse than I thought.

There are audible gasps from the gallery. I feel a weight on my arm. I look down to see Aiden's hand clutching me tightly. I look at his face, and realize he may not even realize he's doing it, so I do not stop him. But he looks down, realizing he is holding onto me and let's go.

The judge bangs the gravel against his bench. "Keep sound effects to a minimum in my courtroom," he warns. Then he brings his attention back to the opposing counsel and says, "Counsel, please state your rationale for such a harsh punishment."

Chris explains, "Mr. Kim's actions show a blatant disregard for human life, and for the rules on which Eden is built upon. As a result, a human who may have lived well into old age, lost her life before her time. Mr. Kim should face the harshest punishment possible."

I turn to glare at him. "It sounds more like you are trying to make an example of Mr. Kim, rather than focusing on the facts of the case. This could have happened to any reaper."

"But it wasn't any other reaper. The fact is, Ms. Parker, that Mr. Kim is directly and solely responsible for—" There's a loud bang and we both turn towards the judge to see his gravel in his hand.

"Both of you need to wait until trial to argue your cases. Not here. Trial is set to begin two weeks from now." The judge turns to address Aiden, "While your case is active, you are to no longer assign deaths or collect souls."

He hits his gravel and stands.

"Please rise for the honorable Judge Hobbs," the bailiff announces as we all stand and wait for the judge to leave the room. Everything feels like déjà vu in a sense, except for the fact that Aiden hasn't panicked.

Once the judge exits, I glance at Aiden. His face is passive as he stares at the table.

"How are you feeling?" I ask.

He looks at me and arches an eyebrow. "Peachy."

I give him a look. "I'm serious, Aiden. That was a lot." I would be crying right now if I was him. Snot running down my nose, full on ugly crying.

He sighs and crosses his arms. "I don't know what to feel. I've lost all control over my existence. My future is literally in your hands," he admits.

I look at my hands then wiggle my fingers teasingly at him. "They are fantastic hands though."

His lip twitches a little bit. "They are alright."

My face gets serious, and I assure him, "I'm going to make sure you aren't stripped of your reaper position and sent to Hell. Do you trust me?"

He hesitates before he answers me. "I'm not sure yet. Maybe like, sixty percent."

I chuckle. "I'll take it."

He stands, stretches his arms out, and grabs my stack of folders. "Let's go get you back to the office, so you can work."

I blink in surprise. "You are holding all my stuff for me? Wow."

"What? You look surprised, as if I'm not a decent person."

I snort. "You walk in front of me, and call me annoying at least once an hour. If you aren't calling me annoying, you're looking at me as if I'm the most annoying person in the world."

"Because you're everything I dislike in a person: loud, annoying, and reckless." He leans down closer to me, his lips are almost touching my ear. My heart begins to beat a little faster, and the skin on my neck prickles at the warmth of his breath. "I can walk behind you if you want. But I'll probably be staring at your ass."

I gasp and lean back to look at him. "You're a *pervert*."

He winks then walks towards the door. I grab my purse and follow him. As we walk out the doors, I open my mouth to confront him on his comment, but I hear Aiden's name called out from down the hall.

Aiden and I turn to see a dark-skinned man wearing a black suit walk towards us with other people of all races and genders. They are all wearing different suit colors. I reasonably assume they are the directors. They all have a powerful, yet calm air about them. As if they know they are untouchable, which in a way, they are as the leaders of Eden.

"Aiden. How are you doing?" the man wearing the black

suit asks, the suit being a clear tell-tale sign that he is the director of the Collection department.

"Will be better once this is over," Aiden grumbles.

"Ah. That's right. Today, you found out your charges and potential punishment," says a woman wearing a red suit with cocoa skin and a shaved head, gold earrings running down the length of her ears.

"Yes. I did, Director Onai," Aiden replies.

The man wearing the dark suit notices me. "Where are my manners? I am Director Jackson. All these lovely people by me are the directors of the other departments.

I wave at them. "Nice to meet you all, I am Joyce Parker. I will be representing Aiden."

The woman wearing the red suit, who I now know as Director Onai, replies, "What a pretty name. I haven't met a Joyce in years." She smiles kindly at me. Oddly, there is a knowing gaze in her eyes that I do not understand.

"Glad to be the Joyce you get to experience after a long break," I joke. All the directors laugh. The only person who does not find it funny is Aiden.

A beautiful woman with straight dark hair cut into a bob, wearing a white suit, smiles at me. "I'm Director Jia Young, of the Heaven department. Pleasure to meet you, Joyce Parker," she says. Her voice is soft, almost musical.

"Pleasure is all mine. I am hoping to see you again when this is all said and done. Save me a spot." I wink.

She lets out a soft laugh. "You are like a breath of fresh air. I needed some good laughs today, and you provided them. I look forward to chatting with you again soon," Director Young replies. I wasn't joking though. She better save me a spot.

Director Jackson claps his hands once. "Well, we were on our way to a director's meeting. I will see the two of you later. Make sure to send those reports, Aiden."

Aiden nods. All the directors walk away, leaving behind Aiden and I.

"Do you want to grab lunch together?" I ask, not wanting to eat lunch alone.

"I'm eating lunch with a friend." He shakes his head, hands me the files, then disappears. I stare at where he once was, and sigh. He can be such a rude asshole. I grab my phone from out of my purse and call Yirah.

"Hello!" she answers. I love that her energy level is always at full capacity.

"Do you want to grab lunch?" I ask, worried that I am going to be turned down again.

"Do birds fly? Of course, I do!" she exclaims and I smile. She's my favorite person here.

8

CALL ME MS. SHERLOCK HOLMES (OR DON'T)

I GRAB my notepad and walk towards the door. It is day three of being dead. Today, I am going to do some more investigating into Aiden's case. It's time to start collecting all my pieces.

Being a defense attorney is like playing chess. You have to plan and anticipate all of your opponent's moves. My opponent may try to argue that Aiden's mistake was due to him drinking the night before, or because he was behind on work and was rushing. They could come up with any number of reasons. Negligence, incompetence, malicious disregard for human life. They are going to paint him as a villain who deserves to be punished.

However, you shouldn't play chess by reacting to your opponent's moves. You should look at your current position and decide where you want your piece to go—and where you want your opponent to move. I know exactly where I want my pieces to go.

"Where are you going?" Aiden asks, as if he is my prison warden and constantly needs to know my whereabouts. I still dislike him, and I don't foresee that changing. He coerced me into being his lawyer and I'm not about to forget that.

Yes, I get that in a way he is helping me out of my doomed fate, but I'm still salty.

"To mind my business," I reply haughtily, tipping my chin slightly up. He stares at me. I hold his gaze. Ten seconds go by. Another five seconds. I break eye contact. Whatever. I don't have the patience for this. "I'm going to interview some of your colleagues. I need information on the day before the incident and the day of."

He nods and looks back to his laptop. Aiden has been on desk duty ever since the incident occurred. He has been getting caught up on paperwork, and helping his supervisor with filing. I can feel how much he hates it by the extra grumpiness in his voice and the sag in his shoulders.

I walk out the office, heading towards Joey Gomez's office. Well, I *try* to get to his office, but I get lost along the way. There are so many similar hallways. I go to the main lobby and look at the directory on the wall, which, by the way, is a fantastic feature. It's a touch screen, so I type in his name. Surprisingly, clear instructions of how to reach his office pop up.

When I finally arrive at his office, I see him putting on his suit jacket. I may have caught him as he is on his way out. As he is fixing the cuffs, I knock on the open door.

"Excuse me," I say hesitantly.

He jumps slightly and lets out a startled laugh. "*Dios mío!* You scared me," he exclaims.

Joey turns towards me, and I stare with my mouth slightly open. It's embarrassing really. I shut it quickly, trying to not add to the embarrassment. Is everyone here attractive? Does becoming a reaper come with a beautification process?

He smiles at me. "Well, hello there, may I help you?" I do a quick glance up and down, and take in his dark curly hair, full beard, and the way his black suit just molds over his firm body so well.

I place my notepad under my arm and hold my hand out towards him. I clear my throat and introduce myself, "Hello, Mr. Gomez, I'm Joyce Parker. I am the lawyer representing Mr. Kim."

He shakes my hand. "Yes! I heard about you from Aiden. What can I do for you?"

"I need to discuss the events the day before and the day of the incident."

"I would love to talk with you, but I actually was on my way out to do some collections." He tilts his head at me invitingly. "Would you like to join?"

Would I like to join him on his journey to collect souls? Hell to the *yeah*.

I smile and clap my hands. "I would love to!"

Joey rubs his hands together with excitement. "Alrighty then," he gestures to his shoulder, "put your hand on my shoulder."

"Why?" I question as I slowly move towards him.

He grins and winks at me. "You'll see." When I am close enough to him, I reach up and place my hand on his shoulder.

Similar to the feeling of when Aiden teleported me to Eden and Yirah took me to lunch, everything melts away quickly. I close my eyes, and when I open them, I am blinded by sunlight.

"That always feels so strange," I say as I take a step away from him. I glance around and see that we are in front of a hospital. It has felt like forever since I've been in the real world. In actuality, I died only three days ago.

"You'll get used to it." He looks at his phone. "The soul we are collecting is a twenty-year-old woman. Her name is Jessica Wallace. Sadly, she is dying of cancer. A different reaper already assigned her death, so we are here to collect her soul in ten minutes." That is just so disheartening.

We walk through the front hospital doors. "I saw you look at your phone for the information on the woman. How does that work exactly? How does Eden have cellphone service?" I pause. "Do reapers have a phone plan?"

He chuckles. "I'm not quite sure of the mechanics of how my phone works. Reapers can teleport, but your concern is about the *phones?*"

"You all really don't ask the important questions."

"I ask important questions when I need something," he says with a wink. I try not to smile but fail. He's just so damn hot. I cough and continue with my questioning. "How long have you been a reaper?"

"About seven years," he replies, as he places a hand on my lower back to guide me since I am distracted with writing his replies on my notepad. We pass by doctors and nurses, but no one seems to notice us. Probably because they are busy working.

"And have you always worked for the Collection department?"

"Yes, I have. I enjoy this department a lot, and the work we do." He stops us outside of a room. I peek in and see that there is only one patient inside. It is a young girl, lying on the hospital bed. An older woman and man stand beside her bed. The older man is holding her hand, and the woman is weeping. I assume they must be her parents.

Joey continues talking. "The Collection department is the core of Eden. Without our department, there wouldn't be work for the other departments to do. We assign deaths and collect them when it is time. We guide frightened souls to their afterlife. Not everyone is cut out for this job. It's much harder to get into our department than the others, but it's a job worth doing."

It sounds like propaganda to me, but I don't say that out loud. I jot down what he said and look at my list of questions. I deviate from the list a little, because I want to learn more about Eden. "How does one become a reaper?"

"It's not as simple as putting in a job application. When someone dies and goes to the Soul Directory department, their good and bad karma are calculated. When there is an equal amount of good and bad, you are assigned as a reaper. You go through training and learn about each department. Then you apply for the department you want to work for, and the department head must personally select you."

"Which department is in charge of managing the new reapers?"

"The Reaper's Resources department."

"So, Taevian, the department head, selected you?"

He looks at his watch and then inside the room before he replies, "Yes, he did. We have five more minutes before its game time." That's a little morbid to call it 'game time'. But again, I do not say this out loud.

"Did Aiden drink a lot the night before, or on the day of the incident?"

He firmly shakes his head. "No, he had maybe two drinks the night before, and he never drinks on the job. I honestly think he just made a mistake."

I look at him curiously. "Why do you think he made a mistake? Have you made a mistake like this before?"

"No, but we were all human once. I feel as though it was bound to happen sooner or later. I didn't think he would make a mistake like this, but he's still good at his job."

Joey pauses to sigh. "I think he got confused. They were identical twins, with similar names—Amanda and Alex. They worked at the same place. If he didn't double check the file, then I could see how this happened. It is unfortunate, because once a death is assigned, there is no taking it back. The twin who was supposed to die, but did not, will continue to live until her death is assigned to her again."

That does suck. What sucks even more is that the opposing counsel is allowed to bring Alex, the twin who wrongfully died, onto the witness stand. I saw a report on Alex's life, and she had a husband and a daughter. She had many goals and plans that she cannot do now. The opposing counsel is going to have a field day with that information, I'm sure.

"It's my understanding that since Aiden is on suspension, you have taken over his role as supervisor?" I ask as I glance in the room again. Those poor parents don't even know what is about to happen in two minutes. A doctor walks past us and into the room. *Strange.*

"Yes, but I honestly didn't want to. I told Director Taevian to select someone else, because it didn't feel right. But he told me I was the best person for the job. Of course, it's not permanent if the court finds Aiden not guilty."

I can understand the hesitation of taking a friend's position. I wouldn't feel good about it either. Seems like he's doing well in the position, so far.

"Okay, that's all I have for you." I flip my notepad to the first page. I will type up all this later. My plan is to conduct some more interviews and collect more information, then try to piece together a solid defense.

He nods. "Perfect, because it's time to go in." He winks at me and reaches for the door handle.

I grab his arm before he opens the door, "Wait, aren't the parents going to see us?"

He chuckles. "No, we aren't visible to humans. One of the powers we have as reapers is that we can decide when and how someone sees us. I am using my powers right now to make you invisible. Sometimes I change my form to someone from the soul's life that would bring them comfort." He grabs the door handle again and slides the door open. "Right now, we won't be seen by anyone except for Jessica."

That explains why no one looked at us as we walked through the hospital, and why the doctor did not acknowledge us when he went into the room.

As we walk in Jessica is flatlining, and the nurses are trying to comfort her wailing parents. Jessica sits up from the bed and looks around with confused eyes. She looks different. On the bed, she looks frail and sick. But now, she looks healthy and vibrant.

"Mom? Dad?" She reaches out to touch her mom, and her hand goes right through her. She loudly gasps and climbs off the bed. That is when she finally notices us.

Joey looks at his phone, then his watch. "Jessica Walker.

Caucasian woman. Born January 29, 2000. I'm sorry, but your life has come to an end. You need to come with us."

She looks at us curiously and asks, "Who are you?"

"I am Joey, and this is Joyce. I am a reaper here to help you on your next steps." He points his thumb at me. "Joyce will be assisting me today. I'm sorry but your time on Earth has come to an end. Don't be afraid. Your next steps may be a new beginning."

I wish Aiden would've been this polite. He just told me that I'm dead and that I had to go with him. When I refused, he walked up to me, put his hand on my shoulder and we were in his office. It's a wonder why Aiden is Joey's supervisor and not vice versa.

"What about my parents?" she asks as she glances back at them. When she looks back to us, there are tears rolling down her cheeks. He walks up to her and places a hand on her shoulder. Touch is one of the ways reapers can teleport with other people. But I also think it is a way to bring comfort to souls.

"You will see them again one day, if fate allows it," he says in a calming tone. She nods her head and wipes her tears. After a few seconds, she takes a deep breath and exhales. The way she collects herself is inspiring.

"Okay," she replies, and looks back to her parents. "I love you both. See you soon." From what I learned, she may or may not see them again, depending on their karma.

"Time to go," he says as he touches our shoulders. I widen my eyes with realization of an idea.

"Wait!" I yell. "Before we go, can you do me a huge favor?" I plead with my hands in a prayer position.

He smiles at me with an arched brow. "Since you've been

great company, sure. But we have ten minutes to get her soul to the Soul Directory department. Can it be done within that time frame?"

I nod and tell him what I want. Both Jessica and Joey smile at me. Joey touches both of our shoulders again, and off we go.

See? Way nicer than that bitter reaper back at Eden.

9

YOU COMPLAIN A LOT FOR SOMEONE WHO NEEDS A LAWYER

I AM BACK in my apartment at Eden going over my notes from my conversation with Joey. But I am also reading the history of Eden from a book that was provided to me my first day. There is no exact clarification of how Eden was established, or who did it. The history is mostly about the evolution of the departments, and the effect of the advancement of technology on Eden.

I also learn about different devices and tattoos they have for specialized projects, and about banned weapons. There is a weapon called 'The Obliterator', which is fitting considering that is exactly what it does—obliterate a human soul. That means no Heaven, Hell, reincarnation, or becoming a reaper. Your soul is gone forever. It was used on people who committed such awful deeds, that the only fit punishment was to cease to exist forever.

However, they banned it, as it was deemed a heinous form of punishment. At least they banned it *after* they used it on Hitler.

Reapers also get number tattoos depending on what

department they are in. So, there should be seven numbers. Each department's tattoo gives them certain capabilities to fulfill their jobs. The numbers also coordinate with the floors they are on. It makes it very convenient when trying to remember where to go. I think I saw Aiden with the number three tattoo on his wrist.

I look at the notes I took while talking to Joey, typing them up to add to the timeline I'm creating. I need to ask Aiden if he can get me a white board, as I work better when I physically put up all the evidence. Most of Joey's answers help me understand their job better and his relationship with Aiden. Joey seems a decent enough guy, but then again, the bar is in Hell after meeting Aiden.

When Joey and I left the hospital, I asked him to take me to my cats to make sure they were okay. Turns out, that asshole *Richard* had my cats. I could not allow that. We did what any reasonable person would do in my situation—we stole them.

Well, is it really stealing if they are mine?

We brought them to Ms. Jean's house, who was not there when we arrived. But she did have some rum cake resting on the counter, which I snagged a couple of pieces from for Yirah and I to enjoy later.

I kissed my babies goodbye with the promise of seeing them again one day. However, I became concerned. I have yet to see an animal in Eden and no one has mentioned it. Do they have separate entities that take care of them? Are there cat grim reapers? These are important questions that need to be answered.

After I said goodbye to my cats, Joey, Jessica, and I left. I was happy to know my cats will be loved by my neighbor.

Hopefully, she'd fatten them up and give them a good life. When we got back to Eden, we took Jessica to the Soul Directory department, where she was told to be seated until her name was called. The department has reapers who sit down with souls and explain why they are either going to Heaven, Hell or becoming a reaper.

I push those thoughts aside, take a deep breath and get back to work. I am writing down a list of other witnesses to talk to, and departments I need to visit, when there is a knock at my door. Considering I know like only three people, I can only guess who it may be. When I open it, I am surprised to see Joey. Perhaps it's not so surprising, considering the number of times I caught him admiring my ass. He wasn't even embarrassed by it, he just smirked and winked.

Joey doesn't wait for my invitation to come in, he just walks into my kitchen and starts unpacking food.

"I didn't think you ate yet, so I brought some food for you while you work. I can't stay for long, but I just wanted to check in," he says as he opens cabinets. Looking for the dishware, I assume.

"It's the last cabinet closest to the fridge," I inform him, watching as he strides over to the cabinet. He opens it and pulls out a bowl. As he is reaching up, I notice a tattoo on his hip. I don't get a good look at it, but it looks like an infinity sign. He sets the bowl on the counter for my meal. It's nice of him to bring me food.

"Why are you bringing me food this late?" My brows tug together.

He sighs and turns to me. "Aiden is one of my closest friends. I want to make sure you are serious about this and doing all you can to help him."

Ah, so he wants to scope me out to see if I'm doing my job well enough.

I smile at him, despite wanting to tell him to fuck off. "Don't worry, I am taking this very seriously. If I lose, Aiden goes to Hell for a hundred years and I go right with him. Maybe they will let us be cellmates." He smiles back as he pours the soup.

I glance at the food. *Are you joking right now?* I swallow down the vomit that I swear is rising in my throat. The problem isn't that it's soup. The problem is that there's *mushrooms* in it. I absolutely—with every fiber of my being—*hate* mushrooms. I am not being dramatic, either. The way it looks...the texture...even the *smell* makes me want to puke. Who the hell picked up a mushroom from the ground and said 'yeah, let's eat this'? Especially considering that some of them are poisonous. It's amazing that humanity lasted this long.

I don't want to be rude because he did go out of his way to bring me food, so I smile politely and lie through my teeth.

"Thank you so much for the food. I'm not hungry right now, but I will eat it later." Is this why I'm going to Hell, because I lie too much? Technically, I'm lying to not hurt his feelings, isn't that a good deed?

But what do I know? If you ask me, I think the whole system is rigged.

As he is pouring the soup into a bowl, he glances at me. "It's no problem at all. I got this from my favorite restaurant."

Once he finishes, he wipes his hand with a napkin. He can see the living room from the kitchen and lifts his chin in the direction of my paperwork spread.

"I see you're still working. Any progress so far? Do you know what you are going to argue?"

"Not really. I still have a lot more work to do. By the way, I don't know the standards for lawyers in the afterworld, but where I'm from, we are not allowed to talk about our client's case."

He nods. "I don't know the rules here either, but I respect what you say." He clasps his hands. "I'm going to head off. Make sure to stop by my office tomorrow and say 'hi'. Maybe we can go on collections together again, perhaps every once in a while? It would be an honor to be accompanied by a beautiful woman."

I grin. "Yeah, sure. I will. Thanks again for the food. I'll see you tomorrow."

I wouldn't mind going on another collection with him. He opens the door, just as Aiden is about to knock. Aiden tilts his head and slightly narrows his eyes at me over Joey's shoulder, before greeting Joey himself. Aiden needs to pull that fat stick out his ass. It appears all I have to do is breathe, and I irritate him. I can't understand why he's upset, seeing as how I met Joey *today*.

"Hey man," Aiden says as they do that special handshake that all men do when they greet each other, as if it's a sacred male ritual. At what age do they learn it, and how is it so universal?

"Hey, you doing good?" Joey asks, patting Aiden's shoulder. "I know it must be a lot on you right now."

"Yeah, I'm doing all right. Hopefully this will be over soon, and I can get back to my full duties." Aiden makes it a point to look at me as he speaks. I roll my eyes at him. *Yeah, yeah, I get it*. I have to win, or I'm going to Hell.

"Good to hear, man. Well, I will catch up with you both later." Joey says, closing the door behind him. As soon as we hear the click, Aiden turns to me.

His lips curve downward. "So, you let just anyone into your apartment at eleven at night?"

I smile at him and taunt, "Only the ones I think have potential to be in my bed."

He scowls at me. His voice hardens as he says, "Now is not the time to find potential fuck-buddies, Ms. Parker. You have a job to do. That's it."

I smirk. "I'm just kidding. It's so easy to annoy you. You take the bait so easily."

He looks up at the ceiling as if praying for patience. I don't know who he's asking, though. Apparently, there's no one listening.

"Why was he here?" Aiden asks.

I point towards the kitchen. "He brought me food. It's mushroom soup. Also, isn't he your friend?"

He glances in that direction. "He's *my* friend, not yours. You shouldn't have time to make friends with you needing to do your job." He tilts his head in confusion. "And you hate mushrooms."

I scrunch my eyebrows. "How do you know that?" Better question is *why* does he know that?

He shrugs. "I just do." He lifts a bag in his hand that I did not notice until now.

"I brought you some food." Aiden walks into the kitchen and grabs the plates. Unlike Joey, he already knows where the plates are, even though I haven't had him over yet.

"How do you know—" I start to ask, but he cuts me off.

"Where are you with my case?" Straight to business as

usual, I see. He opens the bag of food and pulls out sushi. I can get down with that.

"I am still looking into things. I am getting familiar with how Eden works, talking to your co-workers, going through paperwork, and other things. I'm really trying to see where we are at."

"What do you mean where we are?" He doesn't look up from organizing the food onto the plate in neat rows.

It takes everything in me not to get frustrated. "It's only my second day as your attorney. So, I meant what I just said —trying to figure out where we are at with your case. There's two ways to approach this. One, accept that you did it and come up with a reasonable defense. Or two, deny any of it is your fault and prove that it wasn't."

Aiden tilts his head. "Is that possible?"

"I'm not sure. You said that you swore you saw the correct name that day. It is possible it could have been a glitch in the system or something."

He scoffs as he places the plate of food on the table in front of me. "The chances of it being that is like point zero five percent."

I nod my head. "Exactly. There is point zero five percent of it being a glitch. Which means I am exploring it."

"I'm not so sure that is the best argument to go with."

I give him an annoyed look. "Listen, let me break this down for you, since you don't seem to understand the position you are in. But after this bite." I put a little wasabi on it, dip it into the soy sauce, then take a bite. At the taste, I close my eyes and groan in satisfaction. It is my favorite type— spicy tuna roll. When I am done appreciating my little bite of heaven, I open my eyes and see Aiden staring at me.

"What?"

He blinks a couple of times. "Nothing. I was just daydreaming of when you'll tell me how you can solve this case and leave."

I narrow my eyes and point my chopsticks at him. "Do you have an issue with me? You don't even know me."

"I know enough," he mutters. "You were going to explain the position I'm in."

I look up to the ceiling asking for a God—who I just recently found out isn't real—to give me patience.

"Here it is, Mr. Kim—you're fucked. Sideways. Up and down. All around. Fucked." I pause to take another bite before I continue my explanation. "You are being charged with violating not one or two, but *three* rules. All of which make sense. Am I still going to file a motion to try to get at least one dismissed? Definitely. Will it work? Not a fat chance in hell. Besides all of that, there are witnesses and direct evidence to show that you did indeed assign the wrong person death and by doing that, collected the wrong soul."

He clenches his jaw. "When are you getting to the part where you actually do something of value as my lawyer and get me out of this."

I wave my chopsticks in the air and shake my head. "The legal field is like chess. The attorneys are on opposite sides of the board. While we are moving our own pieces, we are studying our opponent. The arraignment showed me Chris' opening moves. It was aggressive and tactical. Therefore, it is not smart for me to attack head on, especially with jack shit."

I pause, examining his blank face. I guess he's not a chess player. "In other words, I'm not getting you out of anything with all this evidence stacked against you. I'm trying to get you through it. Chris can only really prove negligence. My best defense right now is to attack their evidence against you and point out the flaw in the system itself. I am hoping, by showing the flaw in the system, they will lessen your punishment or dismiss it."

He gives me a once over and shakes his head, disappointment written all over his face. "I should've hired a different lawyer."

"You should've. Cause then I wouldn't have to deal with your constant complaining," I snap. I finish my last piece of sushi and push my plate away from me.

Aiden runs a hand through his hair. "I'm sorry. I'm just frustrated."

"I understand that." I cross my arms and lean back in my chair. "Going forward, I will send you email updates of your case so that you can stay informed. But I only need one thing from you and that is to trust me."

"How could you understand me? Have you ever had something happen that could possibly ruin everything you worked for?"

"It didn't possibly ruin everything I worked for. It *did* ruin everything," I snarl. He doesn't know me as well as he thinks. I know he made assumptions and ran with it, but I don't owe him an explanation.

He looks taken aback by my statement. "What happened?"

I'm honestly glad that information on souls is limited depending on which department the reaper works for. It would be annoying for Aiden to know everything about me. He would probably look at me with pity.

I shake my head. "I don't talk about it. *Ever.* Plus, you're the last person I would confide in about it."

He opens his mouth, then closes it. "Fair."

"So, do you trust me to handle your case?" I ask. This won't work unless he trusts me.

We stare at each other. I don't know how much time passes before he replies, "Yes. I do."

The corner of my mouth lifts. "Good. Now get out. I have some work to do." I look down to my notes, effectively dismissing him.

Aiden lets out a chuckle as he stands. He gathers the plate and walks into my kitchen, where I hear him quickly rinse the dishes. After a couple of minutes, he comes out of the kitchen and looks at me.

"I'm going home now. Call me if you need anything..." he pauses, then says, "... actually, don't need anything." Before I can reply, he is out the door. I let out a soft chuckle.

He really can't help himself.

10

YOU HAD ONE JOB. LITERALLY.

I GASP and shoot straight up into a sitting position in bed. I lay my hand on my chest, feeling my heart pounding. It's the same nightmare I always have. I take some deep breaths and glance at the clock. It's 6:55 a.m. My alarm is set for 7:00 a.m.

I think one of the worst things in life—I am not sure if that's the proper word to use, considering I'm dead—is waking up slightly before your alarm is supposed to go off. That is five more minutes of sleep I could've had. But alas, if I go back to sleep, I would wake up at lunch-time and to an angry Aiden.

Tossing off my cover, I climb out of the bed and to my bathroom. I shower, letting the warm water wake me up, and get ready for the day. I choose an emerald-colored suit with nude heels. Too lazy to do my hair, I do not undo my twist out. I just oil my scalp and fix my edges. I quickly do some light make-up, as I refuse to leave this apartment if my eyebrows are not perfectly done.

I head out the door and towards the elevator. It's a couple of days after sharing sushi with Aiden, and I am still trying to build a solid defense. It's hard to do that when I have crumbs for evidence. Luckily, the first day of court is not until next week. Therefore, I will have had about two weeks total to prepare.

Waiting by the elevator, Aiden is leaning on the wall holding a cup in each hand.

"Good morning, Ms. Parker," he says as he hands me my morning coffee *and* a mimosa. This welcome offering makes me wonder if I'm starting to warm up to him. I grab both eagerly, not giving him a chance to take them back.

"You can call me Joyce, you know." I take a sip of my coffee, then wash back the taste with the mimosa. Now, *this* is Heaven.

"I'd rather not," he replies immediately, heading towards the elevator.

"Uh, why not?" I ask, following behind him. He's in his black suit again with the signature silver lapel chain that no other Collection reaper wears. I'm well acquainted with his back, since he always walks in front of me instead of beside me.

I don't mind though.

His ass is like two perfectly shaped buns that were just pulled out the oven. His walk doesn't scream egotistical asshole, it's laid back. As if there is no question about who he is, where he's going, or whether people like him or not.

"I only call my friends by their first name...and I'm not quite sure what you are yet. I just know you are my lawyer, who I now trust." Yeah, I spoke too soon. I am most definitely not warming up to him too much.

I step into the elevator and sip my drinks in silence while sneaking glances at him. He's staring at the elevator's doors, sipping his own coffee. Today, he is not wearing a tie. The first two buttons of his shirt are undone, providing me a view of a silver chain I never noticed before.

He rolls his eyes and looks down at me. "Why are you looking at me?"

I shrug, pretending to not be embarrassed that I got caught staring. "It's true what they say, the devil comes in a pretty package."

He narrows his eyes and opens his mouth to speak, but the ding of the elevator door cuts him off. That's a good thing. His comebacks can be brutal.

As the doors open, my eyes widen in shock. What a way to start the morning. The floor outside is complete and utter *chaos*. Reapers of every suit color are running in every direction, papers are flying everywhere, and did I just see a *freaking bird?*

What in the hell is going on?

I take a step out the elevator first, just as a man is running towards me. He roughly knocks into me, sending me flying towards the floor. My coffee and mimosa fall from my hands and splatter on the ground. I brace myself to hit the ground, but never feel the impact. I look up to see Aiden holding onto me with his arm wrapped under my back, his hand curled around my hip. He helps me upright, then lets me go, taking a step back. The reaper that ran into me mutters a panicked apology and continues on his way.

"Are you good?" Aiden asks with a bit of concern in his voice. I nod at him, looking around the lobby.

"What is going on?" I ask, "Is this normal?"

He shakes his head firmly. "Not at all." As another reaper

is running by, Aiden reaches out and grabs him by the collar to stop him.

"What the hell is going on?" he demands.

"The system went out, and a bunch of souls from Hell were released. Everyone is scrambling to figure out how it happened, and what to do. The directors are meeting to try to plan and make decisions, but they are arguing. This has never happened before, and no one knows what to do." He pants. "They are from the *third tier*," he whispers aggressively. His face is red and his chest heaves.

Aiden lets him go and shoos him away. He drags a hand down his face, shaking his head in frustration.

"How the hell did they lose souls?" Aiden asks no one. Well, I assume no one, because I certainly don't have the answer.

To bring humor into the situation, I reply, "They forgot to cherish them." I chuckle and peek a glance at him. He glares at me in response. I thought that was funny. He does not share that sentiment.

Whatever. A sense of humor is a vastly underappreciated lawyering skill.

"Now is not the time to joke. Let's get to the office." He waits for me to start walking and follows behind me.

From my readings last night, I know division three souls are no joke. They are the worst of the worst. The souls who are to never be reincarnated. The souls that if 'The Obliterator' was still allowed, it would be used on.

Once we get to the office, he closes the door, and we walk to our respective desks. When he reaches his, he immediately starts clicking away on his computer. Before he even gets the chance to do anything, the door to his office opens and the director I met the other day walks in.

"Whatever you are doing, stop right now," he commands with his finger pointing at Aiden. Seems as though he predicted Aiden would not be able to idly sit back and watch other people search for the souls.

Aiden lets out a breath of frustration and slams his phone on his desk. He turns towards the man, glaring at him. "I am just trying to help. You know I am the best at finding a runaway soul."

Director Jackson shakes his head. "Now is not the time to do anything. You need to stick to paperwork and lay low. Every department is scouring Eden and Earth to find these souls. Focus on your case. This is not me asking, either. *This* is a direct order." Aiden stays silent, not moving an inch. The director, not paying any attention to Aiden's brooding, walks over to his black couch and sits down. He finally looks over to me, smiling as he gestures to the chair across from him.

"We previously met. I'm Director Taevian Jackson."

Aiden glances between us from his desk and then sits in his chair, roughly shuffling through his paperwork. I walk over cautiously and sit down.

"Yes. We did meet. After Aiden and I left court." I reach out my hand for him to shake. "Joyce Parker, sir." He gently takes my hand and shakes it. He holds onto my hand a little bit longer than I am comfortable with, then lets it go.

"Pleasure to meet you again, Ms. Parker," he says.

"Oh, please call me Joyce, Director Jackson."

He laughs. "I'll call you Joyce, if you call me Taevian."

"I think I can do that, Taevian." I smile at him. Despite looking strong enough to rip my arms off with minimum effort, he seems very gentle. Something about him feels...familiar.

"How is your stay at Eden so far? I am thankful you took on helping Aiden with this."

I let out a humorless chuckle. "He didn't leave many options."

He tilts his head in confusion. "What do you mean by that?"

"Well, it was either help him, or suffer in Hell. After my brief stay in Hell—which, by the way, was traumatizing and I would like a therapist—the choice was clear. If you can even call it a choice." I glare at Aiden as I say the last sentence. His mouth twitches into a smile. When Taevian turns to Aiden, that smile fades from his face.

The director's glare is venomous as he says, "He sent you to Hell, huh? I will have a talk with him later. That was *not* supposed to happen."

"Oh, that is not necessary." I'm already on Aiden's bad side. Last thing I need is to get on Aiden's worse side. While we aren't fond of each other, there is no need to be at each other's throat.

"If that's what you want. I have to go meet with the other directors about this situation." Director Jackson stands, and I do the same.

He holds out his hand to me and says, "It was nice meeting you, and I will see you both soon."

He gives me a gentle smile then turns to walk out the door, throwing a glare at Aiden as he walks out. Once the door clicks shut behind him, Aiden picks up his phone and taps away at the screen. I walk over to my desk and sit down.

"What are you doing?" I ask curiously.

Without looking up from his phone, he says, "Minding my business, you should try it sometimes." Seems as though he took a page from my book of attitude.

"Until your case is complete, and I ascend into Heaven, your business is my business." He ignores me and continues typing on his phone. I stand and walk over to his desk, tapping my foot with my hands on my hips.

I repeat my question. "What are you doing?" Still no reply. I nod, then lean over the desk and yank the phone out his hand. He tries to grab it, but I'm too quick. I look at the screen and see that he was looking at a list. Before I can scroll, he leans over and grabs back his phone.

I bet all of my wine bottles that was the list of the missing souls. Why can't we just relax? Mind our business? Not get involved? Is that too much to ask for?

Settled back into his chair, he points a finger at me. "Try that again and I'll send you to Hell for a week." He would've been better off threatening to cut off my supply of mimosas.

I shrug. "You're bluffing. Not only would Director Taevian not allow that, but you would only be hurting yourself. You have an active case going on."

He narrows his eyes. "Try me and find out if it's a bluff." We stare at each other for ten seconds. I shift under the weight of his stare before I roll my eyes.

"Whatever you plan on doing, I'm coming with you." If he is going to do something reckless, I'd rather be there as a witness to his actions and to control the situation. Last thing I need him to do is make his current case worse.

"Absolutely not. Stay here and work. I'll be back." He walks towards the door, and I run to block his way. What era does he think this is? *Stay here and work.*

"I'm coming with, or I'm telling Director Taevian. Your choice." I smirk at him. His whole operation would be over before it began if the director found out.

"Those aren't great choices."

"Well, now you see how it feels to not have great options."

He runs his hand over his face, staring down at me. "Or here's another choice. I will drop you off on a deserted island until I am done." Damn. He could do that, but—

I cross my arms. "When you bring me back, I'll tell the director. So, either way, you'll be getting in trouble. Not only for going against a direct order, but also for leaving me on an island."

He thinks about it for a couple of seconds, then sighs. "Fine. You can come along. But stay out of my way and don't talk." I nod in agreement, even though we both know I will probably be in his way, and I will definitely be talking.

He walks out the door with me trailing him. "What is your plan?" I ask.

"Catch the escaped souls and bring them back to the Hell department." I roll my eyes at his obvious response.

"I can feel you rolling your eyes."

I let out a laugh. "I was not trying to hide it. But like, what is the plan for how you are going to catch the souls? You don't know where any of them are."

"We are going to have to use our brains. I pulled up the reports of all the missing souls on my phone. They were released onto Earth, so we are going to have to hunt them down." He stops in front of a silver door and scans his tattoo at the sensor. The sensor turns green, and the door slides open.

"You all don't have a device that can track them?" I ask. That would make things way easier.

"Yes, but the device tells us the general area. Not exactly where they are at. Also, souls can teleport about ten to twenty feet, so it can be hard trying to catch them. That is why we are here."

"And where is here?" I glance around. I see a room with racks of different weapons with a scanner at the side. I turn to my left and see a huge golden sword. Without realizing it, I've moved towards it, but something tugs at the collar of my suit jacket. I look behind me to see Aiden holding onto me. I try to pry myself out of his grip, but his hold on me tightens.

"Don't touch anything, and stay next to me," he warns, still holding onto me.

I pout. "I wasn't going to touch it. I just wanted to—"

He raises an eyebrow. "Why am I always repeating myself to you?" I huff and cross my arms, not saying anything in reply.

"The easiest way to catch and store multiple souls is by using a scythe. Since you are coming with me, you will get one too," Aiden informs me. *Oh, I am so freaking excited!* I will be like an unofficial reaper. Maybe being a reaper was my dream job. The only requirement is dying and neutral karma.

Not bad.

Aiden finally releases me with a pointed look. He walks up to the wall, scanning his tattoo, and a locker opens. Inside are a couple of scythes. I would be amazed, but the problem is that they are the size of a pen. This has got to be a joke, and yet again, not a funny one.

I place my hands on my hips and sarcastically ask, "What

the hell am I going to do with a pen sized scythe? Write them a love letter?"

Aiden smirks and holds out the scythe. "Scythe, extend," he commands. Like magic, the scythe goes from pen-sized to a full-on scythe.

"Holy shit!" I exclaim. Now *that* is a weapon. I hold out my hand in excitement. "Gimme."

He chuckles and hands me the other pen sized scythe. I am going to kick ass with this.

Holding the scythe in my hand, I command, "Scythe, extend." The pen expands into a full-blown scythe in my hand. I am admiring it when a thought comes to me.

"Wait. How do I get it to shrink?" I ask, looking up at him to see him already looking at me.

He holds out his scythe. "Scythe, retract." I watch as his scythe turns pen-sized again.

I repeat what he said, and mine retracts. We both place our scythes inside our suit jackets. Aiden moves to place a hand on my shoulder. I quickly dodge it, startled by the sudden movement.

He rolls his eyes at me. "Joyce, I don't bite." He smirks. "Unless you want me to."

My eyes widen in embarrassment. "Uh, w-what," I shake my head and clear my throat cause no way am I going to let a man fluster me. "I was not expecting you to do that. It was a reflex of mine."

Aiden lips twitches, "Okay, well. Let's try this again." He places his hand on my shoulder and teleports us behind a building, then takes a step away from me.

11

WHO HASN'T MADE MISTAKES?

AIDEN PULLS his phone from his pocket. I watch as he scrolls, a frown on his face as he focuses. His face slightly relaxes when he finds what he was looking for.

"Got it," he announces, not yet looking up from his phone.

"How are we doing this?" I ask.

He looks up to me, arching his brow. "I thought we agreed on no talking during this activity."

I shrug my shoulders. "I lied."

"Exactly why most lawyers go to Hell. You all just lie," he grumbles.

I squint my eyes at him. I don't entertain his comment since there is no proof to suggest otherwise. I, myself, am a lawyer that was going to go to Hell until he intervened. Therefore, he may be right.

"My question still stands," I say.

He lets out a deep sigh and tilts his head, motioning me to come closer. I step near him, and he shows me his phone. It's a picture of a forty-year-old man with dirty, blonde hair and wrinkled lips that reveal he was an avid smoker during his life.

"The first soul is Robert Smith. He seems to be in Florida. Somewhere in the Tampa area. When I searched up his last known address before he died, I saw he used to live here twenty years ago. He may be just trying to go home to see family or friends, or something. He could simply have nowhere else to go. Let's start at his house."

I grin. "See, that wasn't so hard to use your words to explain, right?"

He gives me a look. "This particular soul is in Hell for robbing banks."

"I thought the souls that were released were tier three, meaning the worst of the worst," I say.

"Yeah, he killed everyone in the bank without a second thought when the police had him surrounded, including children. So, twenty people died," he informs me.

My eyebrows jump up in shock. "That will do it."

Aiden places a hand on my back and guides me around the building. Once we are at the front, he points to a small yellow house that looks like it hasn't been maintained in years. The grass is overgrown, the paint is chipped, and one of the windows is busted. The house is unlivable.

We walk up to the front door of the house, finding it ajar. Aiden pushes it all the way open. We walk in with him leading the way.

"Hello?" I yell out. Aiden stops and turns his head to look at me.

"You think a missing tier three soul is going to happily reply back?" he sarcastically asks.

I shrug. "It was worth a try."

Aiden points to me then does a zipping motion over his mouth with the same hand. "Seen, not heard," he states.

I roll my eyes. "Fine." He nods, then faces forward. Our journey through the house resumes. It smells horrible. The furniture is dusty and moldy. We search through the whole house, but find no traces of Robert.

"I guess he is gone. Where should we look next?"

At the sound of creaking floorboards, I swivel my head around. Neither Aiden nor I moved at that moment, so we are not the cause of the noise. Aiden places his index finger on his lips and tilts his head to signal me to follow him. We walk quietly in the kitchen and he points under the sink.

I nod and mouth, 'Okay'. I lean forward, placing my hand on the handle of the lower cabinet. I throw open the door and my eyebrows jump in surprise. I look at Aiden and say, "Wow. You're good."

He winks. "I know. I'm good at *a lot* of things." I roll my eyes. We both turn to the soul who is staring at us. He somehow figured out a way to fit his huge frame in the lower cabinet. It is impressive.

"What do you want?" Robert yells, his eyes wide in fear.

"It's time to go back." Aiden informs him.

"And if I don't?"

Aiden looks at me and rolls his eyes. "Why do people think they have a choice?"

I shrug. "I mean, it's human nature to look for alternatives." No one wants to voluntarily go back to Hell. That defeats the purpose of escaping. I certainly would rather be in Heaven right now.

Robert—who is still in the cabinet—crosses his arms, defiance written all over his face. "I'm not going. I'd like to see you try to take me. I don't deserve to still be in Hell. It's been years!"

I look at him deadpan. "You killed over twenty people, including children."

"Who hasn't made mistakes?"

Aiden and I look at each other, then to him. Aiden replies sarcastically, "I have never killed twenty people by mistake."

Robert doesn't reply. A calculating look crosses his face for a split second, then he disappears.

I swivel my head around. "Where'd he go?"

"He couldn't have gone far. Split up. Remember just use the scythe and cut it through him, it will suck him in," Aiden says. We run outside and veer off in separate directions. I walk a couple of houses down when I spot Robert hiding in one of the neighbor's cars.

I walk up and stare at him. "Get out."

"No."

"I can see why Aiden asks why people think they have a choice, because why do you think you have a choice?"

I open the car door, surprised to find it is unlocked. He isn't the smartest cookie. His eyes widen and he teleports out of the car. Before I can turn, I feel a kick in my butt, propelling me awkwardly inside the car. I push myself back out to see the soul in a fighting stance.

"Let's tussle!" he yells. "I'm not going back."

"Oh yes, you are." I pull out the pen sized scythe and command. "Extend." I crack my neck and shake my shoulders.

"What the hell is that?" he asks.

I smile. "The weapon of your ending." I swipe out the scythe to hit him, but he teleports back to dodge it. *Damn.*

This is going to be hard. At least he can't teleport more than fifteen feet. I run towards him, waving the scythe in the air, but he keeps avoiding it. He teleports behind me and yanks my hair, hard. I'm getting angrier with every second that passes. He pops up and kicks me from behind again, causing me to fall to the ground on my hands and knees. I use the scythe to help me stand up.

He is pissing me the hell off.

I keep trying to swipe him while at the same time studying his teleporting habits. He's not that smart. He teleports the same way depending on which side I'm coming from. If I swipe left, he teleports right and vice versa.

This time, I fake as if I am going to come from the left, but switch directions at the last second. Surprised by my change, he doesn't have enough time to teleport. My scythe goes through his body, and I watch as his soul gets sucked inside.

"Retract." I command, then I let out a deep breath. That was harder than expected. But, like I always do, I get the job done.

I hear clapping and turn around to see Aiden leaning against a tree with a smile on his face.

I bristle. "You were watching the whole time?"

"Yes, I was. My favorite part was when he kept teleporting and messing with you. That kick in the back looked like it hurt." It most definitely did. While we were fighting, I hadn't had time to stop and feel the pain. But now it is radiating all over my body.

"Why didn't you help?" I seethe.

He grins. "I prefer watching you get your ass handed to you by a soul." I would like to hand his ass to him at this moment.

"You're an asshole."

His grin widens. "So, I've heard." He points to his shoulder. "Let's go collect some more souls." I begrudgingly place my hand on him.

Aiden and I spend the next couple of hours finding and collecting souls. Sometimes they come willingly, realizing there is nothing left for them here. However, a lot of them run away, throwing any object they can at us.

It is surprisingly fun.

I enjoy the rush of chasing after the souls and seeing what crazy things they will do to get away. I always try to talk to them first, of course. But alas, why would they want to voluntarily go back to Hell?

We teleport around the world searching for the loose souls, stopping in Brazil for some mouthwatering food. By the time we finish, five hours have passed. As I sweep the scythe through the last soul, Aiden announces, "That is it. We collected half the souls."

"Half?" I ask, in awe of our own abilities. There are a bunch of reapers searching for souls and we did half the job with one percent of the manpower. We are a *good* team.

I raise my hand in the air for a high five. "Up top!" I yell. He high fives me. I move my hand lower and yell, "Down low!"

Aiden presses his lips together. "I'm not doing it. Once was enough."

I drop my hand and stare at him. "My god. You're so—"

"Don't start."

12

HAVE YOU SEEN MR. INTIMIDATOR?

AFTER WE DROP off our scythes to the Hell department, Aiden teleports us back into his office, just as the door bursts open. I dart my eyes in that direction, watching as Director Taevian walks in, his face stoic. I can feel the anger rolling off him in waves. If looks could kill a reaper, Aiden would be imploding. I scoot away from Aiden so that I am nowhere near the direct line of fire.

Aiden raises his hands in the air. "Taevian—"

Taevian points a finger at him, and Aiden immediately stops talking.

He scolds, his voice laced with rage as he says, "You are being charged with breaking the most sacred rule in the Reaper's Code of Conduct. A rule that no reaper has ever broken. The court ordered you to do desk duty, so you tell me..." Without giving Aiden a chance to reply, Taevian continues by yelling, "*Is hunting souls what you should be doing?*"

I pipe in, "In his defense—" Taevian turns to me, shutting

me up with one look. *Yeah.* This is something I should just observe from over here.

With a hard edge to his voice, Taevian informs me, "I'll get to you in a second." I shouldn't have opened my mouth. But I mean...we did catch like half the souls. That's way more than everyone else. If I'm anything, I am most definitely competitive. Aiden knew exactly how to track the souls and we got it done quickly, saving the other reapers time. He should be thanking us, if anything.

Director Taevian turns to look back at Aiden. "Not only did you go against my direct orders, but you brought Joyce with you in your reckless escapades."

Aiden points at me. "I told her to stay here, but she started making all kinds of threats, so I had no choice." *That rat bastard.* I peer at him bitterly. I just tried to defend him, and then he snitches on me. I motion my thumb across my throat, signaling that he's dead meat. He smirks. I stop when I feel the room get fifty degrees warmer under the weight of the director's anger.

Taevian looks between us two and in a low, threatening tone, says, "You both think this is funny?"

"No, sir," Aiden and I reply at the same time. We make eye contact, both our lips twitching.

Director Taevian points to me and accuses, "You're his lawyer, isn't it unethical for you to aid your client in doing something the court ordered him not to do?"

Now may not be the best time to be a know-it-all, but I just can't help myself. "I mean *technically* it's not against the court order. The court said he cannot engage in the collections of passing souls. The souls we collected have been dead for a while now," I reply.

He shakes his head in disappointment. "It seems as though you both need to learn a lesson." He points at me. "Those mimosas you drink in the morning," I gasp in shock. *No! No, he can't!* "Yes, I know about them—don't bother looking for champagne. It will all be gone for five days." I grab my chest in pain. Not physical pain. But soul wrenching pain. *That's so unfair.*

The director turns his finger to Aiden. "I am also suspending your teleportation abilities for five days."

Aiden's mouth drops open and he shakes his head. "Wh-what? No, I use it to get food from the Living World." I stick my tongue out at him. Aiden glares at me.

"Guess you'll have to settle for whatever is here. I don't care. You guys decided to disappear for five hours, so deal with the consequences." On that final note, he turns and walks out the office, the door slamming behind him.

I look at Aiden and glare at him. "This is all your fault. I told you we should've minded our business."

He looks at me, his eyes filled with annoyance. "No. *You* should've minded your business. I would've been quicker without you."

"That's complete cow shit. I helped you. You would've taken forever without me."

He crosses his arms. "I'm not doing this back and forth with you."

I cross my arms too. "Then don't."

"Fine," he replies.

I stick my nose in the air. "Fine."

The door to the office opens, and Yirah pops her head in. She shoots us a lopsided grin as she looks between us. "Another lover's spat, I see."

Aiden and I look at each other, then to her. At the same time, we exclaim, "No!"

She rolls her eyes. "Everyone is going for drinks. Are you guys coming?" *Do cows go moo?* I would never turn down a drink.

"N—" Aiden begins.

"Yes!" I yell out, interrupting him.

Aiden sighs. "Yes. But I won't be able to teleport for five days."

Yirah shrugs. "No problem. I'll take you both there and bring you back. You both live next to each other so it won't be a hassle."

I jump up and grab my purse. I walk quickly over to Yirah, throwing an arm around her.

"How are you, my Yirah?" I ask her.

Yirah puts an arm around me. "I'm great, Joy Joy. Ready to get my drink on!"

A wide grin spreads across my face. "A woman after my own heart."

"Oh wow, I didn't know you had one of those," Aiden mutters sarcastically as he removes his suit jacket and places it on the back of his chair. He rolls up his sleeves, providing me the perfect view of his shapely forearms. Aiden's arms are proof that God is a woman. But then again, maybe only a man would put such an ungrateful personality in a gorgeous package.

I flip my middle finger at him. He lets out a low chuckle and walks over to us, putting an arm on Yirah's shoulder.

"Alright, let's go!" Yirah exclaims. The world flickers and in the next moment we are in an alleyway. Aiden removes his hand from her to walk ahead of us. Yirah and I follow him while chatting about our day. I tell her how I kicked ass collecting souls, and that I should be a reaper. She tells me about the priest who made a whole scene when told that he was going to Hell. I was confused, until she explained that he was stealing money from the church donations to gamble. He tried to explain to her how he begged God for forgiveness each time. Guess that didn't work out for him.

We turn the corner and walk a block before arriving at the bar. Aiden disappears inside, but I stop Yirah before she enters.

"Where exactly are we?" I ask, looking around the busy streets and skyscraper buildings.

She stretches out her arms and does a twirl. "Darling, we are in New York City! The land of rats, dreams, expensive parking, and weird smells everywhere you go. But the vibes are always immaculate. I've always been interested in humanity's love for this concrete jungle."

I laugh. "You say that as if you weren't once human."

She smiles in return. "You're right. It just feels like a million years ago." She grabs my hand and pulls me into the bar behind her. I couldn't tell you the last time I've been inside one of these. The music is loud. Everyone is drinking and laughing. We walk past a group of people in scrubs taking shots. Yirah guides me to a table in the back with Joey, Aiden, and a couple of other reapers I've never met.

I lean in to Yirah and ask, "How is it possible that you all can just come out and drink? Shouldn't everyone be working? What if someone from your past life recognizes you?"

She laughs and pats my hand. "We all have schedules for when we work. There are always reapers working, but we take shifts. Could you imagine if we had to work all day, every day? To answer your other question: reaper's faces are perceived differently. Everyone sees us uniquely. No one will ever be able to recognize us. Since you are working for us, your face does this, too." I nod in understanding. That makes sense. Looking at it, being a reaper is no less than being alive.

A waitress comes over and stands near Joey and Aiden. "What can I get y'all to drink?" she asks the table. Well, it's more like she asked Aiden and Joey. Yirah and I don't exist for her.

"Uh, let me get an old-fashioned. Top shelf," Aiden requests without looking up from the menu.

She leans in close to him. "Anything else, honey?"

He looks up and gives her a dazzling smile. "That's it for me."

I roll my eyes at his response. She winks then takes Joey's order, flirting with him too. The only difference is that Joey asks her what she is doing later. When the waitress is done flirting with Joey, she begins to walk away towards the bar. She didn't even bother taking Yirah's and my order. I begin to open my mouth, but Yirah beats me to it, clapping her hands twice to get the waitress' attention. The waitress turns in our direction, her face slightly confused at the sight of us. *Nice.*

"You didn't take our drink orders," Yirah states, her brow arched.

"Oh," the waitress grumbles. "What do you want?"

Yirah replies, "Six green tea shots, four lemon drops, and two beers. Bring them in that order too." She pauses. "Oh! And an order of fries, mozzarella sticks, and spinach dip."

I blurt, "Goddamn, Yirah. Are we drinking for pleasure, or getting smashed?" Because if I drink all of that, I will be on the floor.

Yirah looks at me, innocently confused. "Are those not one and the same?" I stare at her. Then blink. A smile spreads across my face and I grab her hand.

"You were made for me," I declare. She smiles in response and winks. As we wait for our drinks, Yirah and I chat about everything. Every time we talk with each other, it feels like we're old friends catching up on our lives. It feels nice to have someone to talk to. Someone to trust.

Aiden and Joey are watching and chatting about whatever sport is on the television. I don't see Aiden smile much around me, but he does it a lot with everyone else. I just get sarcasm and frustrated sighs. I mentally shrug. You can't always be everyone's cup of tea.

"If you could marry anyone who's alive right now, who would it be?" Yirah asks.

I purse my lips in thought. I snap my fingers when I come up with my answer. "Idris Elba."

She laughs. "He's already married."

"You didn't say that they couldn't be married," I counter.

Yirah rolls her eyes. "Stop playing and give me an answer."

I immediately reply, "Daniel Kaluuya. Have you seen him in Black Panther? Absolutely scrumptious."

She nods. "That should've been your first answer."

I nod. "You're right. Your turn. Who would you marry?"

"Daniel Kaluuya."

I frown at her. "I already chose him. He's my husband now."

She shrugs. "We can be sister wives." We both laugh as the waitress arrives with our drinks. From the corner of my eye, I see Chris walking up to us with a drink in his hand. I roll my eyes at Yirah. She snickers and takes a shot.

"Well, hello, Attorney Parker. Pleasure to see you outside the courtroom," Chris drawls.

I look him up and down. "I can't say the same," I reply.

He leans in. "Come on. Don't be like that. I'm just doing my job."

"Yeah, and in the process, fucking over Aiden," I remark.

"Let's not talk about work. You're a beautiful woman. Let's talk about us," he says, his eyes running over me and landing on my breasts. *Men.* They are all the same. Complimenting me on my looks. What about my insane intelligence?

"Let's not talk at all, actually." I wave him away. "Go talk to someone else. The only time you and I should be speaking is in the courtroom."

"Or maybe the bedroom?" he suggests. My lip curls in disgust. I open my mouth to spew a couple of well-chosen curse words at him, but close it when I hear Aiden speak.

"I'm confused, Chris. You heard what she said, and yet you are still standing there," Aiden drawls, taking a sip of his drink as he waits for Chris to respond. Chris opens his mouth, but Joey interrupts, with a loud whistle.

Joey raises a shot glass and remarks, "Let's have a drink to all the hard work everyone put into catching those escaped souls! A huge thanks to Aiden and Joyce for doing half the work by themselves!" Everyone cheers. I shyly look down at my cup. Yirah bumps my shoulder and raises her glass for me to clink.

Joey announces, "Salud!" Then, he tips his head back and takes his shot.

Aiden and I look at each other, making eye contact as we throw back our shots. I slam my glass on the table, still looking at him as he licks his lips. My heart speeds up. Well, not exactly my *heart*. It's much lower than that, and it's beating with need. She's such a traitor. I break eye contact with him.

It's the alcohol, Joyce. Plus, you haven't had sex in like, two years.

I don't want Aiden; I just want sex. I let out a deep breath as Yirah yells to the waiter, "Another round!" Good thing I no longer need a well-functioning liver.

I moan loudly as I wake up. Sadly, it is not out of pleasure. Rather, it is in absolute despair at the painful pounding in my head. How is it fair that I'm dead, but I still get a hangover? I understand wanting to keep reapers as close to their humanity as possible, but damn.

There's a knock at my door, and I whimper at the thought of having to move. Struggling, I slowly rise from the bed, attempting not to throw up. I stumble to the door, tripping over everything in my path. I am barely making it there in one piece.

As I pass by the mirror in the entrance way, I get a glimpse of myself. Drunk me did not do her nightly duties. There is no bonnet on my head, which means my hair is a flat frizzy mess. I may break down in tears just at the thought of having to do my hair again. I need to find somebody here who can do proper braids. With all these reapers here, there is bound to be someone.

When I finally open the door, it's Yirah standing there.

Usually I'm excited to see her, but she looks too bubbly for someone who was drinking just as much as me yesterday. Her appearance is well put together, with her cream pants and matching tank top. She's also holding the holy grail, my one true love—also known as coffee.

That might be the only reason I widen my door and let her in. She smiles as she skips—*literally*—into my kitchen and I kick the door closed.

"Good morning, Joy Joy. How are you feeling?" she teases. Following her into the kitchen, I reply with a grunt.

Her smile widens. "Yeah, we drank a lot. Aiden took you home alright, I see. I ended up dropping you both off by your office because you kept rambling about getting your favorite pen."

Ah yes.

My comfort pen, Megan. Her long frame. Wide torso. She fits perfectly into my hands.

I pause and squint my eyes at her when I realize she said Aiden's name. What does she mean Aiden took me home? I don't remember—

Oh crap.

Aiden did take me home, and I totally embarrassed myself. After we got drunk at the bar, Yirah tried holding me up, but she was tipsy herself. Not drunk. I am not sure how that is possible, considering we drank the same amount. Aiden had to carry me on his back. I don't remember all that I did, but I do remember telling him to 'lay one on me'.

As in a kiss.

I told him to *kiss me.*

If that wasn't bad enough, I told him that I haven't had sex in two years. It probably got worse from there, but I can't remember it all.

I slap my face and groan in embarrassment. I lean forward, resting my forehead on her shoulder.

"There, there," she says as she rubs my back. She reaches for my hand and places the warm cup of coffee in it. I lean back slightly and take a healthy sip. The aroma blesses my nose as the smooth java runs down my throat like a waterfall on a sacred island. I feel it warm every inch of my body. This is a little piece of Heaven. This is what I am slaving to get to.

Yirah's voice breaks the cosmic connection I am having with my coffee. "Take these pain killers, and drink up so we can have brunch." She hands me two white pills from a Ibuprofen bottle that she pulled out of her purse and I plop them in my mouth, washing it down with my coffee.

"With mimosas?" I question, glancing over the edge of my cup. You can't do brunch without unlimited mimosas. I haven't removed my cup from the proximity of my face. I have to keep this piece of salvation as close to me as I can.

Yirah rolls her eyes. "You don't ever seem to learn. But yes, with mimosas." I pump my fist in the air, gently, of course, to avoid spilling my coffee.

With excitement buzzing through my body, I say, "You, my reaper, are a keeper."

A slow grin spreads across her face. "Did you just rhyme reaper and keeper?" Of course, I did. I am a poet of sorts.

I inform her, "If T-pain can rhyme mansion with Wisconsin. I can rhyme reaper with keeper."

She giggles and waves me away. "Go take a shower and get dressed. You smell like a bar, friend."

I sniff myself. Yeah, I don't smell the best. I plop the coffee on the sink and head to my bathroom. Thirty minutes later, I am dressed, and ready to impress. I'm wearing a cream satin skirt and white cropped blouse with nude heels and gold accessories. My hair is unrevivable, so I put it up into a pineapple and fluff it out the best I can without ruining the curls even more.

"Yirah!" I yell as I walk into the living room. "I'm ready—"

I gasp and race towards her. I drop to the floor. She's laying on her stomach, a little bit of blood seeping from the back of her head.

I turn her over and shake her gently. I know she can't be mortally injured, but it must have hurt. When she doesn't wake up, I reach into my purse that I dropped next to me and dial Aiden's number.

"Hello?" he grumbles, probably as hungover as I was.

"Aiden!"

"What's wrong?" he demands. "Where are you?" I hear him moving around.

"I'm in my apartment—"

I jump as the door to my apartment is thrown open. He's wearing sweatpants, a t-shirt and no shoes. He moves to where I am and squats. He runs his eyes over Yirah then me.

"Are you okay? What happened?" he questions, still examining me.

I nod. "I'm fine. But something happened to Yirah. I went to get dressed, came out and saw her like this."

He rubs a hand over his face. "Okay, let's call—"

Yirah groans and opens her eyes. She blinks a couple of times then tries to sit up.

"Don't move too much. You're injured," I say, tightening my hold on her.

She ignores me and sits up. "I'm fine. It just stings a little. They were probably trying to knock me out."

I frown. "Do you know who did this?"

"If she knew, she probably would have told us by now," Aiden replies dryly.

"I was talking to Yirah. Not you," I fire back.

"Well, sorry you lack—"

"Now is not the time," Yirah cuts in. She looks at me. "Whoever came here was not expecting to see me. They were wearing a mask, goggles, gloves, and tracksuit. They did not want to be identified. But I know for sure it was a man."

"What could he have wanted with Joyce?" Aiden asks.

Yirah points to my dining room table. "He hit me from behind. Before I passed out, I saw him grabbing the files that were on that table." She looks down to her lap. "I'm sorry, Joyce."

I stand and rush over to the table. All the files for Aiden's case are gone. Not a single paper left. I had brought them all home with me. This is not good. The opening statement I prepared, my notes from all my interviews I conducted, and my list of potential witnesses. All gone, and the first day of trial is tomorrow. Why would someone take them?

"How would they have known the files were here?" I say out loud. I don't expect them to know the answer. I'm just shocked that someone stole all of my papers for the case.

"My concern is if you were here alone, would they have settled for the files?" Aiden says. I turn to face him, crossing my arms over my chest.

I smile at him. "You are worried about me?" He turns his body to face me and mimics my stance. We are only about one foot away having a standoff.

He replies, "Actually, I'm worried about my case. It probably would've been more effective for them to snatch you rather than take the files if they were trying to mess with my case."

I huff in annoyance. "Gee, thanks. Next time, you should provide them with a strategy to make their crimes more effective."

He grins. "I'll make sure to do that—"

Yirah interjects, "Can you both relax for five minutes so we can figure out who did this, and why." She stands from the floor and touches the back of her head. She winces when her hand makes contact.

I walk over to Yirah and grab her hand. I pull her into my bedroom and gently push her to sit on the edge of my bed. I walk into my bathroom for first aid supplies. When I enter the room again, Aiden is standing in the doorway.

I approach Yirah and say, "Turn your head for me, please."

She turns her head. I pull out the wipes from the kit and pat her wound gently. She flinches, but doesn't make a sound.

"You will stay with me," Aiden states. I pause at his statement. Is he crazy? He can barely stand to share an office with me, now he wants us to live in the same apartment. No way. I enjoy my little piece of sanity.

"I'll stay with Yirah," I say.

"I don't recall offering," Yirah retorts immediately. I yank her ear lobe and she lets out a yelp. She looks up to glare at me, but I turn her head forward. *Traitor.*

Aiden sighs. "What about what I said makes you think you have a choice?"

I look up from Yirah's head and narrow my eyes at him. "I'm Joyce Parker. I always have a choice," I say haughtily.

He smirks and replies mockingly, "Yet here you are. As my lawyer. Even though you refused."

"You coerced me," I accuse.

He raises a brow. "I helped you. But you seem to have a habit of being ungrateful."

"And you have a habit of being a dick. Guess we both have things we need to work on."

Yirah sighs loudly and flicks my hand away from her head. "Within the time you both were bickering, my head has already healed." She stands and flattens her hair. "I enjoy my peace. Therefore, I do not want either of you in or near my apartment."

Aiden nods. "So, it's settled."

I nod in return. "Yes. I'll sleep in the office." There is a bathroom in the office that has a shower. I can live there. I'll miss my apartment though. It was perfect.

Aiden looks to the ground then to Yirah. He calmly says, "You talk some sense into her. I am five seconds away from strangling her."

Yirah shakes her head and laughs. "Have you ever tried to talk sense into Joyce? It's like telling a five-year-old that they cannot drink dish soap just because it looks like juice."

"*Hey!*" I whine. "I'm not that bad." Funny. I *was* that child who tried dish soap because it looked like juice.

Yirah raises a brow. "Then, stay with Aiden until we figure this out."

I sigh in defeat. "Fine. Where am I sleeping? You only have one bed." I want as much distance as possible.

"You can take my room," he says.

I hope he's a clean person. I've been in some men's homes, and it looked like a frat house. Nine times out of ten, their cars are squeaky clean though. That's how they tricked me. A clean car, I've learned, does not equate to a clean home.

"Alrighty then," I say, looking around my room. "Let's pack up some things."

We all begin to move around my room, collecting my belongings. We don't pack up too much of my stuff because I'll only be staying with him temporarily.

I turn and see Aiden opening the drawer next to my bed. I let out a scream and run over. I shove him away and slam the drawer. Yirah pops her head out of my closet.

She asks, "You okay, Joy?"

I nod. "Yes. Everything is fine." She smiles and resumes her packing in the closet.

Aiden looks at me, a humorous glint in his eyes. "What is your problem now?"

"Uh, nothing. I'll pack anything I need from this drawer."

He waves his hand dismissively. "I got it."

I shake my head feverishly. "No. It's okay. *Really.* Thank you for offering."

He gives me a lopsided grin that I feel straight in my chest. "Are you trying to hide the Intimidator from me?" With those words, that feeling vanishes. He did not just say the name I gave my new toy. How would he even know?

My eyes widen. I stammer, "W-what? What are you talking about?"

He chuckles. "Last night when you were too drunk to even know your name, you showed me your toy. I was impressed at the size." He leans down until his lips are by my ear. "Let me know when you want something bigger."

My mouth drops open. I swear on my afterlife, I will never get drunk again. I will never pick up another alcoholic beverage. No more mimosas for me. I have never been so embarrassed in my entire existence. A decent person would just act like that never happened. But not Aiden. Nope. He has to open his big mouth.

I point to the door. "Get out. Yirah and I can pack the rest. Take what we have packed and kindly go away."

His smile widens. "Sure thing, Mrs. Intimidator." I flip him off as he walks away chuckling. Once I hear the front door close, I let out a low scream.

Yirah comes out the closet with a suitcase. "Honey, what is wrong with you?"

I yank open the drawer and pull out my vibrator. "He fucking saw this." I wave it in the air between us.

She chuckles. "You should find better hiding spots."

"How could I have known someone was going to break into my apartment, whack you, and steal my files. *Hm?*"

She holds her hand up. "Woah there. Why are you so riled up? You usually don't care what Aiden thinks."

"I *don't* care what he thinks. It's just—it's just embarrassing!" I sputter.

"Well, get over it. *Quickly*. You'll be living with the man."

"Because of you," I accuse.

She grins and shrugs. "I like my alone time. While I do love being with you, I prefer not to be Malcolm in the Middle when Aiden comes around."

"He told me to let him know when I want something bigger!" I yell.

Yirah's mouth drops open and she fans herself. "*Girl*, if you don't tell him you want a test ride *now*."

I roll my eyes at her antics. "Not only do I still dislike him, but he's my client, Yirah."

"I don't think you dislike him, nor do I think it's relevant that he's your client. I think you want to take a trip to the carnival and jump on that *big* ride."

I point at her. "How old are you?"

She shrugs. "I don't know. I forgot my birthday and I've stopped counting the years."

"So, you're old enough to understand how childish you sound right now."

"Wow. That hurts, Joy Joy."

I bang my head on Aiden's dining room table. Nothing I write sounds good enough. Opening statements are crucial for a case. They set the tone for the rest of the trial. If you have a crappy opening statement, chances are you have a crappy case.

I finished unpacking my stuff into Aiden's place a couple of hours ago. It came as no surprise to walk-in and see no colors in the apartment. I can manage it at the office, but I absolutely cannot live here without splashes of color. We had an argument about my throw pillows. But I explained to him how I won't be able to function, and we will lose the case. He eventually caved, although he is not happy about it at all. I didn't do too much, I just put some throw pillows in his room and the living room, then placed some candles around the house. It feels better already.

Aiden will be sleeping on the couch. It pulls out so he will be fine. I will be sleeping in his room. He changed the covers for me already. However, they still smell like him. Despite not wanting to, I love the way he smells.

I tap my pen against my head, begging it to work so I can write this statement and go to sleep. I close my eyes and take a deep breath. When I open them again, Aiden is setting a plate of food in front of me—a square of lasagna, the cheese on top perfectly browned. I glance at the food, then to him, with wide eyes.

He raises a brow. "Despite what you think, I'm not a total dick."

"And despite what you think, I'm not ungrateful."

The corner of his lip lifts. "That's still up for debate." I laugh and throw my pen at him. He catches it deftly, placing it on the table.

"Don't damage your favorite pen," he jokingly warns.

I reach over to pick up my pen from the table. I cradle it gently into my arms as if it was a baby. My pen, Megan, followed me into the afterlife. When I died it was in my pocket. She's a true ride or die.

I glance up to see Aiden looking at me. His face is gentle and relaxed. He is always so tense, it's nice to see him relax a little. I place the pen on the table when my stomach growls, signaling that I should really take a bite of the delicious smelling lasagna. I lift my fork and place it in my mouth. I moan in pleasure and shock at the taste. This man can make a damn good lasagna. It is cooked to perfection.

I raise an eyebrow at him. "Wow, you cook very well. Who taught you?"

"No one. I grew up in the system and learned how to cook

to be able to feed myself." That is the first real piece of information I've learned about Aiden. I wouldn't have guessed that he also grew up in the system. At least we have that in common.

"I grew up in the system, too," I admit.

He nods. "I'm glad you enjoy my food. I usually cook for myself, or Joey." I smile at him. He hides his kind side, but the more I've spent time with him, the more I've seen it come out.

"What do you do all day since you can't collect souls?" I ask curiously. The gentle look on his face turns to frustration. Damn, I ruined it.

"Usually, reapers must file a report on the collections they did and update the soul's profile. I am double checking other reaper's reports and updating the profiles. That's it, really. It keeps me busy because we collect a lot of souls within an hour," his voice is full of disinterest.

I can tell he hates it. But he respects his role as a reaper too much to ever complain. Eden comes first for him. I wish I had as much work ethic as him when I was alive. I just let my respect and passion for the legal field dwindle into nothing.

"We will get you back to doing what you love," I promise him.

He smiles a little. "I'm going to get some rest."

"I'll try not to be too loud. I'll head to the bedroom once I'm done."

He waves dismissively. "No problem. Take your time."

I glance back at the blank paper and sigh. *It's going to be a long night.*

13
IT DOES NOT PLEASE THE COURT

"Tell me what you want," Aiden whispers in my ear. He kisses his way down my neck as his hand trails down my stomach. I moan in anticipation of his destination.

"I want you, Aiden," I breathe, my heart beating faster with every second that passes. God, I've been waiting forever for this moment.

He grins. "Anything you want, baby." His mouth slams down on mine. I make a noise at the back of my throat, lift my hands, and curl my fingers in his hair. His tongue sweeps inside my mouth, taking control over me.

He tastes so damn good. I whimper his name into his mouth as he rubs himself against me and—

Tap.

I groan, ignoring the touch against my forehead. My dream is way too good for me to wake up.

Tap.

This time it is much harder. Irritated, I open my eyes. I glance up to see an impatient Aiden. He is about to use his index finger to tap my forehead again, but stops when he realizes I am awake. Aiden in my dreams was much more tolerable than the real version.

"What do you want?" I grumble, lifting my head from the dining room table. I wipe the drool from the corner of my mouth and lick my lips. I glance around and realize I fell asleep working on his case.

Aiden stares at me for a moment then taps his watch twice. "It is 8:30."

I furrow my brows. "At night?" I question, not understanding why he is interrupting my beauty sleep.

He gives me a look and replies, "In the morning, Ms. Parker."

I give him a blank look. "And?"

He presses his lips together then lets out an exasperated sigh. "We have court at 9 a.m."

I stare at him for five more seconds, then jump up. *Shit!* We have court in thirty minutes. Aiden is already dressed in his signature black suit and silver jewelry, which means I have the bathroom all to myself. I grab my suit and my undergarments and rush into the bathroom. Fifteen minutes later, I am showered and dressed in a dark purple suit and matching purple heels. I am standing in front of the mirror brushing my hair back into a bun when Aiden appears in the bathroom doorway. I watch through the mirror as he leans against the frame, his body taking up the majority of the space.

"Are you ready for today?" he questions with an arched brow. His dark hair is parted on the side, and neatly fixed with no strands on his forehead. I prefer when his hair covers his forehead. Either way, he looks good though.

I bite my lip. "As ready as I can be. I stayed up preparing."

I am trying to gel down some fly away hairs. My hair is very stubborn today.

He nods. "What were you dreaming of earlier?"

I pause. "What do you mean?"

He smirks. "You said my name. Was it a good dream? Were you trying to take advantage of me? Because I must be honest, I'm not that into you."

I roll my eyes and snort. "In your dreams, Aiden Kim, would I want your grumpy ass."

He winks. "No, Ms. Parker. Not my dreams. But apparently in yours."

I ignore him and finally finish my hair. I look at the time on my phone. With ten minutes left to spare, we still have time to stop by the lounge to get coffee. No mimosa for me today. It's game time. I need my mind to be on point for my opening statement.

I walk into the bedroom, grabbing my tote bag from the bedside table.

"Let's go," I say. Not waiting for him, I walk through the apartment and out to the elevator. We would've teleported to save time, but Aiden's teleportation abilities are still suspended. I hear his footsteps trailing behind me. When we reach the elevator, I jab a finger on the down button and cross my arms, tapping my feet impatiently. Neither of us says a word.

The ding signals the elevator has arrived. We step inside and turn to face forward. I run through my opening statement in my head again. Lawyers are allowed to read their opening statement off a laptop or notepad, but I find that lazy. By memorizing it, I can move around the room and make eye contact. I can put on a performance.

When we reach level seven, the Reaper's Court floor, we step out of the elevator. We dart straight for the lounge and quickly collect our coffees. With five minutes before court is in session, we walk into the courtroom. I settle into my seat and take out my notepad and pen.

The opposing counsel, Chris, walks in and gets comfortable at his table. He is wearing a navy-blue suit with his dark hair fixed to perfection. Not a single hair out of place.

As soon as court is over today, I am kidnapping Yirah for some drinks. I am exhausted. I think I got less than four hours of sleep. That is not nearly enough. If Aiden didn't wake me up the time he did, we would've been embarrassingly late.

Chris is presenting his case first, which gives me time to get my shit together. I told Aiden he could trust me with this case and I meant it. The more time I spend with him, the more I understand how important this job is to him. It doesn't hurt to keep in mind that his fate also determines mine.

Yirah is sitting in the gallery directly behind us. She aggressively whispers my name, and I turn to glance at her, my eyebrow raised. She gives me an excited thumbs up. "You got this!" she loudly whispers. I smile at her and turn back around. She's right, I got this. But for some reason my brain cannot get with the program.

"All rise for the honorable Judge Hobbs. Reaper's Court is now in session," the bailiff announces. Everyone stands, watching as the judge makes his way into the courtroom. He settles into his seat, organizing the contents on his bench.

"Please take your seats," he commands. The judge clears his throat and says, "Good morning, ladies and gentlemen. Calling the case of Eden versus Kim. Are both sides ready?"

"Ready, your honor," Chris confirms.

"Ready for the defense, your honor," I also confirm. Chris stands and walks to the center of the courtroom, his notepad in his hand. He angles his body to ensure both the judge and the audience can see him.

He clears his throat, looks down at his notepad, then begins, "Your honor. This is a case about a soul that was wrongfully assigned death by a reaper. When we all become reapers, we swear an oath to promise to uphold the Reaper's Code of Conduct. Those who fail to do so must be held accountable. Aiden Kim should be held responsible for his actions. We will present evidence to show that his carelessness caused a soul to wrongfully lose their life too soon. Thank you for your time." He moves to his seat.

I take a deep breath and stand. Like Chris, I move to the center of the room. Internally, I am freaking out. It is not like I haven't done a trial before. But this time, it is in the afterlife and my client is a Grim Reaper. The game has totally changed. New rules and new competition. I hope I am ready for it.

I look at Aiden. He winks and mouths, *'You got this'*. I straighten my shoulders and clear my throat. "If it pleases the court," I request. The judge nods his head in approval.

I take that as a sign to continue. "Your honor. This is not a case of whether a soul was incorrectly assigned death. We all know that happened. This is a case of whether my client," I point towards Aiden. Everyone turns to look at him briefly, then back to me. "Mr. Aiden Kim—intentionally, knowingly, or negligently did it. The evidence and testimony you will hear during this trial will show that Aiden most definitely did not intend to assign the wrong death, nor did he know his actions would cause a soul to lose their life too soon. It will also show that his actions do not amount to negligence. This was a mistake not negligently done, but rather as a result of a system that is in dire need of change. This could've happened to any reaper. Unfortunately, it happened to my client. We hope to show you that with more safeguards in place, something like this would not have occurred. Defense is asking for these charges to be dropped. Thank you."

Judge Hobbs waits until I am seated to say, "The prosecution may call its first witness."

And so, it begins.

The first witness is going to be no other than Alex Cole. It's the most obvious choice. She is the reason why we are here today. Chris requested special permission to have the Heaven reapers bring her to Reaper's Court. This also makes trials different for me. In the living world, a victim who loses their life cannot come to the stand. Because, you know, they are *dead*. But now we get to hear firsthand accounts from the victim.

"Your honor, we call Mrs. Alex Cole to the stand." The door to the courtroom opens and Mrs. Cole walks in, with a sad, distant look on her face. She keeps her eyes to the ground as she walks past everyone directly to the witness stand.

"Raise your right hand. Do you promise that the testimony you shall give in the case before this court shall be the truth, the whole truth, and nothing but the truth, so help you, Reaper?"

"I do," she replies.

"Please take a seat," the judge commands. Once she is settled, Chris jumps into his questions.

"Please state your name for the record."

"I am Alex Cole."

"Can you tell us why we are here today?"

I stand and announce, "Objection! Narrative." It's my second favorite objection. It stops a witness from telling a story of their whole life, since it can lead to irrelevant and even inadmissible information. My first favorite is relevance.

Chris smirks, and before the judge could reply, he says, "My apologies. Let's get to know you better. Where are you from?"

"California."

"Did you have a family?"

"Yes. A husband and a beautiful daughter. All she has is her father now."

"What did you do for work in California?"

"I was a general surgeon," she states. I know exactly where he is going with this, and it is not a place I want to go.

Chris cocks his head. "You saved lives?"

"Yes, I did," she replies proudly.

"Your honor. Because of the actions of Mr. Kim, Ms. Cole lost time with her family. His actions affected not only her life, but the potential lives she was supposed to save. Ms. Cole was not supposed to die that day. She was to make a recovery and continue her valuable work as a surgeon. A domino effect may have begun. People who may have lived, will die. People who could've gone on to do great things themselves or have a child who would have cured cancer."

Yeah, he is aiming straight for the heart strings.

Chris finishes, "That is all my questions for the witness, your honor."

He takes a seat, and I stand to begin my questioning.

"How many general surgeons work in the hospital?"

"I do not know the exact number. But there is a big group of us."

"But there is enough that with your absence, lives will still be saved, correct?"

She pauses. "Yes."

"When you have done a surgery, do you follow a specific... method to complete it?"

"Yes. I do."

"Using this system, has an unforeseeable mistake ever occurred that made you rethink the system in place?"

She nods. "Yes."

"Did that mistake result in the loss of a life?"

Her eyes get sad as she answers, "Yes."

"Do you regret it?"

"Everyday."

"Did you modify the way in which you did your procedures to avoid repeating the mistake again?"

"Yes. I did."

I turn to face the judge. "Your honor. Mistakes are natural. It's the way of the world. I have made mistakes. Ms. Cole has made mistakes. Aiden has made a mistake. However, should Aiden be the only one at fault? Or do we need to take a deeper look into the actual system in place?"

I pause as something clicks in my head. I don't know why I didn't think of this until now. "Take for example, the souls who went missing. Never in Eden's history have souls from tier three Hell been released. Yet, it happened...isn't it possible that the same error could've happened to Aiden? Opposing counsel has a burden, your honor. A burden to prove that Aiden is solely responsible for what occurred. As we have seen, that is not the case. Thank you." I take my seat and mentally pat myself on the back.

That was good. I'm getting my footing a little bit.

Chris goes on to call the director of the Soul Directory department, and the woman who sent Alex Cole's Information to Aiden. They both testify to the system being effective the way it is. I'll just need to provide more evidence to prove my point.

14

MISERY LOVES COMPANY

I WAKE up bright and early. It is a couple of days after the first day of trial. I don't want to see Aiden this morning. Not because he did anything wrong. It's just that I would prefer not to see anyone.

Today is a day that I wallow in self-pity every year. I want to crawl into a hole, never to be heard from again. But work must get done. I'm hoping I can get it done early then drink and eat my misery away.

I quietly get dressed so as not to disturb Aiden. I opt out of wearing a suit today. I throw on jeans and a Purple Rain t-shirt with a pair of Nike sneakers. I fix my hair into a bun. I cannot be bothered with my hair today. I mean, I still look cute, just not as glamorous as I usually look with my suits.

I tiptoe through the department. Aiden is fast asleep on the couch, tangled in the sheets. I take a moment to watch him as his naked chest rises and falls. When he slightly shifts, I hold my breath, hoping he does not wake up. When the coast is clear, I exit out the door and slowly close it.

When I get to the office, I start working on Aiden's case. I have been spending time re-doing my notes ever since all my stuff for the case was stolen. At this point, it seems as though I have everything prepared. Prosecution has finished presenting their case, so I am just working on my questions for the witnesses who I will call to the stand.

I work for the next two hours. When I am almost done, Aiden teleports right in the middle of the office, his back towards me. He spins to see me already staring at him with confusion.

"What the fuck, Joyce." Wow, that's the first time he has called me by my first name. I should've recorded that. I *so* have to tell Yirah about this.

"What?"

He glares at me, annoyance radiating from him. "Don't I always walk with you to work?"

"Yeah?" I reply, not understanding what his issue is.

He blinks, then tilts his head back to look at the ceiling, giving me a great view of his neck. Something about a man's Adam's apple just screams manly. I should probably ask him about Adam and Eve. Were they real? Cause if that's the case, I have a strong theory of what really went down. I think Adam ate the apple first, then gave it to Eve and had her take all the blame. Hence, the Adam apple in men's lying throats. However, I shove my thoughts aside—for now—and focus on Aiden.

Still looking at the ceiling, he whispers, "If there was a God to pray to, I would pray for patience."

I laugh for the first time today. "You need a whole lot more than patience." He looks down to me, his face set in annoyance.

"Yeah. Because of you, I probably need therapy too."

I shrug. "Not everyone can handle all that I am." I turn my attention back to my computer. He walks up to my desk and takes a seat.

"A lot of stuff has been happening at Eden and when you left the apartment, I got worried," he admits.

Without pausing from my typing, I mutter, "I'm just not in the best mood today."

He leans forward. "Why is that? I have to admit, your mood isn't how it usually is. You've barely dished out much attitude."

"I don't want to talk about it. I just wanted to get work done and go home."

There is silence for a moment. Aiden stands abruptly and announces, "We are going out."

I look up at him with confusion. "Going out? What do you mean?" My heart starts to speed up. I contemplate the possibilities of what he means, but then shake off those thoughts. It's Aiden. He does not mean more than what he usually says. Also, why is my heart speeding up? I barely tolerate him. Or do I? *Shit.* Can you blame me? He's hot, and can speak in complete sentences.

The bar is in Hell after all

"We are going out into the Living World. I am going to take you to places you've never been before." I know one place I'd like to go, and we don't even have to leave this room to go there. I mentally slap myself at my dirty thoughts. He is off limits. I'm his attorney.

I roll my eyes. "I'm busy with work, Aiden."

"And I'm sort of your boss. What I say, goes. So, let's go."

"Aiden, I don't—"

He walks around the desk until he's at my side. "Get up,

Joy." He raises a brow. "Or I'll lift you up." We stare each other down until he moves towards me.

"Okay, okay." I jump out of my seat. "I want to change my outfit though."

"What's wrong with your current outfit?"

"It's summertime. I want to put on a dress. Take me to my apartment. I didn't pack any dresses."

He rolls his eyes. Seems like he does that a lot with me. "Okay, Princess Joyce. Let's take you to your castle." He grabs my hand and teleports us to my living room.

"I'll wait out here," Aiden says. I nod and quickly head into my room. Maybe this will provide me with a much-needed distraction.

I want to put something on that shows off my curves and my ass. I've been having dreams of Aiden and I'm sick of just dreaming. I should be enjoying my afterlife, that includes sex. So maybe I can tease him a little. I throw on a yellow halter top bodycon dress with some white sneakers and white cross-body bag. I put on gold hoops and fix my bun so it is a little more neat. Checking the mirror, I look fine as hell. I turn to get a glimpse of myself from the back. The back roll is rolling today. I hope everyone got some butter, 'cause she's coming out hot.

"I'm ready!" I yell as I walk into the living room. Aiden is sitting comfortably on the couch, laid back with his eyes closed. As he hears me approaching, he looks at me, slowly dragging his eyes down my body as if he is trying to memorize every curve.

I slowly twirl so he can see the whole dress, "How do I look?"

He raises a brow. "Like your usual self."

I roll my eyes. "You are my biggest hater."

He chuckles, then his eyes soften in a way I've never seen before. "You look like your usual self because you always look beautiful."

Goosebumps spread across my skin and something in my chest twinges. Ignoring my reaction, he stands up and reaches for my hand. I snap out of my trance and grab his hand, my excitement growing with every second. I feel the tingling throughout my body and in the next second we are surrounded by colorful buildings. I gasp at the sight around me, shocked that people are just walking by as if the architecture itself isn't art.

"It's beautiful," I say. "Where are we?"

"Spain is a beautiful place."

I look from the building to Aiden to see him already looking at me. I've always wanted to go to Spain.

"How did you know I wanted to go to Spain?" I question.

"When I was helping you clean up your apartment after it was broken into, I found your journal." He raises his hands defensively when I squint my eyes at him. "I didn't open it. It was already opened to the page where you said you wished you could've traveled when you were alive."

I look him up and down and cross my arms. "I guess you're off the hook."

"Oh, thank goodness. Wouldn't want to experience the all mighty wrath of Joyce Parker."

"Damn straight." I look around and clap my hands with excitement. There is so much for us to do. First things first— food. I grab Aiden's wrist and drag him behind me. Off we go on an adventure of an *after*lifetime.

Aiden and I are laying on a blanket near a river. His eyes are closed, so he may be sleeping. Which is well-deserved since he used a lot of energy to teleport us to all those places. We spent the rest of the day visiting so many countries that I lost count. We went to Haiti, Ethiopia, Peru, Australia, Japan, Canada and so many more.

We even made a stop in Jamaica to get my hair braided. I've grown tired of doing my hair every day and with everything that is going on, I don't have the time to do it. The good thing is that it didn't take long because five women were working on my hair at the same time. I now have knotless braids that fall past my waist. While my hair was being done, Aiden sat on a chair nearby and played candy crush on his phone, talking to the locals who stayed next to him the whole time. He smiled and joked with them as they fed him all kinds of food.

A breath of deep contentment leaves my mouth. Today was the best day I have ever had, and it's thanks to Aiden. He still confuses me. Sometimes we are cordial and other times he seems as though he'd rather be anywhere else than with me.

No longer wanting to debate what he thinks of me, I turn to look at him, placing my hand under my head for support. He is laying on his back, eyes still closed, his face peaceful.

I whisper, "Are you awake?"

He turns his head to look at me, making some of his hair fall over his forehead. "Yeah."

I hesitate. "Can I ask you a question?"

His brows tug together. "Go ahead."

"Why does it seem like you don't like me sometimes? Like I understand my hostility with you at first, 'cause you coerced me into being your lawyer. But what issue do you have with me?"

Looking taken aback at my question, he doesn't answer immediately. He turns his head to look at the sky. I continue to look at him.

Finally, he replies, "You've been thinking about this for a while, huh?"

I nod. "Yeah, I just chalked it up to you being upset with me for saying 'no' to being your attorney, and maybe my personality. I'm not sure. There's been a lot of mixed signals."

He presses his lips together, as if he is debating on whether to tell me. Fortunately, he decides to share. "I don't dislike you. Well, at least I don't dislike you *now*. Maybe I never disliked you. I may have misunderstood you." He pauses. "My parents were immigrants. They came to the states when I was around seven. But they were murdered when I was eight and the people that killed them were never caught. I was placed in the system like you. I was so angry with the world that I kept getting into fights, and moved from one home to another. Finally, a teacher told me to take that anger and make a change. To fight for people. I decided I wanted to be a lawyer. I wanted to be a prosecutor to ensure that the victims of crimes got the justice they deserve. Because *I* never got justice. When I was on my way from taking the entrance exam for law school, a drunk driver hit me and I died on impact. He was hammered at noon on a *Tuesday*. Director Taevian was the one who collected my soul. I was devastated, and he brought me a type of comfort that I haven't felt since my parents died. He is the reason I joined the Collections department. Being a reaper gives me purpose. There's nothing more important to me than my position. When I collect souls, I bring them back to Eden where they go to Heaven, because they lived a life of kindness, or to Hell, to suffer the consequences of their actions."

We had the same goals as kids. Only I got the chance to get there, while he didn't even get the chance to start.

He continues, "You achieved so much during your life, but you decided to live as if you were dead already. I was hostile to you because you had everything I was fighting for when I was alive, so I thought you were ungrateful. But the more I got to know you, the more I realized you are caring, funny, and full of life. I just don't understand why you hated being a lawyer enough that when I gave you the opportunity to just represent me, you chose Hell."

I forgot that reapers don't know everything about every soul. Each department only knows enough to complete their duties. The Collection department only knows enough about a soul to assign them a death before collecting them. I contemplate whether I should tell Aiden. Usually, I could care less about what people think of me, but now I care about what Aiden thinks.

I turn to look up at the sky. I've never really talked about this before. I kept it in because when I tried to tell Richard about it, he told me to get over it, that it is the job we signed up for. So, I shut down, holding in all my emotions.

I let out a deep breath, and finally open up about the thing that causes my recurring nightmares. "I used to love being a lawyer. I wanted to fight for people the way no one fought for me growing up. It's cliché, but it's my 'why'. After I graduated law school, I became a prosecutor. Everyone talks about becoming a defense attorney to represent those who are innocent. But not everyone who is charged with a crime is innocent. I wanted to amplify the voices of the victims who suffered at the hands of a bad person. There was this one case I was assigned to—a sexual assault case. She was nineteen years old and had nobody. Her name was Sam and she worked at a strip joint to get money for her education. She had this big dream of one day being a pediatrician." I shake my head in defeat. "One late night, her boss attacked her and ruined her life. She didn't report it until a month later but by then most of the evidence was gone. She took pictures of herself, but she didn't have a rape kit. A lot of evidence was circumstantial, but I was set on getting her justice."

I pause to allow myself a second to pull it together enough to finish the story. "We brought charges against him, and I was the lead prosecutor. My supervisor told me I wouldn't win, but I didn't listen. I went in headstrong, and fought tooth and nail. But it wasn't enough. He was found not guilty. After he was let go, he...he *killed* Sam. He was finally locked up after that. But it was too late for Sam." My chest tightens, and I feel a tear fall from my eye.

Aiden looks at me with sympathetic eyes. "Oh Joyce, I didn't know. I'm sorry for assuming."

I don't reply immediately, because it felt good to say all of that out loud. I finally reply, "It's okay. It's human nature for people to assume. But now you know. That is why I was not in the mood earlier today—it's the day she died. I think about it every year."

His eyes are gentle. "Lawyers can suffer from trauma too, you know. Did you try to see a therapist? Take time off? Even reapers need a day or two off sometimes."

"No. I wasn't the real victim. The victim was who I was supposed to get justice for, and she died. If I had gotten the court to lock him up the first time, then—"

Aiden cuts me off, "Joyce, do you know what is the most common way that humans get bad karma?"

I shake my head. "No."

"Regret. It weighs so heavily on the soul that it affects the choices you make, which leads to more bad karma. I finally understand why you almost went to Hell. It wasn't who you represented that almost got you to Hell, it was the pain that you held on to." He takes my hand. "It's time to let it go, Joyce."

I sigh. "I don't know how."

He uses his thumb to rub circles on my hand he is holding, comforting me. "One day, you will."

He smiles at me. I smile back, my throat tight with emotion. Maybe he isn't that bad, after all. We lay in silence for five more minutes, both of us staring at the sky, with him still drawing circles on my hand.

Aiden lets go, then stands and holds his hand out to me again. I take it and he pulls me up with ease. He doesn't let go of my hand, and I don't move away either.

He grins at me and asks, "Shall we end the night with a bang?"

I tilt my head back to look up at him, "What do you have in mind?" I know exactly how we can end the night with a bang. But his idea is way different than mine.

He winks at me, then teleports us to a karaoke bar where we get a private room. We spend the rest of the night drinking and singing our hearts out. By the time he takes us back to his place, I feel better than I've ever felt on this day.

15

NO OFFENSE, OF COURSE

"HEY, WAKE UP," someone softly whispers.

My shoulder is gently pushed against. I yawn, stretching out my arms. I drop them on the blanket and open my eyes. The hint of light coming from the living room shines on Aiden's face. He is looking down at me, his hair disheveled.

I blink my eyes, attempting to shake off sleep. I turn my head to the bedside table and glance at the clock. It's one in the morning, two days after our impromptu trip. Aiden and I have been spending more time together. We even did a movie night yesterday with Yirah and Joey. Aiden had never seen the movie 'Poetic Justice', which is almost criminal. We rectified that issue and I got to introduce him to the love of my life —Tupac. But, let's not forget about the amazing Janet Jackson. Those two have my heart.

"Get dressed in something, quickly. I want to show you something." The first time he showed me something, he sent me to Hell.

I give him a look. "Can you show me something during normal business hours?"

"*No.* Get up," he replies sternly. He grabs my arms and pulls me out of bed to my feet. I groan in annoyance.

He runs his eyes slowly over me. "Is that *my* shirt?"

I look down at myself. I am wearing one of his oversized t-shirts and just my panties. I haven't washed my clothes, which meant I needed something to wear. Aiden's clothes were easily accessible since I'm in his room.

"No," I lie. It is too late for me to come up with a better excuse. My brain has not turned on yet.

A slow grin spreads across his face. "Yes, it is. If you wanted to borrow a shirt, all you had to do was ask."

I roll my eyes. "Fine, can I borrow your shirt? I haven't washed my clothes."

"Sure. But you'll owe me."

I cross my arms. "And what exactly do you want?" I demand.

He shrugs one shoulder. "I don't know yet, but when I do, you'll be the first to know."

I bet I will.

I move towards the closet and close the door. I change into shorts and a sweater. I yank off my head scarf, slide my feet into my sandals and walk out of the closet.

"Ready," I announce.

"Good. Let's go."

He leads us out of the apartment and to the elevator. Surprisingly, he clicks the first floor—the Heaven department.

I open my mouth, but he beats me to it. "You will understand soon. For now, just trust me," he says. I chuckle softly at how he already knew what I was going to ask. When we arrive, he guides me out the elevator to a room down the hall.

This is my first time being on this floor. The Heaven department has pearly white walls, with silver and gold décor. It is elegant and clean. Uncomfortably clean. As in, I wouldn't know where to sit because I'm too worried about dirtying or breaking something.

We walk past a woman reaper wearing an immaculate white suit. She nods at us as we pass her and continue along. At the end of the hallway is a reaper that I've never met before. He is the same height as me, lanky, and wears glasses. He has short, tight curls with blonde tips.

"Aiden, long time no see." He looks at me and smiles. "It's nice to finally meet you, Joyce. I'm Mac."

I smile. "Nice to meet you, Mac."

Aiden shakes hands with him. "Thank you so much for doing this for me." During the handshake, his sleeve pulls up a little, revealing an infinity tattoo. Seems to be a trend around here.

"Anything for you, Aiden. You helped me through the toughest moment of my life. This is the least I could do." I'll have to ask Aiden later what he is referring to. That is, of course, if I remember.

"Of course," Aiden replies.

"You can walk through this door. You'll find what you are looking for." He opens the door and waits for us to walk through. A bright white light blinds me, and I cover my eyes. Once my vision adjusts, I can't believe what I am seeing.

Tears fall past my lashes as I stare at Sam baking pies with her grandmother in a cozy kitchen. They are smiling and joking around. I watch as they pull out a freshly baked pie and share bites with each other. She looks happy. At peace. My chest tightens as I am overwhelmed with emotions. All the years of regret, and feeling like a failure, come rushing through me. I turn to look at Aiden and see him already looking at me.

"Thank you," I whisper, tears running down my face. "Thank you for showing me this." I feel a weight lift off me. I couldn't help her, but at least she is at peace now. She deserves it.

He pulls me into his arms as I quietly sob. "You're welcome," he whispers back, pressing his chin onto the top of my head. "I hope this can help you let go. You deserve to."

After two minutes of us watching them and me crying, I feel a familiar strange sensation. I lift my face from his chest, looking around our surroundings.

Confused, I ask, "Where are we?"

"Behind a bar," he states.

"Why are we behind a bar?" I let go of him and wipe my face with the sleeve of my sweater.

"You need a drink, Joy. Also, no offense, but you're an ugly crier," he jokes.

I sniff. "And you're just ugly all the time. Must suck. No offense, of course."

He throws his head back in laughter. I watch him laugh with a smile on my face. When he's done, looks back at me with a wide grin.

"Let's take some shots," he says, pulling me into the bar. We take a seat in the corner and give our orders to the waiter. Eight shots of tequila. We decide to only do shots to get the buzz quicker. Four shots are sure enough going to make me feel something.

"Tell me about your parents," I say, wanting to learn more about him while we wait.

He smiles faintly. "My mom's favorite color was pink. Every outfit she wore was some shade of pink. I never thought twice about the color until she died. Now every time I see the color, I think of her. It's like a constant reminder. A good reminder." He pauses. "She was always in the kitchen cooking. While she rarely said the words 'I love you', she showed her love for us through food." This is the most vulnerable I've ever seen him.

"And your dad?" I ask.

He sighs. "We had a...difficult relationship. Even at a young age. He was tough on me. I remember coming home from school, proud of the B+ I received in math. He took the paper from me and said, 'You shouldn't be happy unless it's an A'. He was harsh, but he wanted the best for me. I didn't understand that until I had to face the world by myself."

"Have you tried sneaking in and seeing them in Heaven?"

He shakes his head. "No. I can't."

"Why?"

"Because when given the choice between Heaven or reincarnation...they chose to reincarnate." I think it's amazing that souls designated for Heaven have a choice. I thought about reincarnation, but I'm trying to relax.

I hesitate. "But...how will they find each other in the next life?"

"They tied their souls," he says softly, love glinting in his eyes. That's so beautifully heartbreaking, and I feel weepy again. Aiden may never have them as his parents again, but they will always find each other.

"That's so beautiful. To be sure of someone so much that you tie your soul to them forever."

He nods. "Even if I don't get to be with them, at least, in

every lifetime, they will unconsciously search each other out." Soul ties are a tricky, but amazing concept. They will always feel a pull towards each other. However, that does not guarantee that every time they are reincarnated, they will find each other. One of them could die early. They could get married before finding the other person. There's so much that could go wrong, but there is still the chance that it could go right.

"I'm happy you had them. Even if it was a short period of time. I wish I had that," I gently say.

"You'll have it one day. Whether in this life or your next," he assures me.

I smile at him, not replying because I don't know what to say next. We silently stare at each other, saying a million things with no words. The silence is comfortable. I don't feel the need to ramble to fill the gaps. The waiter brings our shots. We take up a glass and raise them in the air.

"To us. To letting go of the past. And to hopefully finding something as special as your parents one day," I say softly, never losing eye contact with him.

"To us," he says as we throw our shots back and reach for the next.

16

ABOUT DAMN TIME

AIDEN TELEPORTS us back into the middle of his apartment. I'm a little tipsy, so the quick movements make me trip against him. As we both start to fall, he moves me to make sure I'm on top of him. We land on the ground, and he lets out a grunt. I look down at him and start to giggle. I try to move my braids out of his face, but I can't see clearly enough to do it. He smiles and lifts his hand to my lips, rubbing his thumb against them softly, as if he is trying to trace the shape of my smile.

My smile slowly starts to drop as we gaze into each other's eyes. With one hand, Aiden moves my hair onto my back. His hand slightly caresses my back, making me shiver. I look at his lips then lick mine in anticipation. I've thought about those lips every day since I laid my eyes on him. I run one of my hands through his hair, enjoying how soft it feels against my skin.

Before I realize what I'm doing, I am leaning down and pressing my lips against his. After a few seconds of feeling no reaction from him, I pull up and look at him. He doesn't say anything. He just looks at me.

Feeling embarrassed, I look away. The drinks must be getting to me. I must have imagined the way he was looking at me. And it has been a while since I've gotten some.

I start to apologize. "I am so sorry."

He hesitates. "We can't...you're my lawyer and you're...it's just not right."

I bite my lip, not saying anything. He may be right. If we were in the Living World, I would face discipline by mixing business with pleasure. But we aren't in the Living World. What do we have to lose?

He closes his eyes and lets out a frustrated sigh. When they open again, there is a newfound determination burning in them.

His jaw rolls as he holds my gaze. "Fuck it," he growls. He grabs my nape and brings me down to him, slamming his mouth against mine, thrusting his tongue in my mouth.

Oh. My. God.

This isn't a kiss. That seems too simple of a word to describe it. He takes over my mouth like he is starving and finally getting his first meal of the day.

Aiden easily lifts us off the floor and walks towards the bedroom without losing contact with me. When we are in the room, he drops me onto the bed. I lean up on my elbows and watch as he pulls his shirt over his head, revealing his perfectly sculpted chest. His pants and boxer briefs follow immediately after.

Good *God.*

I've been waiting to see what was under his clothes

forever. Any self-respect I had disappears the moment he takes off his boxer briefs.

Holding eye contact, Aiden lifts me forward off the bed and rips my shirt over my head, throwing it onto the ground. He slides my shorts off leaving me in just my panties. Holding eye contact, he traces my slit with his fingertip and groans.

"You're already so fucking soaked. I've been dreaming about you since the first time you sat across from me in my office," he softly says. "I thought about bending you right over that desk and fucking the attitude out of you. I once told you to choose Hell or me. Well, baby...welcome to both." I let out a moan, rubbing myself against him.

"*Aiden,*" I beg. I don't even know what I'm begging for. I just need a release.

I just need him.

He presses his fingers against me, moving them in a deliciously slow motion. "Tell me what you want," he demands in my ear. He uses his other hand to roll my nipples causing my body to tighten.

I'm already on edge. So close to my release and he has barely touched me. The power this man has over my body.

"Tell me what you want, Joy," he repeats, his hands continuing the motion and driving me insane. I need him inside me as much as I need my *next breath.*

I pant and squeeze my eyes shut from the pleasure. "I want you, Aiden," I moan.

He yanks my panties off and a gasp escapes my lips from the unexpected action. His hands leave me, and I moan in protest. I open my eyes to see as he climbs in the bed, moving between my legs until I can feel how hard he is.

Once he centers himself, he asks, "You want me to do what, baby?"

I huff in annoyance. "I already told you." Now is not the time for a pop quiz for fuck's sake. I need a release, or I might start crying.

Aiden smirks, climbing off me. He places his hands under my knees and lifts my hips up to his face. Then his mouth is on me. My legs jerk from the pleasure, and I can't control myself. I start panting and wiggling to get away from him. But at the same time, I do not want him to stop. He is not just eating me out. He's sucking, licking, *feasting* on me like he has been starving for months. He plunges two fingers in me while he sucks hard on my clit. Right as I am about to find my release, he stops.

He *fucking* stops.

He looks up to me, his hair falling over his forehead, making him look so incredibly sexy. He climbs on top of me, positioning himself, then he slowly slides in. Stretching me. Filling me. I open my mouth, but no sounds come out. A few seconds later and I realize he hasn't moved. He places his hand around my throat and squeezes a little.

"I asked you before, Ms. Parker. *What do you want?*" he demands softly.

Finally understanding what he's doing, I give him what he wants. I lean forward so my lips are to his ear and whisper, "I want you to fuck me, Aiden."

He licks his lips. "Good girl."

Then, he slams into me. He gives me no time to catch my breath before he's pounding into me. Every thrust hitting that sweet spot deep inside me. I close my eyes; it's all too much.

He stops thrusting, and I feel his hand at my throat again.

"Open your eyes. I want you to watch me fuck you. I want you to see what you do to me."

Oh, my gawd.

I open my eyes and gaze into his. He begins thrusting again. This time, harder. Faster. I didn't think it was possible to go faster than he already was. His hips roll, his eyes never leaving mine.

"That's it, baby," he rasps. I whimper in response. His hand on my throat squeezes as he feels me begin to shake.

He brings his lips to my ear. "Don't come yet." I clench my hands in the sheets, my whole body tightening as I try to follow his command.

I pant, "But I—" his hand squeezes at my throat again and I get the message. *Don't come yet.* He brings his lips down to mine and devours my mouth, his other hand going down to my clit. My body begins to tremble, my legs squirming with the need for a release.

"Fuck," he groans, shifting his hips as he grinds into me, my body trembling with every thrust.

I moan out, "I *have* to come." I really can't control it any longer. I can't fight against my body's reaction to him. From the minute he touched me, I was undone.

He whispers against my mouth, "Not until I say so, baby." He is thrusting into me with a merciless rhythm.

"*Aiden,*" I gasp. My head is spinning. What he wants is impossible. I can't hold on.

I can't.

I try to hold on for a few more thrusts, but my body has other thoughts. I tremble and let out a silent moan against his mouth. My back arches and I swear—*this is the hardest I've ever come in my life.*

Too quick for me to realize what's happening, I'm flipped onto my stomach and my hips are pulled up. I gasp when I feel a sting in one ass cheek, and then another. I let out a groan of pain and pleasure. I fall forward into the bed from being too weak to hold myself up. He spanks my ass four more times. Every slap makes me quiver.

He rubs my spanked cheeks and growls, "Why don't you ever do as you're told?"

Too out of it to even speak, I let out a soft, pleading moan. I feel him pressed against me from behind, his tip rubbing against my slit. His hand goes around my throat, and he pulls me up until I'm on my hands and knees.

He leans over me; his lips drag up my throat to my ear. He whispers, his voice a raspy growl, "You shouldn't have done that, baby."

I squirm, eager for whatever punishment he's ready to give me. My reply is shaky, but I want to goad him. My voice still bears a hint of attitude. "I *told* you I couldn't—"

He slams into me, and I cry out. He starts to feverishly thrust into me, still holding my throat.

"Don't stop... oh my... please," I beg. Over and over again. His hand at my throat tightens causing my vision to get blurry as I revel in the pleasure of him, doing my best to stave off the build towards another release.

It's too much for me. I can't. With every thrust, I can feel him pressing against my already sore ass. I didn't think I would come again, not this quickly, but it's building up. *Fast.* If he tells me to hold on again, I might die.

Aiden's breath fans across my neck. His breaths are heavy. "This time baby, you come *with* me," he orders into my ear. A shiver shoots through my body at his words.

"Yes," I breathe, he could ask me to do anything at this point and I would agree. I'm too focused on trying not to black out from the pleasure. His hand wrapped around my throat loosens, leaving me gasping for air.

"Who's fucking you, baby?" he growls.

"*You*," I cry out as he thrusts into me with a merciless rhythm.

"Who?" he demands.

"*Aiden*," I moan.

"And who's about to make you come?" he demands again.

"*Aiden*," I cry out again. My voice trembles, completely at his mercy. He wants me to say his name? I will say it. I will scream it. Just don't *stop*.

"That's right." He slaps my ass hard, causing me to gasp from the sharp pain. With a strangled growl, he commands, "Now."

Aiden fully buries himself in me and lets out a groan with his release, emptying himself inside of me. Hearing his release, feeling it inside of me, I let out a cry as I let go too, gripping the sheets tightly. I fall forward, flat onto the bed. Aiden falls forward with me but catches himself before he crushes me. The only noise is the sound of us trying to catch our breath.

After a minute, Aiden moves off me and walks in the direction of the bathroom. When he comes back out, he drags his hand gently up my leg, massaging me as he goes. "Turn on your back and spread your legs for me." Oh god, I can't go again. I will pass out.

Seeing I'm not moving, he says, "Joy, baby." With a groan I turn over and open my legs for him. *Oh, thank goodness.* He just has a washcloth. He gently wipes me, kissing my thighs as he does it. When he's done, he tosses it in my laundry basket and climbs into bed next to me. I move to get up and he grabs my hand.

"Where are you going?" he gently demands.

"I need my head scarf. It's in the bathroom," I tiredly mumble, closing my eyes.

He pecks my hand with a kiss. "Lay down. I'll get it."

My stomach does a little flip flop. I didn't know men like him existed. Aiden gets out of bed and quickly goes in and out of the bathroom. He climbs back into bed and places my head scarf on my head. He pulls me towards him and kisses me on the forehead. He rubs my back as I run my fingers through his hair. We don't say a single word. We just fall asleep embracing each other.

I sigh awake and smile, pleasantly sore and remembering last night. I reach my arm out to my side and feel the bed is empty. A humorless chuckle escapes my throat. I see men dead or alive, still like to pull a hit and run. *Well, fuck that.*

I push up from the bed, letting the blanket drop from my chest. Just as I am about to climb out of bed, the bedroom door opens. In walks the man himself, dressed in a t-shirt and sweats... with breakfast and a mimosa.

Aiden stops at the end of the bed and squints his eyes. "How do you already look angry when you just woke up?"

I bite my lip then reply, "I thought you left and were going to give me crap about it all being a mistake."

He chuckles and raises a brow. "A mistake? Baby, I was there. That was most definitely not a mistake," he says, as he ogles my bare chest. He shakes his head as if trying to get himself to focus.

He continues, "But we *should* talk. After you eat, though." He hands me the plate and places the mimosa on the bedside table.

I look at him. "What about you? Aren't you going to eat?"

He takes off his shirt and climbs into bed. "I made an omelet for me and ate it before I cooked yours, to give you more time to sleep. You've been working long hours." He tips his chin towards my plate. "Eat."

I begin eating the bacon, eggs, and avocado toast he prepared. It is absolutely delicious. I know it's a simple meal, but it tastes better knowing he made it for me.

Anxious about what he wants to talk about, I devour the food in three minutes and sip on my mimosa.

Satisfied, I place the plate on the side table and move to lay my head on his chest.

"What do you want to talk about?" I ask as I draw circles on his skin, under his shirt.

"Us," he says hesitantly. I go still at his words. "You will leave at the end of your contract. I think we should either keep this casual or end it."

Shocked, I ask, "Was it just sex for you?"

He shakes his head. "No. I definitely feel something more for you but... you will leave, and I don't think we could handle it if we caught any more feelings for each other. That's why I'm setting the boundaries now."

I can understand where he's coming from. I'm not a reaper. I will not have a choice but to go to Heaven once the contract is up.

I nod in agreement with him. "Okay, I think we can keep it casual. No expectations."

He looks at me for a second, before he nods. "Alright. Now that we got that out of the way," he says as runs his eyes over my chest again, his hand moving down my stomach. "How about you open wide and feed me breakfast again."

And I do. I do open wide, and I let him have his second breakfast.

Boy is he hungry.

17
"I WOULD NEVER TELL A LIE."
– A LYING LAWYER

I AM AWAKENED by the banging at the front door. I groan and move my forehead from Aiden's chest to look at the time on the bedside table. It is a quarter past six. I shove at Aiden's chest to wake him up so he can get the door, but he does not budge an inch.

"Aiden. Get the door," I mumble. He lets a frustrated breath slip through his lips. He kisses my forehead then climbs out of bed, grabbing his pants from the floor. I close my eyes, forcing myself to drift back into the dream of meeting Tupac. His smile does it for me every time. I hope I can see him in Heaven when it's my time.

I hear Aiden open the door. At the sound of feet pounding against the floor, my eyes pop open to see Yirah standing at the bedroom door, shock written all over her face. She is dressed for work, in her emerald suit with her signature gold jewelry.

"Why did a shirtless Aiden just answer the door?" She pauses and squints her eyes. "And why are you in his bed naked?"

"Yirah. It's six in the morning. Why are you here?" My tone is even, my voice dry. It's way too early for me to be having a conversation.

She ignores me and gasps. "Are you cheating on me?" Aiden walks past her and lays back in the bed, pulling the covers over himself to get comfortable.

"Is it cheating if she was never with you?" Aiden asks her, closing his eyes. I poke him on the side as a warning. He knows he's getting her riled up. A faint smile forms on his face.

Yirah grabs her chest dramatically and leans against the door frame. "I'll never forgive you, Joyce."

I roll my eyes. "*Oh, shut up.* You were pushing for this to happen since day one."

Still holding her chest, she hangs her head in defeat. "Doesn't mean it hurts any less."

I sit up, holding the covers to my chest. I lean over the bed and grab Aiden's shirt. I pull it over my head then climb out of bed and head into the bathroom to brush my teeth with Yirah on my heels. If she is here this early, there must be something wrong.

"Yirah, babe. Why are you here?" I pick up my toothbrush, wet it, put on the toothpaste, then wet it again. Because only psychopaths put toothpaste on a dry toothbrush.

As if a light bulb went off, she says, "Oh yeah! The whole Eden system is down. We need all hands on-deck. I know today is your day off, but Director Taevian needs you to discuss with the reapers the do's and don'ts of their departments to avoid any possible violations of the RCC."

"How am I supposed to know?"

"You are the only one familiar with this new Reaper's Court." She leans in and whispers, "Everyone is worried about ending up like Aiden."

I pause brushing my teeth and reply dryly, "Well, they need to relax and worry about themselves. Not Aiden."

"Wow. You really aren't a morning per—" She is cut off by the sound of her phone ringing.

She pulls it out of her purse and answers, "Hello, Director Young?" I finish rinsing my mouth and begin to wash my face.

"Yes. I can let her know. Okay. Goodbye." She ends the call then says to me, "Seems as though every department wants you to brief them on how to approach this in order to avoid going to Reaper's Court."

I pause from washing my face to give her a look of exasperation. "Why doesn't Reaper's Court brief everyone on how to avoid going to Reaper's Court. You would think this is the first time this has ever happened."

"Actually, yes. It is. Since Eden has existed, this has never happened. Everyone wants to get the job done, but we rely on technology to do it. A lot of the reapers are new, so they aren't familiar with how things used to work. Also, Reaper's Court is packed with cases, and we have no reapers to spare. So, it's you."

No wonder they are all freaking out. There has yet to be a boring day since I've arrived. First, Aiden is accused of breaking the RCC. Then, souls are released from Hell. If it couldn't get any worse, someone breaks into my apartment and steals all my materials for Aiden's case. Now, the whole Eden system is down. Something is not right here. Sure, it could be all a coincidence. But four coincidences? This is becoming a pattern. But what would be the motive behind all of this? Destroy Eden? And then what? That would be the stupidest plan in the world, with zero benefits. I haven't mentioned any of this to Aiden yet, because I have no solid leads. To him this might all sound like conspiracy.

"How long have you been a reaper?" I ask curiously, because she has never really talked about her life before Eden. I dry my face and do my skin care routine.

"Oh, you know. It's been a while. I don't even remember the year at this point. I lost count after twenty," she replies. Damn, she's way older than me. If she lost count after twenty, who knows how long she's been a reaper. But it's also interesting that she cannot remember the year she was born. Who forgets their birthday? I table that thought. I'll push her for answers on her age on a later day.

Using this opportunity to learn more about her, I ask, "How did you pass away? If you don't mind me asking of course."

She grips the bathroom counter, and her eyes lower in sorrow. She replies softly, "Someone I love betrayed me." She said love in present tense, meaning she still has those feelings for them. Hopefully, one day she trusts me to share.

I place my hand on top of her hand gripping the counter. "I'm so sorry, Yirah."

"It happened. All we can ever do is move forward." She smiles brightly at me, her eyes telling a different story.

"So, I need to brief every department?" I ask, changing the topic. I don't want to push on what seems like a touchy topic.

I take off my head scarf and part my braids down the

middle. I thank God every day that my hair is braided. Once I get to Heaven, my first request is braids that last forever.

"Yes. They are waiting on you before they continue their duties with the system down," she says as she fixes her hair and touches up her lipstick.

I nod. "Oh alright. I'll get dressed and start with the Collection department."

"Quickly please. People are dying. Souls aren't being collected or processed. The whole order of everything can collapse."

I roll my eyes at her dramatics. "I said alright. I'll meet you at my office." She winks at me, then disappears.

I walk into my closet, quickly get dressed, then head over to the bed where Aiden is asleep and tap his forehead.

"Aiden," I whisper. He opens his eyes, blinking away the sleep. He wraps an arm around me and pulls me down on top of him. I lean back to look at his face, into his dark brown eyes. His hair is wild, with some strands laying on his forehead.

"Why are you dressed?" he asks softly. My belly does a little flip. His morning voice is the smoothest, sexiest sound I've ever heard.

"All the systems are down in Eden, so I have to go talk to all the departments about how to avoid ending up in Reaper's Court," I tell him as I run my hands through his hair, moving it from his eyes.

He arches one of his eyebrows in question. "What happened?"

I climb off him and grab my bag. I walk over to the door, leaning against the door frame.

"I don't have time to explain. I need to get to the office. Meet me there when you can, okay?"

"Okay, baby," Aiden replies as he places one of his arms behind his head, causing his muscles to flex and giving me a clear view of his chest. I feel my heartbeat, but not in my chest. I shake my head to get me out of the trance.

"Stop doing that," I demand.

"What?"

"*Looking* like that," I grumble.

"Like what?" he says as he pulls the covers slightly down, giving me the clearest view of his v-line. I bite my lip as I run my eyes over him. I shake my head again then cover my eyes with my hand. I back away slowly, then turn and run out of the room.

"Don't do anything stupid!" he yells after me.

"I won't!" I yell back as I exit the apartment.

When I get to the office, I am smiling like a goofball. But the smile is wiped right off my face as soon as I see the number of reapers in my office and lingering outside.

I ignore the reapers as I walk to my desk, quickly taking a seat and typing up some of the basic information they should keep in mind. When I am done, I hit print just as Yirah pops up beside me and arches her brow in question.

"How do you want to do this and how can I help?" she asks. I honestly don't know what I would do without her.

I take a deep breath, turn to her, and say, "Have everyone exit except for the Collection department. I'll start with them because they are the most important right now." I pause in thought. "Then, send in the other departments in the order that you think is best."

Yirah salutes me. "Ma'am, yes, ma'am."

She turns to the room and yells, "Everyone! May I get your attention please!" The conversations stop, and they all turn to look at her.

Yirah continues, "All departments except for the Collection department need to exit the premises and wait in the hallway for your turn." She points to the door. All the other reapers grumpily exit the room, leaving only the Collection department reapers. I look at everyone, and see Joey and Director Taevian talking.

I walk over to the printer and pick up the stack of papers. I clear my throat to get everyone's attention.

Holding up the papers, I say, "I printed out a basic guideline that you can follow to ensure your compliance with the Reaper's Code of Conduct. This paper also includes steps you should take in the event that you do not know what to do." I pass out the papers and they all take a second to read over it.

Director Taevian smiles. "This is wonderful, Joyce."

I smile back and reply, "Thank you." I continue to speak to the others. "For your specific department, I think the best thing to keep in mind is that extra due diligence is required. You all are the bridge between Eden and the Living World. It is of utmost importance that you all triple check the souls you are assigning death and the souls you are collecting. Got it?"

"Got it," they all reply at the same time.

"I hope we aren't taking too much of your attention away from Aiden's case," Joey says.

"Of course not. I have Aiden's case handled."

Joey's eyebrow raises. "You think you will get him off all charges? I'm impressed. I know you were a little behind due to the events in your apartment." How does he know that? Oh wait, Aiden probably told him.

"I'm not at liberty to say, but I was a pretty good lawyer when I was alive." I wink at him. He grins back at me, but doesn't say anything else, which is good because I cannot reveal anything from Aiden's case.

All the Collection reapers file out of my office and Yirah calls in the next department. I go through each department, giving them the papers and explaining to them what they need to keep in mind for each department.

Once I'm done, I fall into my chair with a breath of relief. I am about to pick up my phone to ask Aiden where he is, when Joey walks into my office.

"Hi, Joey."

He sits in the chair in front of my desk and positions himself comfortably.

"I just got back from doing a lot of collections, but we are still a little backed up." He leans forward, a sly grin comes on his face. "I know you helped Aiden collect those missing souls. Since you got the experience, do you want to come and help me?"

"I, uh, don't want to cause any issues."

He waves dismissively. "You'll be with me, plus we need all hands-on deck, and we are down a reaper since Aiden cannot help during his trial."

"I'm not sure—"

"As your friend, I'm telling you that you need to get out of this office. Get some fresh air. Some new experiences before you go to Heaven."

I contemplate his offer for a second. He taps his watch as a signal that we have to go soon.

Hm.

I'm a grown woman. I can make solid decisions. Why not play reaper for just a little longer?

I give in with a sigh. "Why the hell not? Let's do it." I jump up from my chair and walk over to him, placing my hand on his shoulder. He teleports us in the middle of a rundown neighborhood.

"Okay, Joyce, you are going to collect Mr. Thomas Johnson. He just died a minute ago. I texted you his location." He points in the general direction of where I should go. "Once you get him, meet me here. The soul I am collecting is in the opposite direction."

"I don't need a scythe?"

"You shouldn't. The report didn't show him to be hostile," he says. "You'll just need to bring him over here and we will bring them to Eden."

I nod. "Got it."

Joey smiles. "You'll do great. Let's go collect some souls." We head in opposite directions as my phone rings in my back pocket. I pull it out and check it before answering.

"Hey."

"Everything okay over there?" Aiden asks.

I nervously glance around my surroundings and bite my lip. "I am still working with all the reapers and completing paperwork."

"Alright, baby. I'll be in the office in an hour to bring you food. I don't want to distract you."

"Okay. I'll see you—"

A car speeds past me, honking its horn loudly.

"What was that?"

"Uh-Nothing! Sorry, gotta go!"

I click the end button and look at the address on my phone. I need to do this quickly before Aiden comes searching for me. My destination ends up being a run-down house. This house must have been gorgeous in its early days. I walk up the steps and look around, not knowing what to do next. Should I knock on the door? Seems a little contradictory.

Hello, may I enter your house? Oh, by the way, I'm here to collect your soul whether you want to come or not.

I decide to knock. The door opens to the last person I ever thought I would see again. Involuntarily, my jaw slackens, my palms become clammy, and my breath quickens.

The soul clenches his jaw. "Joyce Parker?" he hisses. "I thought I killed you."

18

STRAIGHT TO HELL. NO PIT STOPS.

"Mr. Reynolds?" I mumble, still in shock.

He points an accusing finger at me. "How are you here?"

I stare at him. His attire finally registers in my brain. He is wearing a tan button-up shirt and pants. This man was supposed to be in jail.

I narrow my eyes. "Why are you here?" I shoot back.

He shrugs. "I got stabbed in prison. I guess I'm dead. Why are you here? Are *you* Death now?" The system must've messed up the names of the souls. I would never agree to collect the soul of this asshole.

"No. I'm not Death. I am temporarily working for the afterworld and helping with the collection of souls. I'm here to collect your soul."

"No," he states. *No?* He says that as if it is voluntarily. I can see why Aiden thought I was ridiculous.

I sigh. "Listen. You and I both know you have to come with me."

He crosses his arms and taps his foot. "Only if you

promise I get to go to Heaven," he demands. I let out a short laugh. The audacity of this man to demand anything. If I can't get into Heaven, he sure as heck is not getting in.

"What are you smoking? You not only killed your employee, but you also killed me. You are going straight to Hell, buddy. No pit stops."

"Over my dead body," he replies.

I gesture to him. "Newsflash. You're already dead and gone."

He smirks. "Want to see what I can do?"

Before I can reply, Mr. Reynolds disappears from my sight. I look around, searching for where he could have gone but I find nothing. I exit the house and search around the grounds.

"Fuck," I mutter. I already messed up and it's only five minutes of me trying to be a reaper. I have no idea how I am going to get him to Eden without a scythe. Hopefully, Joey comes searching for me soon.

I hear a whistle in the air, then feel something slam against my back. I fall forward onto the ground, the wind being knocked out of me. I roll off my stomach onto my back. Before I can get up, he steps on my stomach and raises a sharp broken bottle.

"You're the reason I died in prison," he accuses.

My eyebrows fly up. "Me? What type of backwards logic do you work off?" Last time I checked, I haven't committed murder. If I could, I would start with this insolent man.

Mr. Reynolds brings the bottle down to stab me, but pauses at the sound of clapping. We turn towards the sound. Standing there with a completely relaxed posture is Aiden, wearing his signature black suit and silver jewelry. His exterior does not reflect the anger that I can feel radiating off him.

"Great performance, Mr. Reynolds. But if you touch her one more time," he warns, "I'll make sure you suffer a fate worse than where you are heading."

Mr. Reynolds turns his full body to Aiden and replies, "I'm not going. I know I will be sent to Hell. I refuse!" I roll my eyes at him. He deserves whatever is coming to him. I hope it's tier three Hell.

Aiden tilts his head. "What about this situation makes you think you have a choice?"

In response to Aiden's words, Mr. Reynolds quickly turns and aims the glass bottle at my chest. I know I won't die again but it's going to hurt like a bitch. Closing my eyes, I brace for pain, but it never arrives. When I open my eyes again, I see Aiden holding him by his throat.

Aiden leans into Mr. Reynolds, his face relaxed with a hint of amusement. "I *warned* you."

He struggles against Aiden's grip. "I didn't touch her!" he yells.

Aiden's face darkens, his voice low and dangerous as he says, "You tried to stab her with a broken bottle, and you already murdered her once before. I was the one who collected her soul. I saw what you did."

Mr. Reynolds begins, "But I—" Aiden throws the soul on the ground and he lands with a grunt. Before he can make his escape, Aiden pulls out the pen sized scythe, commands it to extend, twirls it in the air and swings it through Mr. Reynolds' middle, sucking him into it.

Finally.

I need a warm bath and some wine. No more adventures for me for a while. I let out a groan in pain, then laugh. "That was insane. He was a dirty fighter, which I'm not surprised about." I stand up and brush myself off. I am banged up, but not too badly.

I look at Aiden and immediately stop laughing. His eyes are piercing into mine. Nothing in his demeanor reveals how he feels, but his eyes can't hide it. There is fury burning from them.

"Aiden—" I say hesitantly.

He raises a hand, silencing me. I bite my tongue to stop myself from dishing out attitude. He crooks a finger at me. Wary of his motives, I slowly walk over until I am five steps away.

"Closer," he bites out. I move until I'm one step away. He wraps a hand around my nape and closes the distance between us. In the next second, we are in his apartment.

I try to step away, but his grip tightens. "You lied to me about what you were doing today," he states, his gaze boring into mine.

I purse my lips. "I didn't lie."

Knowing very well that I did in fact lie. But it's only because he would have worried for no reason. I guess now it wasn't for no reason since I almost got my ass handed to me by a murderous soul.

His eyes narrow. "You omitted the truth. Same fucking thing," he says with a sharp tone. "Why would you go to collect a soul without telling me?"

I yank my head away from him and take a couple of steps away before I fire back, "First, I don't have to tell you anything. Second, let me help you pull that stick out your—"

He takes three big steps in my direction and I quickly back away. He continues to stalk towards me until I run into the wall. He places his arms on the wall on either side of me, trapping me in.

"That's where you're wrong, Joy. I don't know what you think is going on between us. But let me make myself crystal clear..." He leans down, forcing me to make eye contact with him. "For as long as you are here, you're mine. Every single inch. I don't like getting to the office and not finding you there. I especially don't like finding out you were trying to collect the soul of a murderer. A murderer who is the reason you died."

"It's not like I can die again. I was trying to—"

"I'm. Not. Done," Aiden bites out. He uses one hand to gently grab my face. He touches the cut above my eyebrow. "And I really fucking hate seeing you hurt." His hand slides down over my stomach to my pants where he possessively cups me, pressing into me. This maneuver causes a tremor to run through me and directly to the area between my legs. Instantly, I'm soaking.

He leans down and I feel his breath by my ear. Softly, he whispers, "I think you owe me."

"Owe you for *what?*" I sputter. I shove him and he backs up a couple of feet. Knowing he is way stronger than me, I figure he let me push him away. I start to inch closer to the door of his apartment. He notices and smirks, starting to unbutton his shirt.

He glares at me. "For my pain and suffering of having to not only save you, but having to deal with your attitude afterwards."

"Nuh-uh," I say as I shake my head, still moving away.

"You owe me for representing you in Reaper's Court. Do you know how many sleepless nights I've had over this case?"

He arches a brow as he removes his shirt and goes to unbutton his jeans. "You're about to have another one," he declares. The amount of sex I've had since meeting Aiden should be illegal.

"Aiden..." I say, licking my lips at the sight of him.

He gives me a half grin as he removes his pants and boxers. My breathing gets harder, but I continue to slowly back away towards the door of his apartment. I start to turn but he's faster. He appears in front of me and roughly pushes me against the wall, my back pressing against his front.

He leans back a little to yank my blouse off me and undo my bra. He presses a hand to my back to keep me still while he takes off my pants and panties. Once I'm completely naked, he takes a step back.

"Turn around," he orders. I turn to face him. "On your knees." I open my mouth to protest, but he cuts me off.

"I didn't say for you to open your mouth and give me attitude. I said, get on your knees." He runs his hand down my back and roughly grabs my ass, hinting at what's next to come if I choose wrong. "Your choice, baby," he warns.

Aiden and these damn ultimatums. First, it was *be my lawyer or you're going to Hell*. Now, it's *get on your knees or you aren't getting off*. Knowing Aiden, he means what he says.

I slowly drop to my knees, defiance written all over my face. He wraps his hands in my hair and yanks my head back as he guides his tip to my lips.

"Open for me, baby," he says. I narrow my eyes. He wraps his hand around my throat, squeezing tightly. I gasp for air, and he uses that moment as his opening to slide inside. I moan at the size of him in my mouth, then I suck and slowly lick him with my tongue, taking the time to drive him insane like he does to me. I hear him groan and I smile as I look up to him to see he is already looking down.

"Stop messing with me and suck me like you owe me," he orders roughly. I ignore him and continue to tease him with my slow pace, slowly rolling my tongue over his tip. I wrap a hand around him, moving it in a rhythmic motion. Annoyed with my antics, his hand in my hair tightens and he takes over the pace. His thrusts quicken and I moan, enjoying it a lot. I feel myself getting wet and I move a hand down to touch myself.

Aiden pauses his thrusts and says, "Look at me." I look up to him to see his eyes filled with pleasure and strands of his hair over his forehead.

"Don't touch what's mine," he orders softly. "I'll get to you when you fulfill your debt. Nod your head if you get me." I nod my head slowly as he uses his other hand to rub my cheek.

"Beautiful," he whispers. He starts to thrust again and I take him in my mouth just like he wants. I feel myself begin to build up, but I don't touch myself. I'm doing exactly what he wants.

His speed picks up. I moan realizing I'm about to come from just having him in my mouth. Just as I am about to be pushed over the edge, he pulls out. I let out a cry of protest, but before I can do anything about it, he drops to the ground and flips me, so I am on my hands and knees.

He guides himself between my wet slit and slams into me.

I immediately come with a bitten back scream. Without a chance to recover, he fucks me. On the hard floor. In the middle of his living room. He goes faster and harder, every thrust deeper than the last. He stops, withdraws, and flips me onto my back, then continues to thrust into me, lifting my legs over his shoulders to get into me as far as he can.

"I want your mouth," he says as he leans down and kisses me, devouring my mouth.

He draws back, swiping his tongue along my lower lip. "My sweet, sweet Joy. Are you going to lie to me again?"

At my hesitation he stops and completely pulls out of me. I cry out in frustration. He collars my throat with one hand and runs his other hand between my slit.

He squeezes my throat. "I asked you a question, baby. Are you going to fucking lie again?"

I smirk. "And if I do?" The probability of me lying again is high.

He chuckles and roughly pulls me closer to him with the hand at my throat. "I know every line, curve, dip, and sensitive spot on your body. I know exactly how to drive you crazy."

He proceeds to prove his point. Two fingers drag along the swollen lips of my pussy. He traps my clit between his fingers and gently squeezes.

"*Aiden, please,*" I moan.

The hand around my throat tightens. "Don't speak unless you are giving an answer." He thrusts his fingers inside and I begin to pant as he curves his finger, hitting that delicious spot with every brutal thrust. I clamp around his fingers as I feel myself about to come. But before I can, he pulls his fingers out. I let out a scream of frustration.

He runs his thumb over my bottom lip. "That greedy pussy. Too bad you don't listen. Have you had enough?"

I let out a sob in response. Pleading him with my eyes to let me find my release.

"Then answer my fucking question. Are. You. Going. To. Lie. Again?" he bites out.

"No."

"That's my Joy," he whispers, then he lines his cock to my opening and slams in. *Deep.* He furiously powers into me, every thrust filling and stretching me.

He gives one last command, "Come," and I explode, gasping for air. He buries himself inside of me and comes, too. When his orgasm leaves him, he lifts me off the floor and carries me to his room. He lays me in the bed, then settles down next to me and wraps me in his protective arms, spooning me. He pulls the cover over us and lets out a deep sigh of contentment.

"Don't do that again, Joyce," he says softly.

I nod and reply, "I won't." He kisses my shoulder then relaxes.

I get it. He was worried. I don't blame him. I put on a brave face earlier, but I was scared at that moment. But Aiden came and helped me. I hear his breathing even out, signaling he is asleep.

Before I close my eyes, I whisper, "For the first time, I feel completely safe and it's because of you."

What I didn't know as I fell asleep was that Aiden was wide awake.

I open my eyes and blink away the sleep. My head hurts less from yesterday's event, but it still hurts. It is times like these that it wouldn't suck to be a reaper, so that I didn't have to feel pain for this long. I turn my head towards where Aiden should have been asleep. I place my hand on his side and feel that it is slightly warm. He must've just gotten up.

I roll out of bed, grab one of his t-shirts from a drawer and throw it on. I go to the bathroom to take care of my business then walk towards the bedroom door. As I am opening it, I hear two voices. Both men. After listening for a couple of seconds, I discern that one is Aiden and the other is Joey. I slowly try to close the door to not intrude, but my ears perk up at the sound of my name.

"If you ever put Joyce in danger like that again, I'll kill you again my fucking self," Aiden warns. He is probably very serious too.

I hear Joey sigh. "The system shutting down made it to where we didn't have all the information. I didn't know he was a murderer, Aiden. I especially did not know he was the one who murdered, Joyce. I really would never put her in danger like that on purpose. I'll have to apologize to her when I see her."

There's a pause. "You still shouldn't have taken her with you without telling me."

I can almost hear Joey roll his eyes as he says, "She's your lawyer and you barely like her. She can do as she pleases, Aiden. What is your issue? You're never this strung up over anybody, especially not a woman."

Aiden calmly explains, "I already told you, Joey. Joyce doesn't leave Eden without me at least knowing, and she sure as hell doesn't collect souls. You know how dangerous it can get. I doubt it would be good for me if my lawyer goes missing or suffers to where she can't work."

"That makes sense." He pauses. "I'm sorry, bro. I just thought she may have wanted a break from Eden and a change of pace. I really fucked up." He is right. I really did want a change of pace. It can get very slow at Eden sometimes.

A couple of seconds go by and Aiden sighs. "Alright. We're good."

"You up to go get some drinks after work?" Joey asks.

"Nah, I've been tired lately. The trial and paperwork really take a toll on me."

"Yeah, me too, buddy," I whisper to myself. But that's not the real reason why he's tired. My body needs a week-long vacation, at least. Especially after last night. Hardwood floors are not the most comfortable to kneel on.

"Okay, I'll see if Yirah and Joyce want to come," Joey says in response.

"I recall Joyce telling me that she was spending tonight resting after work," Aiden informs him despite the fact that I'm pretty sure I never told him that.

"How do you go from barely standing her, to having her schedule memorized? It seems as though you might be warming up to her," Joey says.

Aiden lets out a breath and replies sarcastically, "I'm not warming up to her. You can ask her yourself about her schedule. At least I warned you."

"I will. Let me know if you change your mind, though." Joey pauses and chuckles. "But if both you and Joyce cannot make it, maybe I can get some alone time with Yirah. I'm surprised I haven't ran into her before Joyce got here."

Aiden chuckles. "You like Yirah?"

"I wouldn't say like her...more like looking at the possibility of what could come from being alone with her," Joey clarifies.

I roll my eyes. You would think men would be a little different after death but no. They all still think with their dicks.

"Joyce will destroy you if you hurt Yirah. Just think you should know," Aiden warns him. He's right. I will find some way to ruin his afterlife. I need to pencil in a friend date with Yirah to debrief her on this. If she's interested, then we have to play this right. If she's not, then we have to kick him to the curb.

I hear them briefly do that pat on the back thing that men do as a goodbye. Why wouldn't Aiden just tell his best friend about us? Yirah knows. I hear the front door close, and I rush back to bed, pulling the covers over me. Aiden walks into the room and slides into the bed, pulling me close to him so that my back is to his front.

I feel his face in my neck and he chuckles in my ear. "I can smell toothpaste, Joy. You also took off your head scarf and have a shirt on. I'm fairly certain I left you here naked."

Damn it.

I forgot I did that. I stick to ignorance though and refuse to open my eyes. He slowly runs his hand down my arm to my stomach. I try to keep my breathing even, but I am failing miserably. Aiden rubs his fingers in a circular motion on my stomach then he stops. I think he is going to lower his hand, but I am painfully wrong. He chooses this moment to do a sneak attack when I'm at my most vulnerable. His fingers begin to tickle me, and I squirm like crazy, giggling and begging him to let me go.

"*Stop!*" I screech in between my giggling, but he does not show an ounce of mercy. He climbs on top of me, straddling me, and begins to attack my armpits.

"Aiden! Oh my god!" I try to buck him off me with my hips, but he doesn't move an inch.

"This is what you get for fake sleeping," he says with a huge grin on his face.

"You're so mean," I pout. "You know I'm extremely ticklish."

"I know. It's my new secret weapon to get you to listen to me," he jokes.

"I heard Joey out there," I share. I prefer to not hold things in for too long. I might as well rip off the Band-Aid, rather than let it lay there.

"Ah, you were eavesdropping," he replies to me. He rolls to his back, bringing me with him so that I am now straddling him. I adjust myself on his lap so that I am comfortable.

"No. You both were talking too loudly. I had no option but to hear what was being said," I explain. If I had closed the door, I probably wouldn't have been able to hear them.

Aiden arches an eyebrow. "Well, then you heard that he's going to ask you and Yirah out for drinks."

I nod. "Yes. I also heard you tell him I was going to be busy."

"Because you are going to be busy. With me."

I roll my eyes. "I can't be with you all the time."

He tilts his head in confusion and tightens his hold on my hips. "Says who?"

"Well...me."

His grip loosens and he gives me a lazy grin. "Oh, if that's the case, then I most definitely can be with you all the time," he states.

I decide to leave it alone. Aiden and I can go back and forth all day if we wanted to. I want to get to the part that bothered me.

"I also heard you tell Joey that you aren't warming up to me." I tilt my head. "Why wouldn't you just tell your best friend about us? Yirah knows about us."

"Because, my Joy," Aiden explains, "he tends to let things slip out by accident. I don't want him accidentally mentioning something to Director Taevian. You know how he can be. Also, I haven't told Joey about anything dealing with my case. He can find out like everyone else. I don't want anything or anyone distracting you. Unless, it's me, of course."

I think for a couple of seconds. It would overcomplicate things, and we *are* trying to keep it casual. Director Taevian finding out would only cause him to give us a big speech, at best. I would rather him not threaten my supply of champagne again.

I finally nod. "That makes sense."

"I know it does," he informs me, his mouth in a half grin.

Aiden pulls the t-shirt that I'm wearing over my head and holds it up, leaving me naked again.

"Did I give you permission to wear my shirt?" he questions.

"Um," I mumble. "I don't recall exactly. But I'm sure you did at one point."

He slowly shakes head and smirks. "I didn't, baby," he informs me. He moves my braids out of the way so he can have a clear view of my chest. I move my hands to cover myself, but he stops them.

"Let me show you how you can earn the privilege of wearing my shirt."

He doesn't wait for a reply as flips me on my stomach and places a pillow under me. He proceeds to show me exactly how to earn that privilege.

19
LOVING RAISINS IS A SIN

It's a couple of days later after the incident with the system shutting down. Aiden, Joey, and I are sitting on the couch in the office, eating lunch. We are betting on what famous people we think are in Hell, when the door to our office opens and an influx of reapers walk in. They are wearing beige suits, which means they are from the Reaper's Resources department. It worries me that the director of Heaven, Jia Young, is with them.

Aiden raises his eyebrows at them and begins to ask, "How can I he—"

One of the reapers turns to look at me, ignoring Aiden. "Are you Joyce Parker?" she asks, her voice filled with determination.

There aren't any other ways to phrase it, other than to say she is a very attractive woman—locs that reach past her waist and are a bright ginger color, her eyebrows the same gorgeous shade. Creamy cocoa skin with hints of tattoos peeking from under the suit.

Director Young chuckles. "Please excuse her enthusiasm.

These reapers had some concerns, so I brought them here to hash it out with you, Ms. Parker. I hope you don't mind."

"Of course not," I reply immediately, even though I do indeed mind. Everywhere I turn I see Director Young being nice, or helping someone. Doesn't it get tiring to be that nice? I heard she has never yelled at one of her reapers. I mean, Director Taevian is a nice guy, but even he gets fed up with other reapers' shit. My point is—I don't trust anyone who's too nice. I know she's the director of Heaven, but still. Too nice.

"Excellent. I will leave you all to it," she says as she smiles. She gestures to Joey. "Mr. Gomez, could I speak to you?"

Joey grabs his food. "Of course, Director Young." He winks at us and makes his exit with her. I wonder what's that about.

Aiden turns to look at me, raising an eyebrow as if asking me what I did. I press my lips together and shake my head. I am assuming since they are from the Reaper's Resources Department that they came based on a report filed. *Damn.* Everything really does come to bite you in the ass. I guess it's time I pay my dues.

I drop my head in thought, attempting to encourage myself to face my sins. I take a deep breath to prepare myself for my punishment. What was I thinking when I did what I did?

I look at the group and admit, "I know, *I know.* I shouldn't have stolen the three bottles of champagne from the staff kitchen, but it was an emergency. The bottle of champagne in my apartment broke and I—"

She shakes her head and cuts me off. "Girl, I don't care about the champagne. We need your help."

I let out the breath I was holding and laugh. "Whew. For a second there I thought I was a goner."

Aiden shakes his head. "We talked about this, Joyce. You don't have to steal things here."

I wave him off. "You talked. I pretended to listen." That's truly how most of our conversations go. He is all about the rules, while I believe they are just suggestions. Which is almost comical considering I'm a lawyer who is representing him because he may or may have not broken some rules.

In my defense, I was in dire need of a drink. I would've needed Aiden to take me to the living world to pick up a bottle, and he was busy at that moment. I made a decision that was best for me and I have no regrets.

I turn back to the reaper who I am assuming is leading the cavalry. "What's your name?"

"Valerie Pierre," she replies. I stand to shake her hand, then turn to the other five reapers and shake their hands, too.

"Please come over to my desk. I don't have enough seats for everyone, so some will have to stand," I explain. Aiden continues to eat, just watching the whole thing go down. I'm sad I can't finish my food. He picked us up some pasta from Italy. There's a lot of privileges that come with being a reaper, teleportation being a huge one.

They follow me to my desk. Valerie takes a seat along with one of the other reapers. The rest gather behind them.

I take out my notepad and pen. "What can I help you with?"

"You're the only defense attorney at Eden. They haven't recruited any others. I heard it's because no one wants to do it. Therefore, reapers have just been going into court representing themselves. But we need your help. Our case is serious."

"Are you all being charged with violating the same rule?" I ask. I guess that was the wrong question to ask, because she slaps her hands on the desk making me jump a little bit. I peek over at Aiden to see his eyes are narrowed in our direction. He looks ready to pounce at any second. He reminds me of a cute grumpy cat.

Valerie says, "We didn't break any rules! This is all those other reapers' fault." She seems to honestly believe they did nothing wrong, which would be good because it's easier to defend innocent people most times.

"Let's start from the beginning again, shall we? Why are you here?"

She takes a deep breath. "We all recently died, and our souls were collected. We all went through the same process of going to the Soul Directory. That is where we were all told we were going to be reapers, because our karma was neutral."

I nod. "Okay, what is the issue?"

"Well, now they are saying that there was a glitch in the system before we came, and we were all meant to go to Hell. They said we are being stripped of our reaper positions by tomorrow."

My eyebrows jump up. "No way is that okay."

"Exactly what I said!" she exclaims.

"You want me to get them to not remove you as a reaper?"

"Yes. That, or send us to Heaven for our service."

I shake my head. "It is doubtful that you will go to Heaven, but I may be able to help you remain as reapers."

Valerie leans forward. "Wait. So, you'll help us?" All the reapers are staring at me, hope in their eyes.

I think for a moment. I need a break from Aiden's case, and this may be the perfect excuse. But I need to know something first.

"Have any of you committed fraud, murder, assault, rape, child molestation, grand theft auto, or enjoy raisins?" I ask, my face passive as I wait for their answers. I hear Aiden chuckle in the background. Probably because of my mentioning of raisins. It's a valid question.

All the reapers look at each other in confusion and Valerie replies for the group. "No. I don't think so." But one of the reapers raises his hand nervously.

I point to him. "Yes? What's your name and your sin?"

He stammers, "I-I am Gabriel, and I enjoy raisins." I see a bead of sweat roll down his forehead. Only sinners like raisins.

I shake my head in disappointment. "There's no hope for you."

His face twists in horror. "I'm going to Hell because I enjoy *raisins?*"

I smirk. "No. But you should." Because any person who enjoys dried grapes must be evil. Why don't they just eat a normal juicy grape? Why would they dry it? Also, whose bright idea was it to put raisins in bread, or cookies? I *know* that person is in Hell for sure.

I hear Gabriel let out a breath of relief as Aiden says, "There's nothing wrong with someone who loves raisins, Joyce."

I gasp and grab my chest. I peer around the reapers to make eye contact with him. "Don't tell me you love raisins." I think my voice is shaking a little bit. This would be my breaking point. I can't sleep with someone who loves raisins. I just can't.

He shakes his head. "No, I don't. I just don't think he should be judged. You literally drink coffee then take a sip of a mimosa immediately after. Is that not weird?"

Valerie and I answer at the same time. "No." I like her. A woman with some class.

Aiden looks at Gabriel and sighs. "I'm sorry, man. I tried to help. You'll never hear the end of this." Gabriel just sadly nods, accepting his fate. He's very understanding for a sinner.

I clasp my hands as I glance at all the reapers. "Alright y'all. Let's show the Reaper's Court that everyone deserves justice."

I am printing the complaint that I drafted to turn into the Reaper's Court. I am requesting a hearing as soon as possible, or a delay in sending the glitch reapers—that's what I'm calling them—to Hell while I prepare our case.

Grabbing the stack of papers, I slide them in a yellow envelope, then walk to Aiden's desk where he is updating forms on his computer. I come up behind him and lay my chin on his shoulder, watching as he clicks away at the screen. He uses a hand to gently pat my head, the other still on the mouse.

"You good?" He asks, not pausing from his work.

I lift the envelope to show him. "Yes. I am leaving to turn in these documents to court. I'll be back shortly."

"If you wait two minutes, I'll come with you if you want."

I nod my head excitedly against his shoulder. "Yes, I would like for you to come."

He gestures to the right side of his desk. "Sit right here and I'll be done soon."

I pout. "But I like where I am." He smells delicious. I bury my nose into his neck.

He leans back and looks at me, causing my head to lose contact with him. "You're too close to me and it's causing reactions that aren't appropriate at work."

I look at his lap, then back at him. I smirk and whisper, "We can do some more things." I lean into his ear and place my hand on his thigh. "Things that aren't work appropriate."

His eyes darken. He licks his lips, causing a tingling sensation between my legs. He wraps a hand around my nape and pulls me down to him. Just as our lips brush against each other, the door to the office opens. Aiden abruptly stands causing me to fall backwards. He doesn't even try to catch me as I land on my ass. I glare up at him as he glances down at me with wide apologetic eyes.

Director Taevian walks in and we both turn to look at him. He pauses at the sight of us, his eyes squint in suspicion.

He sighs. "Why are you on the floor, Joyce? Are you two fighting again?"

Aiden looks back at me and raises an eyebrow. "Yeah, Joyce. You need to be less clumsy."

My teeth grind together as I let out an agitated breath. *Oh, he is so in the doghouse.* I stand and dust myself off.

I bore my gaze into Aiden's. "Yeah, Director Taevian, I was clumsy." I raise an eyebrow. "I can promise it *won't* happen again." I place an emphasis to ensure Aiden understands what I mean.

Director Taevian laughs. "You're adorable, Joyce. I came over to see if you're free for a chat. We could go to Paris for a cup of coffee? We haven't had much one-on-one time. I think it's time, considering I'm like your boss' boss."

I pat my chest twice. "You had me at coffee." I point to the documents on the desk. "I just have to turn in these documents to the court first." I take a couple of steps to Aiden's desk and pick up the envelope. I feel him try to grab my thigh and I flick him with my envelope. He looks up at me with puppy dog eyes, but I ignore him. My ass is still aching from the fall.

Director Taevian nods. "Ready to go?"

I walk over to him. "I sure am."

We head out the door. I peek at Aiden to see him mouthing, *'I'm sorry'*.

I flip him the middle finger as we walk out. Taevian and I turn down a hallway and almost run right into Director Young, who's wearing her signature white suit. She loses her balance, but Taevian places his hands on her shoulders to balance her.

She laughs. "Oh dear! That was a close one."

Taevian smiles and says, "That was. How are you, Director Young?"

She smiles shyly at him. "I'm doing alright. How about you?" I look down at my shoes, feeling as though I am intruding on something. Today's heels are my favorite—light pink, pointed toe and sky-high stilettos. I tend to wear more pink now since that time at the bar with Aiden.

"I'm doing well. About to head out to get coffee with Joyce. Would you like to join? Of course, only if it's okay with you Joyce."

I smile. "It's okay with me." Seems as though Director Taevian and Director Young have something going on.

"How about you, Jia?" *Oh*, first name basis I see. I think they would be cute together.

He rubs his hands together. "Perfect. Let's go." Director Young and I take his arms. We appear in an alley. Even from here, I can see the Eiffel tower. I chuckle as I remember the last time I came here. It was with Aiden. He surprised me by taking me to the top of the tower. I almost peed my pants. He just laughed the whole time.

"It's around the corner. Listen, this place has the best coffee and croissants I've ever had, and I've been to a lot of places," Taevian boasts. We walk out of the alleyway and towards the shop.

"You're sounding your age," I tease. He laughs and pats my shoulder.

"With age comes wisdom. Right, Jia?"

Director Young chuckles. "Yes. I've learned a lot in my thousand years."

I stop walking and my eyes almost pop out of my head. They turn to look at me, humor on their faces. "You're a thousand years old!" I exclaim.

"Yes, dear," she replies, a kind smile on her face. "I am the only original director still working at Eden."

"That's impressive," I reply in awe. She has lived through so many different eras. I have a million questions to ask her.

"She is impressive," Taevian says, with a fond smile. We stop in front of a cafe and walk inside. It is beautifully decorated, with a rustic vintage look to it. The scent of coffee beans and pastries bless my nose. We give our orders, then sit down.

Director Young begins, "Ms. Parker—"

"Oh, please call me Joyce," I say.

She smiles. "Joyce, how is your experience at Eden so far?" she asks curiously, taking a sip of her coffee.

"It has been amazing! I have had quite the experience here so far."

"That's good to hear. I'm glad Aiden chose you as his lawyer. You are very special. How is it working with him?"

I shrug one shoulder. "It's been alright, I guess. He's bearable," I lie. He's been more than alright. I completely and irrefutably have feelings for Aiden. What those exact feelings are—I don't know. But I do know that every time he calls me Joy, my chest tightens, and I feel as though I could burst. Every touch feels like warmth covering all my skin, like a blanket. However, I will take these feelings with me to Heaven before I ever tell him, or anyone else. He made it clear in the beginning that this was just a temporary thing. I agreed with him, but little old me had to go and catch *feelings*.

Director Taevian interjects, "Those two are always bickering and arguing. If they could kill each other, they would try." I chuckle and take a sip of my coffee. We still bicker, despite being friends. It can't be helped.

"I'm sure they are growing on each other. You know how opposites attract. Maybe they will grow feelings for each other," Director Young teases as she takes a sip of her coffee, and gives me a wink over the rim of her cup.

I choke on my coffee. Taevian pats my back and replies, "You see. Even the thought of it made her choke. I really do hope you and Aiden can become friends before you leave." Little does he know, we are way past friendship.

The three of us spend the next hour talking about my

cases, the drama at Eden, and some of the things we enjoy in the Living World.

When I walk back into our shared office, Aiden is taking a nap on the couch. I quietly walk up to him and kneel down to stare at his sleeping face. Kind of creepy, but he usually wakes up before me. I never get a chance to really look at him. He looks so peaceful with his usual frown missing from his face.

I run my finger gently across his cheek. His eyebrows slightly furrow. He blinks a couple of times then gazes upon me with those dark brown eyes I adore. His eyes light up when he realizes it's me.

I give him a quick kiss on the lips. "Mr. Kim. Are you sleeping on the job?"

He gives me a lazy grin. "I'd rather be sleeping with you," he replies, a slight rasp in his voice from waking up. Yeah, God would have been a woman if she was real.

I roll my eyes. "All you think about is sex."

"We can cuddle too." He proves his point by pulling me off the floor and on top of him on the couch.

He places a hand at my nape and pulls me down to his lips. He gently runs his tongue along the crease of my mouth. As if my mouth already knows what to do, it opens, and his tongue caresses my own. Before the kiss gets any deeper, he pulls away.

He kisses my nose and says, "There's more of that later, after I feed you."

I lay my head on his shoulder. "Actually, I was thinking of cooking."

He groans. "Reapers can still experience food poisoning. I'd rather not put my body through that."

I sit up to see his face. "Hey!" I exclaim. "My cooking isn't that bad."

He arches a brow. "Just the other day, you burned eggs. Do you know how easy it is to cook eggs? But somehow you seem to do the impossible."

"For that slick comment, you ain't getting nothing from me later." I snap my fingers. "That reminds me. You are so in the doghouse for pushing me off your lap earlier."

He runs his hand down my back and grabs my ass. "I'll bet your left-over cheesecake that I'm getting some." Does he think I can't refuse his charm? *Puh-lease.*

"You're on," I agree.

Safe to say that I lost the bet and my New York slice of cheesecake.

20

NEVER CALL SOMEONE'S GRANDMA A BITCH

TODAY IS the court day for the glitch reapers and I'm going to wrap this case up in a pretty pink bow. I glance at my watch seeing that it's almost time to head over to court. The glitch reapers should be waiting for me. I pick up my purse and walk over to Aiden's desk. He's clicking away at his computer, completely focused.

For someone who is suspended, he seems to always have work to do. I walk around his desk to get behind him. I lean down and kiss his cheek.

"I'll see you later," I whisper.

He looks up and smiles. He turns his chair and moves me so I'm standing between his thighs.

"Let me get another kiss," he replies as he leans in, pressing his lips against mine. He runs his tongue along the crease of my lips then slides his tongue in my mouth. He tastes good, so good.

He's addicting.

His hand wraps around my nape and brings me in closer. He breaks the kiss to lift me onto his desk and lay me flat on the hard, cold surface. I feel a rush between my legs. He moves his hands under my shirt and up my stomach to my bra where he yanks the cups down and curls a hand around my breast. He leans down to my neck and I feel his teeth lightly nip at the skin.

The ringing from my phone breaks the moment. I gently push Aiden's chest and yank my phone out of my purse. I look at the screen, clear my throat, and answer.

"Hello?"

"Hi, Joyce," Valerie says. "Are you on your way over?"

Aiden decides in the moment to suck my nipple into his mouth. *Roughly.* Letting me feel the edge of his teeth. My lips part and I gasp, grabbing his hair tightly. His other hand cups me possessively over my pants. He presses down and gently rubs me in a circular motion. A little breathy moan escapes my lips and I cover my mouth with my hand.

"Joyce? Are you okay?"

I take a deep breath, move my hand and reply with a strained voice. "I'm fine. I just, uh, was drinking coffee and choked on it. I'm on my way over now!" I hang up, tossing my phone on the desk before she can say another word. I use my grip on his hair to pull him up to my lips.

"Want me to take care of you before court?" he whispers against my lips.

"*Yes,*" I beg desperately. He unbuttons my pants and yanks them off. He pulls his chair closer and pulls my hips close to the edge.

He gives me a sexy grin. "Because my Joy asked so nicely."

He leans down and his mouth covers my clit. He sucks it in his mouth, while thrusting his fingers in me. My back arches off the desk and I grab the edges of the desk for support.

"*Aiden*," I moan. He removes his fingers, grabs my legs and tosses them over his shoulders. His fingers tighten around my hips. When I start to get louder, he picks up my panties from beside me and shoves them in my mouth.

"Can't have anyone hearing you," he murmurs.

I dig my heels into his back, moaning his name over and over again. He sinks his tongue in, using it to fuck me while his finger presses against my clit.

"I love how you taste. Like sweet honey," he murmurs against me before resuming his torture. I buck my hips against him as his tongue thrusts deeper, *faster*. His fingers dig into my flesh, adding pain on top of the pleasure. When he tugs my clit with his teeth, my hips jerk violently, my back arches against the desk, and I cry out in pleasure as my release washes over me.

I collapse onto the desk, stuck in a dizzying haze. My wits are absolutely gone. I catch my breath, then finally look at Aiden.

He licks his lips, then his fingers. "My Joy. Always so delicious."

Before I can find my sanity, he unbuttons his pants, dropping them to the floor. He wraps a hand around himself, stroking his already hard cock. I let out a moan as I feel myself tighten with the promise of him filling me.

He grabs my legs, throwing them over his shoulders again. I feel as he drags himself along my swollen slit. Slowly, he guides himself inside, his breaths ragged.

"You feel so fucking good," he rasps. I moan in response, gripping the desk tightly.

When he is all the way in, he wraps his hand around my throat. He gives me a half grin. "Let's see how far I can push you." Then he pulls all the way out and slams into me with such force that it causes the desk to shift.

His possessive and lustful eyes bore into me, "Take it, baby. *Take it.* I want you to walk around Eden knowing who you belong to. Who you'll always come back to." He fucks me so hard, I think we are going to break the desk. Not once does he ease up.

"*Oh God,*" I sob, the words muffled by the panties still in my mouth. His hand around my neck moves to my mouth as he covers it. Every stroke is demanding. Possessive. *Brutal.* Downright savage. The only sound is him pounding into me and his guttural breaths.

He leans down to my ear and growls, "Keep quiet before someone hears how much of a whore you are for me. Now come all over me. Now."

At his words, I come with a silent scream, my body violently shuddering. Aiden continues to fuck me like a madman.

"So fucking beautiful," he says hoarsely.

"I-I can't. It's too much," I plead, tears seeping from the corner of my eyes. I watch as he fucks me. I like it. *No.* I love it. I love that I do this to him.

"You'll take it," he says, a warning in his voice. He reaches up and pulls the panties that I forgot were in my mouth. He covers my mouth with his, his tongue plundering every part of my mouth. I feel his finger trailing up my stomach to my breasts. He gently circles his finger around my nipple, then twists and rolls it.

"Be my good girl and take care of the other one," he

commands against my mouth. I grab on to my nipple and play with it. I feel myself close to the edge, my breaths coming out in shallow pants. Aiden uses the same fingers that were at my breasts to toy with my clit. With one gentle tug, I shatter into a million pieces. He swallows my screams with his mouth as he finds his own release. I feel as he fills me up, my pussy involuntarily milking him. I close my eyes, too tired to do anything else. Aiden is still laying on top of me, both of us breathing hard. He moves off of me and I hear the rustling of him fixing himself. After a few moments, he gently yanks me to my feet. I still haven't said a word.

Aiden chuckles. "While you're recovering, I'll get you fixed up." He grabs my panties and pants and helps me step into them. For the next two minutes he adjusts my clothes.

He hands me my purse then taps my ass twice. "You're good to go, Ms. Parker."

I finally snap out of my daze. I grab his hand and say, "I may need that before every court appearance."

He kisses my forehead. "Whatever my lawyer wants, she can get."

"You honor. I can save everyone time and energy by simply explaining what a unilateral mistake is and why this contract cannot be deemed void just because the Soul Directory made a mistake and the Reaper's Resources department did not catch it," I state.

After my eventful goodbye kiss with Aiden, I finally made my way over to Reaper's Court. All the glitch reapers were waiting for me. Valerie, of course, huffed when she saw me and made a remark about lawyers needing to be on time. I winked as a reply, and she just rolled her eyes.

Opposing counsel starts, "Unilateral mistake does not apply here—"

The Judge raises her hand, effectively cutting off whatever false statement the opposing counsel was about to say. My opponent today is a reaper I have yet to meet. Before court was in session, I learned that this is her first case. I kind of feel bad for her. Losing her first case will be a blow to her pride. Maybe I'll buy her drinks later.

"Continue, Ms. Parker," the Judge instructs.

"As I was saying," I give opposing counsel a look, "when Eden entered into the contract with my clients for them to be reapers, the Soul Directory and Reaper's Resources department made the mistake. In order for the contract between Eden and my clients to be voided, opposing counsel will have to show that my clients should've known they were designated for Hell."

Opposing counsel interjects, "People usually know if they may or may not be going to Hell."

I raise a brow. "That is in no way a fact." I point to my clients. "They haven't committed fraud, murder, assault, theft, or child molestation. If they did any of those...then sure, I can see why they should have known. However, their greatest sin is loving raisins." My lip twitches as I hear the raisin loving sinner let out a sigh behind me.

To prove my point, I requested a copy of their karma. There was no one thing that shifted their karma. It was an accumulation of different things. Nothing horrible, though.

"I disagree. They should have—"

I groan in annoyance. "Listen. You don't have a valid argument. *Okay?* My clients could not have known, or should have known, they were going to Hell. They were supposed to go to tier one Hell, which means that they weren't going to be in Hell for very long anyways, before they were to be reincarnated." I pause, open my folder, and remove a paper that I retrieved from Yirah on the way here. She really is the best. "Have you read some of the things people went to tier one Hell for? It can be very random."

I wave a paper in my hand, then I look down and pick out some of the interesting sins.

I begin to read out loud, "You can go to tier one Hell for calling someone's grandma a bitch every day, road rage, never giving money to someone in need, sticking your chewed up gum under a table, skinny dipping in a restricted area, creating laws in order to control women's reproductive rights—that one is worthy of tier three hell in my opinion—"

The judge waves her gravel in the air, cutting me off. "Okay, Ms. Parker. We get it. They could not have known they were going to Hell. Opposing counsel, do you have any proof that they knew or should've known they were supposed to go to Hell?"

"Well, no—"

The judge raises her hand to silence her. "Ms. Parker, what do your clients want?"

I reply, "They are requesting to remain as reapers. When they choose to leave the position, they would like to be reincarnated."

Opposing counsel begins, "Your honor, in no way—"

The judge strikes the gravel. "Ms. Parker. The court accepts. This case is now dismissed. We got better things to do in Reaper's Court than handle a clear-cut case." The judge moves to stand.

"All rise for the Honorable Judge Williams," a reaper announces.

Everyone in the courtroom stands and waits until the judge leaves. As soon as the door closes behind her, the glitch reapers rush up and wrap around me in a group hug. They all start talking at the same time.

"You are awesome!"

"The way you started listing what people have gone to Hell for was hilarious."

"Let us treat you to drinks!"

I laugh and pat them as a signal to let go. They all take a step back.

"We really appreciate you. You didn't have to help," Valerie says, appreciation evident in her voice.

I wave my hand, all nonchalant. "It's my job as a lawyer to help people. It helped that I believed in your case, too."

"Let us treat you to drinks?" she asks again.

I look at my watch. I'm supposed to meet up with Aiden later, but I have plenty of time. Plus, I'll never say no to a drink.

I nod. "Yes. That sounds good." Everyone exits the courtroom, with Valerie and I following behind them.

She whispers, "You and Aiden are cute together."

I stumble over my feet and stop, looking at her with wide eyes. She stops too and snorts when she sees my face. She could not possibly know about Aiden and I, right?

I stutter, "W-what? Aiden and I aren't together. We are just attorney and client. That's it. We barely even like each other."

She rolls her eyes and lets out a chuckle. "Girl, if that's the story you want to go with, then sure." She begins walking again then says over her shoulder. "But just so you know, you didn't actually hang up the phone and I will never say no to free porn."

I gasp. Absolutely shocked at this information. While I am a little embarrassed, I have other concerns.

I chase after her, yelling out, "*You owe me at least a hundred dollars!*" She should at least pay me for my performance.

21
OBJECTION. RELEVANCE?

"Keep your fist up!" Aiden yells as he throws another right hook at me. I barely manage to dodge it.

"You can go a little easier on me," I snap, breathing hard. We have been sparring for an hour. I am anxious about the trial today, so Aiden suggested we release some stress. I mistakenly thought we were going to be doing a different type of workout.

There is a gym located on every residential floor in Eden. It is equipped with everything a normal gym has in addition to a boxing ring, which is currently where Aiden is beating my ass.

"You claim to know how to fight, yet you have gotten your ass kicked twice since coming to Eden."

I glare at him. "I'm not that bad." I am rusty for sure. I used to go to the boxing gym almost every day, but work got extremely busy.

"You could be better," he says. "I want you to be able to protect yourself."

"I'm not going to be going on anymore collection joy rides. I'll be fine."

"You will be fine, because I will make sure of it. Hands up," he commands. I throw a jab, which he blocks. Before I can pull my arm back, he sweeps his feet under me, and I fall back flat onto the mat with a grunt. I look up to him to see him smiling down at me. I raise my hand for him to help me up. He grabs it and I use the opportunity to kick out my feet to trip him. He roughly lands beside me.

I burst into laughter, rolling to my side to face him. "I guess you're rusty too."

He turns his head towards me and narrows his eyes. "No. You play dirty."

"You think a soul won't play dirty?" I sarcastically reply. In a rush of movements, he ends up on top of me, his arms on either side of me, and his hard body pressed against mine. I run my eyes over his sweat covered face.

"I'm interested in seeing what other dirty tricks you've got," he teases, his eyes drooping in anticipation.

I lick my lips. "Lean closer and find out." He leans down. Just as his lips are about to touch mine, I push my knee up and slam it into his stomach. He grunts in pain. I push my hips up to force him to lose balance, and he lands on his back with me on top of him.

A sly grin forms on his face. "Oh, you're going to pay for that." He rolls us, so that he is on top again.

I arch a brow. "And how exactly am I going to—"

I'm interrupted at the sound of someone clearing their throat. We look in that direction and see Joey leaning against the wall. His sense of timing is horrible.

Joey grins wide as he points a finger between Aiden and

me. "A lot of things that weren't adding up…makes sense now. How long have y'all been at it? Wait, no. Let me guess. It was before the collection's incident. That's why Aiden was all in my ass about it."

"You better not say a word to Director Jackson," Aiden threatens. Hopefully, Joey doesn't.

"Now, why do you think so little of me?"

Aiden gives him a look. "Because you have a big mouth."

"The ladies love it though. Right, Joy?" He winks as Aiden rises off me. He grabs my hand and pulls me to my feet. Joey obviously has a death wish.

"Keep her out of your horny mind, you bastard."

Joey makes eyes at me. "Joy Joy, are you going to let him talk to me like that? I thought we had something special?" Aiden moves towards him, but I stop him with a hand. Knowing Joey is messing with Aiden, I play along.

I pull my bottom lip between my teeth then sigh. "We've been over this Jo Jo. We can never be. We are star-crossed lovers." Joey drops his head to look at the ground. Aiden looks between the two of us, annoyance echoing off his face.

"I hate both of you," Aiden states. Joey and I look at each other, then burst into laughter. It's so fun to mess with Aiden.

"I think I can move back into my apartment," I casually mention to Aiden. It's an hour after our workout session. We showered and got dressed for his second day of trial. Currently, we are riding in the elevator to the Collection department's floor. I need to print out some documents before we go to Reaper's Court.

"Okay, I'll help you," Aiden replies nonchalantly.

"That's it?" I push. I was hoping for some type of reaction. Some sign that maybe he cares more for me beyond being friends and having sex.

He shrugs a shoulder. "No one has tried to break in or harm you and we have found no proof yet. At this point, you are probably fine."

"Oh," I reply, sulking at the fact that he does not seem to care.

He grabs my shoulders and turns me to face him. "Plus, we are usually together. We will take turns going to each other's apartments. I know you miss your colorful apartment," he says. His words bring me comfort that he hasn't grown tired of me.

I smile at him as the door to the elevator opens. We walk to the office and I gather all my materials for court, making sure to also print some documents that I will need.

"When are you putting me on the stand?" Aiden questions. I walk to my desk and organize my files.

"I'm not," I reply, without stopping my preparations. I feel him walk up behind me and wrap his arms around me. He rests his chin on top of my head.

"Why not? I can talk about that day. Show how I did everything I was supposed to do."

With a frustrated sigh, I scrub my fingers over my face. "We all already know what happened that day. The wrong person died. Putting you on the stand will just give Chris the opportunity to attack you."

He turns me around in his arms, his gaze boring into me. "Put me on the stand, Joy. I deserve the opportunity to show that I would never recklessly or intentionally take a life. I'm not like the monster who took my parents' life."

I pull my bottom lip between my teeth. "Fine. I'll put you on the stand. Don't make me regret it."

"I won't," he says with an appreciative grin. I glance at my watch. Ten minutes until court.

"We've got to go," I inform him. He moves around me and collects my files. He waits for me to walk and follows behind me. We head to the Reaper's Court floor, and I feel his gaze on my lower body.

"Are you staring at my ass again?" I admonish over my shoulder.

"My ass," he whispers, and gently slaps it with his free hand. I jump, turning my head to mouth curse words at him.

Aiden cautions, "Joy, watch—"

I turn too late, running directly into someone. Luckily, they catch me before I fall. I look up to see Gabriel, one of the glitch reapers smiling down at me. He is kind of cute. Only kind of, because I still remember that he enjoys dried grapes. The monster.

"So sorry, Gabriel!" I say. He lets go of me, and shyly takes a step back.

He smiles. "No problem at all, Joyce."

"How have you been doing? You look fantastic in that suit! I'm assuming you found your niche in the Soul Directory department."

"I sure did! I've met so many nice people. Thank you again for all your help."

"No problem at all. Just doing my job. I look forward to—"

"We are in a rush, Joy. Maybe you two can converse later,"

Aiden rudely interjects. He jerks his head towards the Reaper's Court.

Gabriel's eyes widen. "Sorry to bother you before court. It was nice seeing you both. I will see you around, Joyce."

"You too," I reply, I watch as he walks away. He seems different. More confident. Even in the way he walks.

"I bet he will," Aiden mumbles under his breath. I glare at Aiden and poke him on the side.

"Stop being an ass," I whisper harshly.

"You were flirting with him."

"I did not flirt with him. I just complimented him on his suit. You know you're the only man I like to look at."

He rolls his eyes. "I bet you tell all your men that."

I chuckle. "Yes. But it's your turn."

He stares at me then turns to walk into the courtroom, not before I see the faint smile on his lips. I know he thinks I'm funny.

Court begins soon after we settle into our seats. Chris calls up his last witness and has them give their testimony about how great Eden is. Like we get it. Eden is great. No mistakes could have ever happened. *Blah, blah, blah.*

"Your honor. The prosecution rests its case," Chris announces, then takes a seat. Now, it is my turn to start questioning.

Today, I am only calling Aiden and Director Jackson to the stand. I will call the rest of my witnesses at the next court day. I will use Aiden to show his good character. His passion for Eden and being a reaper. His careful mindfulness of the rules. Our case is a little shaky right now. Prosecution has a solid case, so I need to put a whole lot of cracks in it. I don't know how yet, but I'll figure it out. It's what I do. Drink mimosas and figure things out.

"Defense may call its first witness," the judge announces.

I stand and clear my throat. "Defense calls Aiden Kim to the stand." Chris' eyebrows jump up. Murmurs begin around the room. Everyone must be shocked by this, not expecting me to call him to the stand. Aiden stands and buttons his suit jacket. He strolls to the witness stand in that nonchalant, sexy way of his that I'm obsessed with.

The bailiff walks up to him. "Raise your right hand. Do you promise that the testimony you shall give in the case before this court shall be the truth, the whole truth, and nothing but the truth, so help you, Reaper?"

"I do," he swears.

"Please, take a seat."

I walk until I am at a decent distance from the witness stand.

"State your name for the record."

"Aiden Kim," he replies with ease.

"How long have you been a reaper?"

"Five years."

I cock my head. "What made you want to work with the Collection department?"

He smiles. "There are many reasons. First, Director Taevian was the one who collected my soul. He helped me through many of the feelings and regrets I went through. I owe a lot to him."

"What else?" I encourage him with a smile.

"I love that Collection reapers are the first ones to greet a soul. We are the beginning of the process. I take that responsibility seriously. I have always loved helping people in their vulnerable moments." He shakes his head. "I would never intentionally, negligently, or knowingly take the wrong person's life."

"Did you deviate from normal procedures the day in question?" I ask.

He shakes his head. "No. I did everything I was supposed to do."

I nod, then direct my attention to the judge. "Your honor. That is all my questions."

As I take a seat, Chris stands and walks to the witness stand. He immediately jumps into his questioning.

"You got into a lot of fights when you were younger, correct?" he asks. See, that's the issue with putting your client on the stand. They testify to how good of a person they are and how they would never do what they are being accused of. It opens the door for opposing counsel to attack the character of the defendant with past incidents. Like how Chris is doing *right now*. That does not stop me from trying to prevent it.

I rise and slam my hands on the desk. "Objection! Your honor. Prejudicial and irrelevant."

Judge Hobbs raises a hand. "I'll allow it." I sit back in my chair and cross my arms.

Aiden hesitates. "Yes...I was an angry child. But my parents—"

Chris cuts him off. "You also got into a fight during college, correct?

"Yes, but—"

"During your probation, you went to collect souls that escaped from Hell against court orders, correct?'

"Yes. I was trying to help Eden," Aiden answers.

"You also collected a soul when the glitch in the system occurred. Correct?"

"Yes, but—" he stops and looks at me. "Yes."

Shit. It was stupid of me to try to help with collecting souls. Now, it is affecting Aiden's case, since he doesn't want to tell Chris that he was actually saving his irresponsible lawyer's ass.

"It's reasonable to conclude that you've broken multiple rules many times, correct?"

Aiden sighs in defeat. "Yes."

"And you have a tendency of being violent and sneaky, which shows that you cannot be trusted, correct?" That is a radical conclusion Chris is making.

Aiden says, "I wouldn't say—" I stand to object, but Chris beats me to it.

"No further questions your honor," Chris interjects, taking his seat and sending me a wink.

Fuck me sideways with a chainsaw. I couldn't have imagined a worse turnout. I shouldn't have allowed Aiden to blur my duties as a lawyer. I knew this was a horrible idea.

Aiden walks over to our defense table, and takes a seat. Chris just threw Aiden's character in the trash and showed that he may not be the most trustworthy. Therefore, his testimony means nothing.

"Who is your next witness, Attorney Parker?"

I stand. "Defense wishes to call Director Jackson to the stand."

Chris stands. "Your honor. May I have a sidebar with Ms. Parker?"

"You may," the judge replies.

Chris walks to me and whispers, "Don't call him. I found

something out this morning. I was not going to admit it into evidence. But if you call him on the stand...you'll leave me no choice." I don't have many witnesses and Aiden's testimony was a shitshow. I need Director Jackson on the stand. I can handle whatever he throws at me.

I shake my head. "Whatever it is Chris, I'll deal with it. I appreciate your...whatever this is." Chris stares at me for a second, then nods and takes his seat.

I look at the judge. "Defense calls Director Jackson to the stand."

Director Jackson rises from the gallery, walks to the witness stand. Once he is sworn in by the bailiff, I begin my questioning.

"Please state your name for the record."

"I am Director Taevian Jackson."

"How long have you been a director?"

"Ah, let's see. I became a reaper thirty years ago. Then, six years later, I became a supervisor. I was promoted to a director two years after becoming a supervisor. The previous director, my mentor, decided to retire and passed the torch to me." I love Taevian, but he did everything except answer my question. I mentally calculate in my head, which takes longer than I am willing to admit.

I nod. "You've been a director for...twenty-two years?"

He smiles. "Yes."

"How many times during those twenty-two years did you prevent a reaper from assigning the wrong death?"

"More than I can count. I pre-approve all the new reapers assignments before submitting them. For established reapers, I do not. However, I always advise them to check it over three times at least."

"Do you think Aiden would have checked in over three times at least?"

Taevian nods his head. "Yes. He's the type to check it over five times at minimum. I truly do believe there was something wrong with the system and not Aiden. He has never made a mistake before on the job. With all the issues occurring at Eden, this could have been a glitch."

I smile. "No further questions, your honor."

Chris walks in front of Director Jackson. He turns to look at me one more time then takes a deep breath and faces the Taevian.

"You've been a reaper for thirty years?"

Taevian replies, "Yes."

"What do you think of Mr. Kim?"

"He is one of the most hard-working reapers I've ever met."

"Attorney Joyce Parker is thirty years old, correct?" How am I relevant to this in any shape or form? He does not need to go around announcing my age for goodness sake.

I slam a hand on the desk then point to Chris. "Objection! This is beyond irrelevant!"

Instead of looking at the judge, Chris looks me in the eyes. "You honor. My next question will show the relevancy."

The judge waves his hand. "Objection overruled." I lean back in my chair. Aiden taps my leg and I glance at him. He points to my hand where I am gripping my pen so tightly you could see the veins in my hand. I let go and take a deep breath. It just annoys me that Chris continues to get away with sneaky attacks.

Chris continues. "I'll repeat my previous question. Attorney Joyce Parker is thirty years old, correct?"

Taevian hesitates. "Yes." I narrow my eyes on him. Why would he hesitate?

"Were you married thirty years ago to Erin Jackson?"

With saddened eyes, he replies, "Yes."

"And she was pregnant when you died? With a baby girl, correct?"

Taevian's face slackens. "Yes."

"And that baby grew up to be Joyce Parker. The daughter who you manipulated the system for to prevent her from going to Hell and disguised it with Aiden's case, correct?"

I hear the courtroom gasp as I roll my eyes. Chris needs to double check this information. The number one rule for being an attorney is to always ask questions you already know the answer to and the answer to this question is an obvious 'no'.

I laugh and turn to Aiden to share this moment of Chris embarrassing himself. But he's not laughing. His face is carefully blank. I turn forward. The courtroom is quiet as they await an answer.

Taevian looks at me. "Yes. She is my daughter."

What the fuck.

No.

That doesn't even make any sense. Why wouldn't he tell me? No, this is a sick joke.

I look at Aiden. "Is this true? Did you know about this?" He does not say anything, but his eyes reveal the truth for him. My breathing begins to turn labored as I struggle to make sense of what is going on.

"You knew," I whisper. "This whole time...you knew." I sit back in my chair, a million thoughts racing through my head. I think back to every moment I spent with Taevian.

Aiden reaches to grab my hand, but I aggressively rise from my chair causing it to fall backwards. Refusing to believe it, I walk around the table, past Chris and directly to the witness stand. I slam my hand on the stand and point to Taevian. I feel tears run down my face, the wetness infuriates me even more. I hate appearing weak in front of people—especially those who would lie to my face. I aggressively swipe at them as I reach for a strength deep inside myself.

My voice is full of steel when I finally speak. "Are you my father?"

"Yes," he whispers, his voice tortured. We stare at each other.

I break the silence. "Fuck you."

Then, I walk out of the courtroom.

22

THE REASON THE UNIVERSE
EXISTS

"JOYCE! OPEN UP THE DOOR!"

Aiden has been pounding on my door for the past five minutes. I've been on the floor in the middle of my living room staring at my ceiling, rethinking through all my interactions with Taevian. Trying to figure out how I felt. I feel an anger in the depths of my chest, clawing its way up. This feels like such a betrayal. How dare they toy with me this way? But, I also feel so much pain. I was alone my whole life, with no family, and they didn't think to tell me who Taevian was?

From the moment I met Taevian, I felt...comfortable. He felt like someone I've known my whole life, so I thought he was just one of those people who form instant connections with people. He is very charismatic, and I appreciate that about him. On multiple occasions, he asked to spend time with me. Again, I chalked it up to his personality. But now I know it was because I was his daughter. I've been here for weeks and he didn't tell me. More importantly, Aiden didn't tell me. I bared my soul to him and he just kept it to himself.

At the sound of the pounding again, I slowly rise to my

feet. I walk towards the door, every step feeling like there is concrete weighing me down. When I am in front of the door, I take a deep breath then yank it open, coming face to face with him. The sight of him makes my chest burn with rage.

He walks past me into my apartment. I slam the door shut causing the paintings on the wall to shift and turn to face him.

"What do you want?" I ask coldly, not even recognizing my own voice.

He looks at me with desperate eyes. "I want to talk to you. I want to ask for forgiveness."

I nod. "Go ahead."

He pauses, surprised at me actually giving him a chance. "Joyce, I'm so fucking sorry. I should have told you." Yes, he should have told me. But he made his choice and I'm entitled to mine.

I stare blankly at him. "Okay."

His eyebrows furrow. "Okay? Do you forgive me?"

"No. I don't. You can leave."

He takes a step towards me. "Baby—"

I raise a hand, stopping him in his tracks. "I have three degrees, you know. *Three*. And you still somehow played me for a fool. You smiled and laughed with me. Held me while I cried over my trauma from work and the emptiness of never having a family. But, you said *nothing*. Nothing that whole time."

"Joyce—"

"You want to know what I've concluded, Aiden?"

He hesitates. "What?"

"That you never truly cared about me. Not in the way that matters." I shake my head. "This was temporary for you."

"That's not true. I—"

I shake my head. "I don't care what you have to say. Get out." I try to walk past him, but he gently grabs my arm. I do a quick maneuver to twist my arm from his grasp.

Stepping out of his reach, I point a finger at him. "That's the last time you ever touch me. Get out."

"Joy—" he tries reaching out to me again. I take a step away back from him, his hands losing contact with me. I wipe the tears from my face that I didn't realize were falling.

"Get the fuck out," I whisper harshly.

He lets out a breath, and says, "Okay, but I'll be back tomorrow."

"Don't bother. You and I are done. I'm your lawyer, and that's it. Once this is all done, I'll be glad to never see you again." I didn't mean that at all. I won't be glad to never see him again. I'll be in pieces. I didn't realize the depth of what I felt for him until this moment.

"Can we—"

I cut him off. "No." I point to the door and hiss, "Out."

He looks at me for another second, then nods. "We will talk when you've calmed down a little bit."

I cross my arms. "I'll be calm when I never have to see you again." Pain flashes across his face and for a moment I regret saying it. Only for a moment though because reminders of what he kept from me instantly floods my mind again.

He looks at me one more time then walks out. As soon as I hear the click from the door, I drop to the floor and start sobbing into my hands. Not even a minute goes by before there's another knock at the door. Softer this time.

"Joy Joy. It's me, Yirah. Open the door."

"It's open," I call out weakly. The door opens and Yirah

walks in. She lowers herself to the ground in front of me and wraps me into her arms.

"My sweet friend. I heard what happened," she whispers.

I nod against her shoulder. "I can't believe they would hide this from me," I tell her. "They weren't going to tell me, either."

Yirah sighs, then chews her lip. "Okay. As your friend, my job is to listen. But I am also here to give you my opinion, but only if you want it."

Trusting her, I reply, "I want it."

"I understand where you are coming from. You grew up without a family. That must have been lonely," she whispers.

"It was very lonely," I agree.

"But let's look at this from your father's point of view, okay? He died before you were born. When he found out you were going to die, he checked your karma—which is against the rules by the way—and did everything he could to prevent you from going to Hell. He has been trying to protect you." I know she's right but the family I longed for all my life has been right in front of me. Taevian was just going to let me move on without ever telling me.

"Okay, what about Aiden?" I fire back. Taevian may have an excuse for keeping it a secret, but he does not know me as well as Aiden. I've shared my deepest and darkest moments with him. He was the one person I thought would understand me.

She bites her lip slightly. "Aiden was probably conflicted on what to do. Director Taevian is not only his boss, but someone he looks up to. He wouldn't want to betray his trust."

I scoff. "What about my trust?"

"Honey, everything is not black and white. There are different shades. We all tend to forget that reapers were once humans. We still feel and experience things like humans do. We make mistakes. We get jealous. We have secrets. We aren't perfect. Aiden is not perfect. Your father is not perfect. No one is. But you have a family right in front of you now. You have a father, you have a man you love, and you have me."

Bewildered by her statement, I aggressively shake my head. "I do not love Aiden."

I don't.

Of course, I have feelings for him. But love? I haven't known him that long. If I loved him, wouldn't I be completely certain of it? When I think of all the people I've loved in my life, the list comes up short. Richard and I exchanged the words three months into our relationship. I didn't feel scared. Instead, I was completely calm and rational. Uncaring even. The stability of us being together is what brought me comfort.

When I think of Aiden and the feeling of love, I'm terrified. Just the thought of it has my heart thumping rapidly in my chest.

She stares at me. "I'm going to need you to be serious right now. It's obvious that you both love each other."

"I just can't be with him. I can't."

"Ah, I get it. You want to deny what you feel for him because you're scared of being hurt. You've never felt this type of love and you're afraid to lose it. Don't get me wrong, I do not know the future. But what's the other alternative? Being alone forever? Never trying to love?"

Feeling overwhelmed by the truth of her words, I stand

abruptly. "I don't want to talk about this anymore. I'm drained from today's events."

Yirah stands and places her hands on my shoulder. "At least promise me you'll talk about this with your father before you go to Heaven?"

I give in. "Fine. I will."

She pulls me into a tight hug and whispers, "I'm so proud of how much you've grown, Joy Joy. You are so special and you are finally figuring it out." I breathe her in, grateful for the opportunity to experience a true friend. Since I've arrived here, she has been nothing but supportive and caring. I hate that we don't have much time left.

I whisper into her hair, "You are my bestfriend."

I feel her smile. She leans back to look me in my eyes. "And you are mine too. Which is why I want you to work this out with Director Jackson and Aiden. You love them. Don't give me that face, Joy Joy. You love your father, and you are in love with Aiden. I see it every time you look at him as if he puts the sun in the sky every morning. What you do not realize is that he looks at you as if you are the reason the universe exists."

23

SO HELP YOU, REAPER

I SAUNTER INTO CHRIS' office without knocking. He is flipping through some files on his desk. I had a restless night, tormented by thoughts of Aiden, his case, and most importantly—my father. But I can only focus on one problem at a time. When I woke up this morning, I decided it was Aiden's case. Everything else can wait.

Chris purses his lips. "Good morning, Joyce. To what do I owe the pleasure?" It is never a pleasure to talk to this man. Unfortunately, I need information.

I cross my arms. "Why didn't you tell me you knew he was my father?"

"I found out right before court. There was no time to talk to you about it."

I yell, "But you didn't have to announce it in court!" I take a deep breath, trying to collect myself.

He opens his mouth to speak then closes it again. When it seems as though he has his thoughts together, he speaks.

"I have no duty to tell you anything. I was doing my job. I tried to warn you, but you didn't listen. That's *your* problem.

Not mine." One thing about Chris, he will always put the job first. I don't know whether to be impressed or annoyed. At least I will always know where he stands.

"Tell me how you found out. You owe me for dropping that secret on me with no warning."

He chuckles. "That's where you're wrong, Ms. Parker. I owe you nothing. I am Chris Dalton, the attorney for Eden. Not for Aiden. And most definitely not for *you*. I wear my suit proudly and represent my department with honor. The minute you understand that, is when you and I will finally be on the same page. But for now, we aren't even in the same book. Please, kindly find your way out of my office. Unless, you finally want to admit your feelings for me."

I roll my eyes. "You're not my type."

He snaps his fingers and smirks. "My fault. *I forgot*. Your type is Aiden Kim." Well, shit. I guess Aiden and I weren't that good at keeping it a secret.

My lip twitches. "How did you find out?" There is no point in denying it. It would just be an insult to Chris' intelligence.

"Well, I suspected it, but I got confirmation when Joey let it slip at the bar after a couple of shots of Tequila. I thought of reporting you, but there's no rule against it. It would've just wasted my time and I need all the time I have to lock up your reckless client." Aiden was right about Joey. He didn't know how to keep his mouth shut. I need to have a stern talk with him after court today.

Chris and I get into a staring contest. Little does he know, I have grown accustomed to it because of Aiden. After two minutes, he caves with a sigh.

Haha!

I always get what I want in the end. He crosses his arms and mutters a name that I didn't see coming. In that moment, my brain pieces together everything that once did not make sense. I not only know where I need to move my chess pieces to win, I also know who is on the other side of the board.

Checkmate.

"Defense, who will you be calling to the stands?"

I rise from my seat. "Your honor. I would like to call Joey Gomez to the stand."

Joey is my last witness before I rest my case. We are almost nearing the end. The testimony from Joey will help me close this case shut since he is Aiden's close friend. Hopefully, I do well enough to prove my arguments.

The judge nods his head and gestures for Joey to move towards the witness stand. Once Joey reaches the stand, they have him raise his right hand.

"Do you promise that the testimony you shall give in the case before this court shall be the truth, the whole truth, and nothing but the truth, so help you, Reaper?"

"I do," Joey says, unbuttoning his suit jacket as he takes a seat, getting comfortable.

The judge nods at me and announces, "Counsel, you may proceed."

I walk to the middle of the courtroom, facing the witness. Since we do not have a jury, I want his attention to be on me.

I begin my questioning by stating, "Please state your full name for the record."

"Joseph Gomez," he replies with ease. He smiles at the gallery, not at all nervous about the testimony he's about to give.

I continue, "What is your current position?"

"I am a reaper for the Collection department."

I nod. "How long have you been a reaper?" It is important to begin any questioning by setting a foundation. It is a way to warm your witness up to ensure they are comfortable with you.

"About seven years."

"Do you enjoy being a reaper?" He opens his mouth to reply, but Chris abruptly stands. I roll my eyes. This is going to take much longer than needed if Chris does not relax.

"Objection, your honor!" he yells. "Relevance." I guess we share a favorite objection.

The judge looks to me to give my reply to the objection.

I sigh. "Your honor, it will be proven to be relevant if given the chance."

The judge thinks for a second then nods. "Objection, overruled."

My lip twitches as I look at Chris. He sits back down and crosses his arms. If I could stick my tongue out at him, I would. But that would be unprofessional.

"I'll repeat the question, Mr. Gomez. Do you enjoy being a reaper?"

He smiles at the audience and judge before he answers. "Yeah, I do. I've loved it since the day I got here. I wouldn't mind working this job for eternity."

I nod my head at his reply. "How long have you been friends with Aiden?"

He tilts his head in thought then replies, "About five years."

I point to Aiden and glance at him. His gaze is fixed on me, eyes not wavering once since I've been standing here. "Would you say he is good at his job?"

"Yes, he was amazing at his job. Truly passionate about his role as a Collection reaper." *Was*. Past tense.

"How does one become a supervisor?"

"The director of the department has to select you."

"Is there a minimum time you have to work as a reaper before you are selected?"

He shakes his head. "No. But it's usually five years."

I cross my arms. "Wouldn't you say that Aiden got promoted fairly quickly then? I mean c'mon. He was a baby reaper. You were already two years in."

"Yeah, but he worked hard. Harder than most."

I look at him confused. "Do you not work hard? Seven years has gone by, and you haven't been promoted. Oh! *My bad*. I mean seven years has gone by and you finally have been promoted."

Chris interjects. "Is there a question coming or is the attorney testifying?"

I smile and raise my hands. "My apologies. Let me ask a question." Now, it's time to get into the meat and potatoes of questioning. I cross my arms and ask, "You felt jealous that Aiden got promoted before you, correct?"

His eye twitches, just as Chris once again stands up causing his chair to fall back.

"Objection, your honor! Argumentative." *Now, he's just throwing out objections.*

I sigh. "Your honor, if he would just give me a chance, it will be proven to be relevant."

The judge replies, "Objection overruled." He gives me a pointed look. "Please get to the relevancy."

I turn back to the witness, arching my eyebrow. "Please answer the last question."

Joey's incredulous smile falters a little bit. *Interesting.* "I did not feel jealous of Aiden. He deserved that promotion."

"You've taken over the role as supervisor since Aiden's on desk duty?"

"I didn't *take it*," he emphasizes. "I was assigned it while Aiden went through trial."

I move to the defense table where Aiden is sitting. I don't look at him as I retrieve a paper showing an email to Director Taevian from three years ago. I provide the opposing counsel a copy, and also to the judge. I slide the copy in front of the witness. He creases his brows as he examines the paper. Then, his face slackens, going pale.

"Do you recognize what's in front of you?" I ask.

He hesitates. "Yes."

"Is it accurate and true? Meaning that it hasn't been altered in any way."

"Yes but—"

I cut him off. "It was a yes or no question, Mr. Gomez."

Reluctantly, he answers, "Yes."

"Your honor, I would like to admit this into evidence." The judge nods and I walk to the clerk, giving them the document so they could officially mark it into evidence.

I can now use this in any way I want to help my case. I

take the paper back and place it on the projector next to Joey. The document is blown up on the screen for everyone in the courtroom to see. I walk back to the center of the courtroom.

I raise my brow at Joey and continue my questioning. "Please identify what's on the paper."

He leans close to me and angrily whispers, "What are you doing?" I don't reply. I just smile.

The judge slams his gravel. We all look to the judge as he says, "Witness, no sidebar. Do as counsel says."

Joey looks from the judge to me. His nose flares as he finally answers, "It's an email."

I tilt my head to the side. "From whom, exactly?"

"Me."

"And to who?"

Joey glares daggers at me before replying, "Director Taevian Jackson."

"Please read what is on the paper, Mr. Gomez."

Joey clenches his jaw. "Director Taevian, how could you promote Aiden over me? I've worked my ass off to get promoted to supervisor and—" he pauses and looks towards Aiden. Aiden's face is stoic, giving away nothing. Joey continues, "—you gave it to Aiden. I deserved it, not him."

I tilt my head. "Didn't you previously state you weren't jealous of Aiden's promotion?" One of the brilliant ways to show a witness is unreliable is to bring up inconsistent statements. It's a direct attack to their trustworthiness and is hard to recover once it is gone.

"I wasn't jealous of Aiden—I was just upset. Aiden is good at his job; he did deserve to be a supervisor." *There goes that past tense again.* As if Aiden is guilty and will face his punishment. Real friends would have your back till the very end, believing in your innocence.

"Hm." I tap my chin. "The day Aiden received the death assignment, you were at Eden, correct?"

I notice Joey's chest starts to rise and fall a little faster. *Just a little.* Throughout my years of experience, I've learned that a lawyer is a performer. We put on a show. Lawyers tell a story that makes people in the gallery scoot to the edge of their seats. We tailor the facts in favor of our client to prove their innocence. If you're good at your job, you can take the smallest of details, the things that most people would overlook, and turn it into your whole case.

And I am great at my job.

"No, I was collecting souls like I am supposed to do, per my job duties."

I walk to my desk and grab the remote to the court room monitors. I really love how high-tech Eden is. I click some buttons and a picture from one of the cameras in Eden pops up, showing Joey at Eden.

"This is you at three in the afternoon on that day, correct?"

"Yes, it is probably when I was dropping off a collected soul at the Soul Directory," he says, picking at his collar to loosen it.

I click the button again. "This is the list of all your death assignments that day. You had none between twelve and four."

"Okay, I can take a break, right? Reapers need to eat too." he chuckles as other reapers in the room laugh along.

I faintly smile at him. "Of course." I click the button on

the remote again. "But here it shows you at the desk of a reaper who sends files to the Collection department."

"Okay, what's your point? I was probably checking my email while waiting for one of the girls who I flirt with occasionally. I didn't do anything wrong, and I'm not the one on trial." Way to throw your friend under the bus there, buddy. Let's see if I've got him nervous enough.

"Can you read the time stamp on this photo," I ask, pointing to the evidence.

"3:05 p.m."

I click the button again, showing the document received by Aiden from the Collection department on the same day that contained the information of Alex Cole. "Read the time on this document, too."

"3:06 p.m."

"Mr. Gomez, do you believe in coincidences?"

He starts, "I—" But I don't give him a chance to finish.

"Do you think that Aiden just happened to get a death assignment the same time you were at that desk?"

"I'm not sure—"

"Do you think it's a coincidence that you were next in line for his position?"

Joey clenches his fist. "I don't know—"

"Were you the one that informed the opposing counsel that I was Director Jackson's daughter?"

"I—"

I cut him off once again. My goal is not to have him answer.

No.

It wouldn't be enough. My true plan is to rile him up. To make that jealousy and hate that he hides so well come to the surface. To press my fingers against all of his buttons and put him in a corner where he has no choice but to move to the exact spot I want him in.

"Did you switch Alex and her sister's names, knowing they were identical, and Aiden would be none the wiser?"

"Why would I do that?"

I stab a finger towards him. "You tell me, Mr. Gomez. You were upset that Aiden got promoted before you. *Furious,* even. You deserved it, but you weren't good enough. You *still* aren't good enough. Director Taevian knew that. You knew that. And now everyone in this courtroom knows that the only reason you have the position now is because he," I point towards Aiden, "is sitting in that chair, and you took over his role. You will probably never be good enough to—"

Opposing counsel slams their hand on the table. "Objection, you honor! She is badgering the witness—"

"*He didn't deserve it!*" Joey yells, his veins throbbing in his neck "*I deserved it!*" He pounds his chest. "*Me!* And he gets promoted before me. I thought I would just wait it out because soon it would be my turn. Seven years. *Seven.* Aiden is here for only a year, and he gets promoted! It was my turn. Now, it is finally my turn." He is breathing hard when he finishes.

Boom.

That's how you do it. Before court this morning, I went to Taevian's office to ask him for access to all communications between him and Joey. The minute I walked in, Taevian tried to talk to me about what happened in court. I did not give him a chance to speak, wanting to focus on this case.

Silently, with Taevian standing behind me, I went through his communications starting the year Aiden arrived.

In those emails, I found all the information I needed. The problem was that I did not have enough to pin it on Joey.

So, I went with plan B.

All I had up to this point was circumstantial evidence. If I wanted to clear Aiden completely, I needed Joey to admit to his disgraceful deeds. Men are easy though. Hurt their ego a little and they have to try to prove something to you. Getting a witness to confess is the most challenging thing a lawyer can try to do. But it's thrilling. It puts not only the attorney on edge, but also the audience.

I smirk at Joey.

Ladies, gentleman, and nonbinary besties—the show is over.

Chris falls back into his chair, shock written all over his face. *Yeah, buddy.* Imagine my surprise when I figured it out. I always felt it in my gut since I arrived that something wasn't right. Every time we spoke about Aiden's case, I sensed Joey was slightly lying when he told me that he hoped I would win. I just couldn't put my finger on it. Then, I kept replaying what Yirah said last night. She said, *we all tend to forget that reapers were once humans. That we still feel and experience things like humans do.*

Joey had visited me at my apartment and started asking about Aiden's case. The only people who have been to my apartment to know where all my case files were is Aiden, Yirah...and Joey. It always nagged me on why the thief only went to my house and didn't ransack the office. The office is the most logical place to search first. Not only that but Joey never seemed optimistic about Aiden getting off not guilty.

Also, when I went to collect souls with him, he just happened to give me a murderer. If I had gotten badly hurt, it would have affected my ability to represent Aiden. Despite all of this, there was one question that needed to be answered... who would benefit the most from Aiden being stripped of the title of reaper and thrown in Hell? The answer was right in front of my face the whole time. When Chris told me that it was Joey who informed him of my father, I finally understood the game that was being played because I knew who I was truly playing against.

I just didn't want to believe that our friend, Joey, could be capable of hurting Aiden to this extent for an unpaid supervisory position. Jealousy is one of the most dangerous emotions. It can lead people to doing the most horrendous things—like killing an innocent soul.

I turn to the judge. "You honor. We request all charges against Aiden be dropped. He did not intentionally, knowingly or negligently break the Reaper's Code of Conduct. He was framed by this man," I point to Joey, "and as result, Joey broke four rules. By violating rule four, which states that a reaper *may never directly or indirectly harm another Reaper or interfere with their duties without written permission from their designated supervisor,* he not only caused the souls to be mixed up and not be collected on time, but he also saved a human life designated to die."

Joey jumps out of his chair in the witness stand and yells, "You fucking bitch!"

I roll my eyes.

Haven't heard that one before.

He starts to move in my direction. Everyone around us moves to stop him. I take a stance to fight him off. But it's Aiden who appears in front of me, grabbing Joey by the throat. The room goes silent, watching the exchange between two people who used to be close friends.

Aiden brings Joey's face close to his. Aiden's face is frigid as he says, "Touch her. I fucking dare you to lay a single finger on her. I'll make you wish you could die again." It's probably not the best idea to threaten someone while we are still in court. However, considering the circumstances, it is understandable. Joey struggles against his hold with no avail. Aiden finally throws him on the ground.

Joey holds his throat, gasping for air. Aiden leans down with a humorless grin. "I hope you rot in Hell for the rest of eternity." He pauses, then shakes his head sadly. "I was your best friend Joey, and you set me up."

Joey coughs out, "I didn't know they were going to punish you by removing you as a reaper. I thought they would've just demoted you."

I chuckle. "Ah, but when you found out he was going to be removed as a reaper, you still said nothing." He could've stopped this madness at any point. But he didn't. He was going to let Aiden suffer.

The judge taps the gravel to get our attention. We all turn to him. "The charges against Aiden Kim will be dropped. Mr. Gomez, you will be detained until your trial." Two reapers grab Joey, and he struggles against their hold.

He sneers. "You'll pay for this, Joyce! If you think this is it, you are wrong."

Why is it that people blame *me* for the stuff *they* do? For example, the client who killed me. I didn't tell him to murder someone. Just like how I didn't tell Joey to frame Aiden. *But yes*, let's blame the person who had nothing to do with it. I'm just doing my job, which is being a kickass lawyer. As I've said before, being a lawyer means everyone is mad at you. All the time.

I smirk at Joey as he is being pulled away and mockingly say, "I guess you'll be representing yourself, huh." Because it sure as hell won't be me. He snarls in response.

Once Joey is gone, Aiden turns to me with gentle eyes. "Baby—"

I cross my arms and look at Aiden, my face void of all emotions. "No. I am no longer your *baby*. I am your attorney —actually, I *was* your attorney, but my job is now done. Which means I am leaving. There is nothing left to say."

Aiden opens his mouth, but reapers from the audience walk over to congratulate us and invite us out for drinks. Gabriel ends up giving me a lift to the bar. When I arrive, I take a seat by the bar and order an old-fashioned, top shelf. I take a healthy gulp, needing to drink away my thoughts. I examine my drink and internally sigh, realizing I ordered Aiden's favorite drink. Before I can continue to drown in self-pity, I feel someone place a hand on my shoulder. I look up to see Yirah smiling at me.

"I heard you did amazing. I'm sorry I couldn't be there," she says as she takes a seat next to me.

I wave my hand dismissively. "Honestly, it was our conversation from last night. What you said helped me put together the pieces."

"No, Joy Joy. That was all you." She smiles and waves down the bartender. I'm still wearing my suit, so I take off the jacket and hang it on the back of my chair. The bartender comes over and takes Yirah's order, flirting with her as he takes it.

I glance around the room and notice Aiden talking with a group of Collection reapers who he used to supervise before being charged. He turns his head in my direction and I divert my eyes, feeling a burning sensation in my chest, but I ignore it.

As I am turning in my chair to face forward, Taevian steps into view. He walks up to me cautiously, as if worried about my potential reaction. I turn to distract myself with Yirah, but the traitor is nowhere to be seen.

Taevian walks up to me, staying two feet away. "Can we talk outside, Joyce?" he gently asks. I wish I could say when I look at him, I feel anger. But all I feel is an extreme sense of hope.

Contemplating it for a moment, I inevitably nod my head. "You have five minutes," I inform him.

He nods and gestures for me to go first. I slide off the bar chair and turn my head in Aiden's direction again. He is listening to another reaper talk, but he is looking intensely at me. I break eye contact and walk towards the door, Taevian in tow. We step outside and into New York's heat.

I turn to look at Taevian and we just stare at each other for a moment. Finally, Taevian breaks the silence. "Joyce. I am so sorry you found out the way you did."

I cross my arms. "But not sorry that you didn't tell me?"

He sighs. "You don't understand. I *couldn't*."

"Explain it to me, then," I demand. Did he expect me to accept an apology without an explanation of why he wouldn't tell me he is my father?

He runs his hand down his face in frustration. "When your mother was pregnant with you, I was walking with her. We had just come from the farmer's market. During her pregnancy, she only ate organic food. She was so careful because she loved you so much, already. As we were crossing the street, a car ran the light and was heading straight for us.

There was no time for both her and I to get out of the way, so I shoved her at the last minute. She only got slightly clipped in the foot. But I...I died, Joyce. Right there on the street. Your mother witnessed the whole thing." My eyes widen. That must have been horrible for her.

He continues, "I have been watching you your whole life since the day you were born. I was there when you came into the world, and I was broken into pieces when your mother left you on the steps of the firehouse. But she was broken, too. There was nothing I could do but make sure you were safe from there on."

He takes a step closer. I notice his eyes swell up as he grabs my hand. "I wanted nothing more than to be your dad when I found out your mother was pregnant. I was also in foster care as a kid, but I was adopted. I'm sorry you had to live in the system your whole life. You're everything to me, Joyce, even if I am nothing to you."

I begin to tremble. All that loneliness I felt growing up is clawing at me. But it turns out I was never alone. He was always there. He was everything to me, too. It's crazy how I didn't know him a month ago and now I can't imagine being without him.

My throat is tight from trying to keep my tears at bay, but I force out the next words. "You were checking on me my whole life?"

He pulls me into a warm, tight hug. "Yes. It is against the rules to check in on family from a past life. It is also against the rules to intervene in a past family member's life. I broke so many rules just to see you."

He rubs my back. "When I saw that you were going to die, I snuck into the Soul Directory department and looked at your karma. I knew you were going to get sent to Hell, so I was trying to figure out ways to prevent that. It just so happened that Aiden needed a lawyer. I convinced Aiden to help me, Joyce. He asked me to tell you so many times, but I stopped him. I didn't want to put you at risk by knowing this information. Please forgive him for me. I can see how much he cares for you."

"How do you know about us?"

He lightly chuckles. "You both are not good at trying to hide it. While I did not like it at first, I noticed how happy you make each other. You should give him a chance, Joy."

I shake my head. "There's no point. I'm leaving soon and we may never see each other again. I think I should just let it be."

Taevian begins to speak, "But—"

"I know you want to help. But no. Please." It already hurts enough that I have to leave Aiden for what may very well be forever.

He nods. "Okay." He leans back to look at me. "Do you forgive me?"

I smile. "I do...Dad." It feels so good to finally be able to say that.

He smiles brightly and squeezes me to him so tightly that I can barely breathe. We hold onto each other as if we are meeting each other for the first time in years.

In a way, we are.

At the sound of clapping, we pull apart to see Yirah clapping and wiping tears from her face. Taevian chuckles at the sight of her.

"I'm so happy for you both," she cries out as she runs and

hugs us. Yirah is one of the funniest and kindest souls I've ever met. I hope we can be friends again in the next life.

I laugh and hug them tighter. "I love you both very much."

We all break apart from each other. I yell out, "Let's get our drink on!"

Taevian pats my shoulder. "I'm an old man, dear. I'm going to get some rest. Especially, since tomorrow is going to be a rough day for me."

"Don't worry. You have a daughter as a lawyer. We are going to get you through this."

He grins. "I know you will. I'll drop by your place tomorrow so we can eat breakfast."

"Alright." I give him a hug and he leaves. I turn to Yirah and smile.

"Let's have some fun!" I grab her hand and drag her into the bar.

At this point, night has come, and reapers have started to leave to head back to Eden. Yirah is playing darts with a reaper I've never talked to before, but he is cute. Valerie and I are chatting about how her time has been at Eden so far.

"Honestly, being a reaper feels no different than being alive. If anything, it's better. Like you mean to tell me, I don't have to worry about bills? I can just work and drink all day? I'll do this for the rest of eternity! Beats my previous life."

I smile. "How was your last life?" We never got a chance to really sit down and talk about each other's lives. Whenever

Yirah, Valerie and I meet up, we are likely drinking and telling funny stories.

"Girl, I worked check to check. I was a starving musician working three jobs. But then one day, I tripped off the stage, hit my head, and ended up as a reaper. Now, I get to remain a reaper because of you."

I brush off my shoulder. "Aren't I the best?"

"Yeah. I got a 'get out of Hell' free card from you *and* porn. Your services are immaculate."

I tilt my head back to look at the ceiling, then back to a grinning Valerie. "You still owe me."

She rolls her eyes. "Sis. I'll sell my left toe to hear something like that again. I mean seriously. It was a performance. I was rooting for you the whole time. I don't blame you though. Aiden is fine as hell. You are too. Let me know when y'all need a third."

I give her a pointed look at the mention of Aiden's name.

She raises her hands. "My bad. I won't mention him again. As a matter of fact..." She points to a tall woman with a huge afro and a nose ring, wearing a red suit. "I'm going to flirt with that reaper. I need to get laid too. Maybe she will call me a *good girl*," she says with a wink. I try to swat her, but she dodges my hands.

As I am about to ask Yirah to take me home, a tall reaper who I've seen, but not spoken to, walks up next to me at the bar and smiles. His smile is sexy and so is he with his dark straight hair that is tied back in a man bun on the top of his head. He also has dark brown eyes. His sleeves are rolled up, showing a sleeve tattoo. This man is a walking sex advertisement and I'm the target audience. This may be just what I need to forget about Aiden.

He leans in. "How are you doing today, baby?" I internally cringe at him calling me baby. It only sounds right coming out of Aiden's mouth.

I lean forward, placing a hand on his arm. I give him a shy grin. "I'm doing better now that you're here."

He looks at my lips, then back to my eyes and says, "I'm Justin. You trying to get out of here?"

I nod, and grin invitingly as he places a hand on my thigh. "I'm Joyce. I'm ready when y—"

One second, he is in front of me, the next he is laying across the bar on his back. I don't have time to react before I am face to face with an angry Aiden. I didn't even realize he was still here.

He turns the bar stool that I am sitting on to face him. Then, he places his hands on either side of me.

"I let it slide when you touched his arm. But you've lost your mind if you think you are going anywhere with him," he says with a hard edge to his voice.

I tilt my head to look up at him. Anger taking over every cell in my body. I shove his chest to get some distance between us, but he does not budge.

Justin yells from across the bar, "What the fuck, man! Who do you think you—"

The bar disappears. Everything melts away and we are in my kitchen.

Oh, I'm going to kill this man.

24

LOCKED OUT OF HEAVEN

"WHAT THE HELL do you think you were doing?" he demands. This must be a joke. I sober up immediately.

"First, if you ever grab me and teleport me away like that again," I narrow my eyes at him, "We are going to have a serious fucking problem. Take me back now."

"Why were you flirting with him?" Why do men think they can demand something, and it will be willingly given?

"What I do is none of your concern anymore. Especially since you've been hiding a huge secret from me since the day I met you!" I yell.

"To protect you, Joyce! Just like I am protecting you from that piece of shit reaper."

I roll my eyes. "Seems like I have a habit of attracting piece of shit reapers."

He narrows his eyes menacingly. "You're acting unreasonable now."

"Oh," I reply sarcastically, "that's golden, Aiden. I have every right to feel the way I feel. Yes, I get it. You were doing what Taevian said. But did you at any point stop to think about me? Was I ever going to find out? Or were you both just going to let me ascend to Heaven without ever knowing my own father. Probably not, because *you don't give a shit about me!*"

He takes four large steps and ends up in front of me. I back away, and he follows me until my back hits the counter. He grabs my hips and lifts me up with ease, setting me on the counter. Stepping between my legs, he places his hands on either side of my thighs.

I shove against his chest repeatedly, "Aiden, I'm not doing this with you. Back up. *Now!*"

He grabs my hands and brings them behind my back, holding them in place.

"Alright I'm going to give you two seconds to move the fu—"

"I can't get you out of my head," he cuts me off. "The way you walk in those heels. The way your suits mold to your body. I can't walk behind you because one look and I'd fall to my knees. Fuck, Joyce. You already have me on my knees. I can't sleep. I can't breathe. I can't go through the day without thinking about you. Whether you ate. If you are sleeping well. Who you are talking to. You've taken over my every thought."

I angrily snap at him, "It's just my body for you, Aiden. You don't care for me. It's lust, and that's okay. But do not play it like it is something else. You said from the beginning, that we shouldn't start anything serious. I agreed."

"You're wrong. It's not lust." He lets go of my hands and gently grabs my face, looking intensely into my eyes. "In the beginning, sure, I could care less about keeping this a secret from you. But only because I didn't know you. Within these last few weeks, you've become my everything, Joy. It became harder and harder to hide it from you. I tried a thousand times to convince your father to tell you, but he wouldn't let up. Can you find within yourself to forgive me? *Please*." Still grasping my cheek, he leans forward and places his forehead against mine. "I'll get on my knees if I have to. I'll do anything."

A lump forms in my throat. "I grew up in the system, with no one to call my own. You *know* what that was like, and you still did it. You disregarded Taevian's orders before, without a second thought, when it was something you cared about. It just feels like I wasn't a concern for you."

He rubs my cheek. "You're my only concern, my Joy. I know your favorite meals. Your favorite perfume. How you like your coffee. Your favorite song. I love your off-key singing. I love how you find humor in everything. I know you love me, and Joyce..." he takes a deep breath, "I love you too. I love you because you exist. I feel like I could've loved you in a past life. But it also feels as though we just met. Your existence in my life has brought me a kind of happiness that I've never experienced before. There are so many layers to you that I want to spend the rest of my eternity uncovering. I thought I knew my purpose, but then I met you. My purpose isn't being a reaper, my purpose is to be *yours*. I love you, my Joy."

I didn't realize I was holding my breath as he spoke. I let out a deep exhale. My heart is pounding so hard that my chest feels as though it may burst. I heard him. I heard the words. But after a lifetime of loneliness and pain, it makes it hard to believe. You don't really realize how much love matters until you've spent your whole life without it. I understand how much it matters now, which is why I was so mad at Aiden and Taevian for hiding this from me.

I did love Richard when we were together. At least I thought so. I think I loved the idea of loving and being loved, but not the actual love. Not the actual person. Richard did not care for me like how Aiden does. The way I feel for Aiden is not consuming. With him it is peaceful. It feels like home. It eases my anxiety and makes me feel safe. I did not fall in love with Aiden. I walked to it and held his hand.

Could I get hurt again? Sure.

But I am already dead, and there's no point in not taking the risk. I am willing to put my heart on the line, because it's Aiden. He has only ever been there for me. Well, minus the fact he made me be his lawyer after I firmly said hell no. But that's in the past.

I place my hand on Aiden's neck and pull his lips down to meet mine. I pull my lips away slightly and whisper against his lips, "I love you too, Aiden."

His eyelids droop slightly in relief. He places his hand on my back, sliding it down till he can grip my ass. Aiden licks my bottom lip and works his way down my neck, licking and sucking as he goes. I shiver against him.

Aiden stops and moves his lips to my ears. His voice is deep and low as he asks, "How much do you love me?" His words send waves of pleasure spiraling through my body. He has barely touched me, and my body is ready for him.

When I don't reply, he squeezes my ass again. One of his hands moves between my legs and he rubs me against my pants. He asks again, "How much do you love me?"

I gasp. "So, fucking much."

He leans back and looks at me as he continues to rub

between my legs. Driving me absolutely crazy with need. I need him in me like I need my next meal.

"Good girl," Aiden purrs. Then he stops, moves his hand back to my ass, and lifts me clean off the counter. He walks us to my room.

When we are by the bed, he gently drops me on top of it. I go to remove my shirt, but he grabs my arm, stopping my movements.

"Let me take care of you, baby." His words cause another tingling sensation between my legs.

I look up to him and whisper, "Okay." Aiden gently pushes my shoulder. I fall back on the bed. He climbs on top of me, his legs on either side. He leans over to me and places his thumb on my bottom lip, gently rubbing it. With that same hand, he moves from my lips to my throat, squeezing it gently.

His hand continues its journey down to my chest. One by one, he unbuttons my top, groping and caressing my breasts as he goes. Once the shirt is unbuttoned, he lifts me slightly to completely remove it, and throws it on the ground. My bra is next. Then my pants and panties. I am completely naked in front of Aiden.

And then he is on top of me, completely taking over my mouth. He drives his tongue into me. Owning it. Owning *me*. Showing me how much he missed me. His hand finds my breasts, his other sliding between my slit.

"Oh, my God," I pant into his mouth.

Aiden drags his mouth away and whispers in my ear, "Not God, baby," He slides his finger fully inside of me, his thumb pressing against my clit, *"Me."* I gasp as his fingers start to pick up pace. I start to ride his fingers, but he moves the hand that was on my breasts to my hip and holds me in place.

He gently says, "What did I tell you? You're mine to take care of."

I feel a build up inside me and I don't even try to hold it in. I moan loudly signaling to him that I'm close. He curves the fingers inside of me, hitting the spot that makes me pant with need.

"Come all over my hand," he demands against my lips, circling his finger around my clit.

At his words, I cry out with my release, my back arches off the bed, and my body shakes in pleasure. When I finally come down, I look at Aiden to see him undressing, never taking his eyes off me.

He lifts his shirt over his head, giving me a clear view of his chest. I watch as he unbuttons his pants and steps out of them. He removes his boxer briefs and is left standing naked in front of me. My breathing quickens as he moves towards me. I feel myself slightly tighten in anticipation of feeling him inside of me.

He climbs on the bed, running his hand over my leg, over my stomach and to my breasts. He leans down and twirls his tongue around one, sucking and biting it.

"The other one is feeling lonely," I pant, running my hand through his hair.

He looks up and does a half grin. "We can't have that," he replies, moving his mouth to the other one, giving her all the attention. He licks, bites, and sucks on my nipple, before giving her a break. Aiden leans away, positions himself at my entrance. I raise my legs and lock them around his hips. He sinks into me with one fluid, rough motion causing my back to bow from the bed as a scream tears from my throat at the sudden shock of penetration.

He feverishly thrusts into me, groaning when he feels my muscles tighten around him. Every thrust is urgent and deep, making me feel drugged with pleasure. I grip his hair and pull him down to me. Our mouths meet in a passionate, desperate kiss.

"I've fucking missed you. You're so perfect," he murmurs against my lips, his voice strained.

"Don't stop. *Oh God. Please, Aiden,*" I beg him, clutching onto him for dear life. I don't even know what I am begging for at this point. He slides a hand between us, rubbing against my swollen bundle of nerves relentlessly. My legs start to quake uncontrollably.

A familiar intense pressure washes over me. My entire body tightens as I cry out, "*Aiden.*"

With a throaty groan, he pulls out of me, flipping me over to my stomach. He pulls my hips back and slams back into me, going so deep I cry out from the intense pleasure. He spanks my ass. Pain radiates through me, but I accept it with a whimper. His hips begin to pound into me violently. I push back to meet every feverish thrust, groaning at the feel of his teeth running along my shoulder to my neck. He kisses up my neck to my ear causing me to shiver.

His breath tickles my ear as he groans. "That's it. Take it. *Take me.* Only I can make you come. *Say it,*" he growls.

"Only you can make me come," I sob. I've lost count of how many times I've found my release. He just keeps going. Proving his point. No one has ever driven me this crazy with need. No one else ever will.

I clamp down on his cock as my mouth opens with a

silent scream, my release draining every ounce of energy from me. He calls out my name, and with one last thrust, buries himself deep and explodes into me.

We are catching our breath, looking at each other as the shudders from our orgasms die down. Aiden turns to lay on his back. He moves me so I am sprawled over him. A thought comes to my head. I chuckle.

Aiden smiles. "What are you laughing at?"

"Now, I understand why you were so despicable when I met you. You like to follow the rules, but Taevian was breaking them by having me be your lawyer." I admit.

He laughs. "Yeah. I was despicable, but you're adorable when you have that annoyed face. Your nose does this cute little scrunch."

I huff. "I don't want to be adorable. I want to be sexy."

He tightens his hold on me. "You're adorably sexy." I roll my eyes.

We silently embrace each other for a little bit. My whole body is left weak from his merciless onslaught. I can't help but worry a little. I'm not a reaper and won't become one. Also, my contract ends soon. Won't I have to leave and go to Heaven? As I open my mouth to mention this, I close it shut. No. I am going to soak this moment in and bring this up later. Right now, I want to just be with him.

I kiss his neck and whisper, "I'm sorry about Joey."

His hold tightens. "Don't be sorry. He is a grown man who let jealousy get the best of him. I'm just grateful I have an amazing lawyer who proved my innocence."

"He's your best friend though."

He shakes his head. "He *was* my close friend. A true friend would never set up their friend like he did, even if he didn't know that I would have been stripped of being a reaper and thrown in Hell for a hundred years. He also killed an innocent woman. That's beyond unforgivable. He deserves everything that is coming to him." He kisses my forehead. "But, I have you now. You're all I need."

I smile into his neck. Relieved that he is doing sort of okay with the fact that his friend betrayed him. I am still thinking back to what Joey said as he was getting detained. He said, *'If you think this is it, you are wrong!'* But I'll table that thought for another day because my stomach is growling.

"Are you hungry?" I ask. I'm getting a little hungry, and want to eat a meal with him.

His eyes heat up and he lifts his hand, rubbing his thumb across my bottom lip. He leans forward and whispers in my ear. "For you."

I involuntarily squirm. "I meant real food."

He chuckles. "I know. How about this—I eat you first, then we both can cook something to eat."

"Wait—" My words are cut off when I feel Aiden's fingers tunnel between my legs again. If we were still alive, I would have died from exhaustion. I gasp when his fingers dip inside.

He gives me a devilish smile and says, "You're already so wet. My Joy is always ready for me."

He moves down my body. When he reaches his destination, I feel his mouth against me. I grab onto sheets on either side of me and open my mouth in a silent moan. This man really knows how to use his mouth.

One hour later, and we are finally making food. One of the things that suck about not actually being in the Living World is that we can't just order take-out.

I am dicing onions as Aiden seasons the ground beef. We are making a worldwide classic, whether you are a reaper or a living being—spaghetti. Since, we are both spent after all the mind-blowing sex we had, we wanted something quick. I finished dicing the onions two minutes ago, but I am distracted by my concerns and keep moving the knife. My anxiety is growing by the second the more my thoughts swirl in my head.

"Aiden," I say hesitantly. He looks at me, happiness glowing in his eyes. I tuck my chin in sadness. My eyes well up with involuntary tears. He stops what he is doing, washes his hands and dries them. He walks over to where I am butchering the onions and gently grabs the knife from my hand, placing it on the counter. He turns me around and places his hands on either side of me on the counter, placing a finger under my chin and lifting my head up.

He leans down and looks into my eyes, his face lined with worry. "What's wrong, baby?"

I pull my bottom lip between my teeth. "I finished your case," I say, looking away as I say the next part, "So, our contract is done. I'll be leaving tomorrow for Heaven."

Aiden turns my head until our eyes meet again. His eyes are filled with so much love and patience.

He taps my nose as if I'm being silly. "Do you think Heaven can keep us apart?"

I tilt my head in thought, then nod. "Actually, I do."

He chuckles. "I can't come with you because reapers are required to do fifty years, but I'll visit. I'm not sure it is allowed, but I'll switch to the Heaven department if I have to."

I blink in surprise. "You'll switch departments? But you love working with the Collection department." He finds such fulfillment in the job he does, and his relationship with Taevian.

"Not as much as I love you."

I gently shove his shoulder. "Aww, who knew you were such a romantic?"

"Nah. I just like doing you. Can't do that if I can't get to Heaven. There's magic in your pus—"

I cover his mouth and give him a look of exasperation. "I miss when you barely talked."

He chuckles and removes my hand from his mouth. He gives my hand a quick kiss, then leans into me and gives me a peck on the lips.

"I love you," he says.

I lean away from him and bite my lip in worry. "Is now the time to tell you that I just want to be friends?"

He narrows his eyes and gently slaps my ass. I let out a laugh. "I love you too."

"I'll never get tired of hearing that," Aiden replies. He hugs me close, nestling his face in my neck. I close my eyes and smile.

When I open my eyes, I notice a reaper in regular clothes. Now, how the hell did he get into my apartment? I look at his hand to see him holding what looks to be a gun pointed at—

I shove Aiden out the way as the reaper pulls the trigger. I feel a sharp pain in my chest, and I look down. There's a red dart sticking out. Aiden looks at the dart with wide eyes. His face twists in anger as he turns toward the reaper. As he moves, five more appear. I try to move, but my body does not listen to me.

The dart must have been laced with something. Darkness creeps in from the corner of my eyes. Before I can even think of saying something, I collapse.

25
WILL WE EVER KNOW PEACE?

I TRY to open my eyes, but I'm finding it hard to do so. When I finally pry my eyes open, I realize I am not familiar with my surroundings. I'm in a hotel room, not my apartment. Slowly I sit up, letting the cover fall down my chest. I'm naked, and by myself. What the hell happened? I remember being in the kitchen and arguing with Aiden. He confessed to me, then we had amazing sex. We started cooking, but then when I looked up, I saw—

Shit!

Where the hell is Aiden? I scramble off the bed and grab the robe on the chair beside the bed. I quickly tie it and am about to search for my phone, when the door opens. Aiden strolls in.

I exhale a deep breath. "Oh, thank God. You're okay. What happened? Where are we?"

I take a closer look at him, and notice he's covered in bruises and cuts. I gasp and run towards him, lifting his shirt and looking closely at his injuries. "Are you okay? Why are you hurt?"

He looks like he got into a brutal fight and barely won. Some of the cuts look slightly healed, which means he was probably in way worse shape.

"Baby, lay back in bed. I have some food for you." He gently pushes me towards the bed with one hand, holding a large bag of food in the other. I sit in bed and pat the area next to me as a gesture for him to sit beside me, which he does.

He leans in for a kiss as I lean away, putting my hand over my mouth. I have not brushed my teeth and would hate to kill him this early in the relationship.

"I haven't brushed my teeth yet," I mumble from under my hand. He smirks and settles for kissing me on the cheek.

"What's the last thing you remember?" he asks.

"That stupid reaper shooting me."

He chuckles. "Yeah, then you passed out and some more reapers came in trying to take us. I fought them off, then teleported us here."

I nod and reach for the food. I'm starving. This whole still-feeling-hunger thing, even though I'm dead, is not cool.

I lift the fry to my mouth and notice a tattoo on my wrist. I hold my arm up in front of me and look at it. It looks like a mini scythe.

"Why do I have this?" I ask.

"It's one of the reaper's tattoos. While you were knocked out, I went to the armory room at Eden and took an old mini machine to be able to put that on you. It will be temporary, but it gives you heightened strength, teleportation, and the ability to make yourself not visible to the human eye. You basically have all the powers of a reaper for a small amount of time. As the tattoo disappears, so will the abilities it gives you. The more you use it, the faster it will fade. So, use it only when you must."

"Got it. Only when I need to." I smile at him, then shove ten fries in my mouth.

His mouth curves upwards. He rubs my hair. "My perfect Joy," he whispers. I swat his hand away. He knows I have a praise kink.

He laughs as he grabs the bag of food and sits next to me, taking out a burger and biting into it.

"Okay, what's the plan?" I ask.

"I'm not sure yet. We still do not know who or what is behind this and why they are tracking us down. But I do know I can't get in contact with Taevian."

"What about Yirah?" I ask, hoping she is okay.

He shakes his head. "I don't think we should involve her yet. We don't know what is going on."

I pull my bottom lip between my teeth then let go. "What if this has something to do with Joey? I mean you heard him as he was being dragged away. He said this was not the end of it."

Aiden contemplates what I said for a moment. "What would he benefit from doing this? He's not the type to do something without a reason."

I shrug. "I have no idea. But they came to my apartment, so they must have been looking for me."

"What did you do?"

I scoff. "Why must I have done something?"

He raises a brow. "You are always getting yourself into some trouble."

"That's a false statement. I do not *always* get myself into trouble."

"Okay, then. You have a pattern of finding trouble," he teases.

"Well, I didn't do anything...this time."

He moves our food to the bedside table and pulls us under the blankets. We are laying on our sides, facing each other. I realize I don't know where we are.

"Where are we?" I ask curiously.

"New York," he states, playing with one of my curls.

"Why New York?"

A gentle smile plays on his lips. "Because you like it." My heart flutters. He remembers every little thing about me. I probably mentioned liking New York once.

I lean in and peck him on the lips. "I love you."

A slow grin spreads across his face. "I love you more," he replies.

"What should we do now?" I ask, glancing around the room.

"Let's go explore New York," he suggests.

I grin wide.

His eyes darken as he stares at my lips. "Before we do that, I think you owe me again."

I blink in surprise. "For what?"

His hands move down my body then under my robe. "For saving you once again."

My eyes narrow. "I saved you first by pushing you out the way."

He caresses his lips against mine then whispers, "Then I owe you, too." His fingers tunnel between my legs then dip inside. I gasp.

"Time to pay up," he whispers.

Aiden pauses. Then blinks. He looks at me. Blinks again. "Are you whoring me out for a slice of pizza?"

"Babe, of course not. You are worth so much more." I pat his shoulder. "I'm whoring you out for two slices of pizza. You have to eat, too."

We can't use Eden's cards, because the reapers who attacked us might trace them back to us. He had some cash that he usually uses to leave tips, which he used to pay for the hotel and meal earlier. We have to budget the money to last us until we come up with a plan. But, it's late at night now and I'm hungry. Aiden might as well use his good looks and charm to flirt with the girl.

We spent all day walking around New York and taking the train. He didn't want to teleport since we are not sure if the reapers could find us that way. My favorite part was the super cheap boat ride we took to see the Statue of Liberty, and the well-known bridges.

Aiden looks at me with disappointment all over his face. "I expected more from you."

"Really?" My tone is dry.

He tilts his head in thought for a moment. "Actually, no. I know you would sell me for unlimited mimosas right now if you could."

I shrug. "I plead the fifth." Because I totally would. Someone has to have their priorities straight.

"You can't plead the fifth outside the courtroom."

I shrug again. "I just did. Plus, I know the law better than you."

He places a finger through one of the belt loops in my

jeans and pulls me in close. He leans down until his mouth is by my ear.

He whispers, "Oh yeah? Let's see if you have all that attitude later, Ms. Lawyer." He leans back to look at me. I bite my lip and he grins. He taps my ass twice before walking into the pizza shop. I stare at his immaculate ass. Hate to see you go, but I love—

I don't get a chance to finish my thought. A hand grabs me from behind, covers my mouth and teleports us to an empty alleyway. I elbow the assailant in the stomach and spin around to face Mac, the reaper who helped Aiden and I sneak into Heaven.

"You're in danger," he stresses. He's late to the party.

I let out a breath of relief that it's him and give him a look. "No, shit Sherlock. Why do you think I'm in New York?"

He chuckles nervously. "I know but—"

"Joy!" I hear Aiden's panicked voice. I open my mouth to call out to him, but Mac covers my mouth. Confused, I try to remove his hand, but feel a sharp pinch in my neck. In the next moment, he teleports us to a different location.

I rip myself away from him. "What the hell was that?" I demand. Mac lifts his hand to reveal a needle with a blue substance in it.

"Can't have you getting away. This serum neutralizes reapers' abilities for at least an hour."

"I'm not a reaper," I inform him.

He gives me a look as if I'm slow. "I see the scythe tattoo on your wrist." Ah, so the serum neutralizes reaper tattoos too. Good to know.

"Why are you doing this? Who put you up to this?"

He puffs out his chest a little. "We are trying to make

Eden great again." Yeah, I've heard a statement like that before. Nothing good ever follows it.

"Who is *we*?" I push. I need more information from him, but he is tight lipped.

"You'll see. I'm waiting on the other reaper to confirm they got Aiden. I'm assuming he will come voluntarily because we have his girlfriend."

I give him a look of exasperation. "I would rather you just tell me. I'm not particularly fond of surprises." I look around, unsure of where I am, but I do know wherever he is going to take me is not a place I want to go.

I knee him in the groin, and he doubles over in pain. Not giving him a second to recover, I punch him in the face then sprint away. I run down the alleyway, not glancing back once. When I almost reach the street, I slam into something. Looking up, I see it is Mac. He roughly grabs me by the throat and throws me onto the ground.

"I was trying to be nice, but you are forcing my hand," he says, then raises a fist and slams it into my head, causing me to blackout.

26

NOTE TO SELF:
NEVER TRUST SOMEONE WHO IS TOO NICE

I BLINK my eyes a couple of times. I look around, trying to figure out where I am, but my eyes are met with darkness. I groan as I try to sit up, which is proving to be a hard thing to do. My arms are tied behind my back, and chained to the wall. My first thought is Aiden.

"Aiden?" I call out. I swear he'd better be alright. I hear groaning, and then movement.

"Joy?" My heart jumps at his voice.

"Aiden!" I try to crawl in his direction, forgetting I'm chained to the wall. The chains painfully yank against my wrists. I fall back onto my ass. "Damn it to Hell. How many reapers are evil at this point?"

"I never expected Mac to betray me." First, Joey. Now, Mac. The question we have to ask is who is *not* going to betray Aiden.

"Seems like a lot of betrayal is going around. What did you do to piss these people off?" I ask, seriously concerned about why we are mixed in the middle of all of this. Seems as though even when I try to mind my business, the business wants to mind me.

"Joyce." I roll my eyes. He can never take a joke.

"Okay, okay. I'm joking. Let's think about this. There's no way a bunch of reapers are just doing this by themselves. There has to be someone more powerful."

"Like a director?"

"Exactly." I stand up. The floor is uncomfortable, and I want to pace a little. There is not enough give in my restraints for me to pace too far, but it's enough.

"Aiden, can't you just teleport yourself away?" I ask.

"I tried the moment I woke up, but it seems like they did something to me." It was probably the serum. In all my readings about Eden, I did not come across anything about a serum.

I lean my head back in irritation. "That's annoying. Who do you think is behind this?"

"Maybe Joey? It's always who you least expect it to be. You mentioned that it could be him when we were at the hotel."

I shake my head. "It's not Joey. He's just a pawn. It has to be a director."

"I hate to say this...but could it be your father? We haven't been able to find him."

There are seven directors. The most obvious answer is my father. He went missing and is in trouble with Eden. But I know it's not him. Not just because he's my father, but because it makes no sense for it to be him. What would he have to benefit?

Until this point, we have been dealing with pawns. My father is very charismatic. Reapers love him and the directors respect him. In chess, he could be considered the king—the most important piece. You take out the king and the game is over.

When it was revealed he was my father, that should've been the end of it. He lost all of his credibility as a director and his position is threatened. But Aiden and I are being held captive, which means he was never the true target...never the true king. If the directors are not being targeted, then the only option left is something bigger than a director. What's bigger than a director? Well, it's the place they are in charge of—Eden.

I just haven't figured out why yet.

"No, it's not him. I know that for sure."

He hesitantly says, "Babe." I can feel him desperately trying to figure out what to say.

I shake my head. "Hear me out. You get set up by your closest friend for breaking the rules. Then, the system glitches causing souls to get released and it affects the Karma system. With the Karma system being affected, the wrong souls got recruited as reapers. To top it off, the system shuts down all together resulting in everyone having to manually collect and process souls. Before we could even take a breather, Taevian is revealed to be my father in court. Lastly, there are, for all *we* know, a bunch of reapers who have turned to the dark side." I pause in thought. "Follow me here...when we think about the directors, who would be negatively impacted by this?"

"Well, the IT department because they control the system. Also, Hell, Collection, Reaper's Resources, and Soul Directory. All those departments had major blow backs."

"Now, which department was the least affected?"

"Reaper's Court and Heaven department," he says slowly, as if it's starting to click for him.

"Reaper's Court was just established, and the director is newly appointed. Therefore, it's unlikely he could have created such an elaborate plan. So, what does that leave us with?" I stop pacing and look in the general direction of where he is. I can almost hear the gears shifting in his head as he mulls over the question that I already know the answer to.

It's well-known in chess that the queen is the most powerful piece—able to move in any direction she pleases, and can easily manipulate those around her. The queen is the piece you do not use until you have developed your other pieces. Aiden and I are the last pieces that need to be developed.

No.

I am the last piece. They were never after Aiden. He just happened to be with me. They need *me* for something...or someone.

"Wait, so it can only be—" he begins to say as the door opens. The lights flicker on, revealing the villainous bitch who smiled in my face while actively trying to harm us and take over Eden.

I smirk. "Speak of the devil and they shall appear," I announce.

"Well, Ms. Parker. You really know how to put those lawyer skills to work," she replies mockingly as she walks in wearing a terrible gold suit. Actually, it is very stylish. I just despise her, which means I have to hate her suit too. "Hello to you, too, Mr. Kim."

I laugh humorlessly. "Well, if it isn't Director Jia Young. You've finally graced us with the other side of your two faces."

I look her up and down. "I knew you were too nice. No one is that nice, unless they are a psychopath."

She rolls her eyes and grimaces. "I'm not a psychopath, Ms. Parker. No need to be rude. I did not come here to threaten you."

Of course, that's what all villains say before they proceed to threaten you when you don't comply with their plans.

I tilt my head in question and retort, "Would you prefer to be called a bitch? I don't have a preference." The grin is wiped right off as her eyes darken and her face hardens.

Ah, there she is.

She takes a step back and makes a gesture towards someone. Two reapers walk in, one towards Aiden and the other to me.

Aiden glares towards the reaper heading to me. "Don't you fucking touch her!"

They ignore Aiden and unchain us from the wall, shoving us to move forward towards the door. Aiden headbutts the reaper, causing the reaper to grasp his head and yell out in pain.

Director Young lets out a sigh of annoyance, grabs something from the other reaper standing closest to her and walks toward Aiden, pressing it against him. Aiden moves to avoid it, but she is faster. He lets out a sound of pain and collapses into the wall.

"Aiden! Are you okay?" I shout but there is no response. I glare at her. "What the hell did you do to him?"

She lifts the device in her hand for me to see. "It's a stun gun. He will be fine. He is just knocked out for a little bit. Wouldn't want him hurting my other reapers."

"I swear I will—"

In a blink, she's in front of me. I gasp at the suddenness. She wraps her empty hand around my throat. "You will what, Joyce? You can't do a single thing. So shut up, or else I'll make sure to hurt your little boy toy even more." She watches me for a beat. I do not do anything, but glare at her. Satisfied with my compliance, she walks away, tossing the stun gun to a reaper. "Get them to the main room."

She looks at me before exiting the room. "I have someone you probably want to see." She winks and walks out of view.

I should've figured out it was her sooner. It makes so much sense. She was one of the first directors at Eden. She is also the most influential director. One thing that stays consistent in humans, whether dead or alive, is craving power. I just don't know exactly how she plans to achieve it.

The reapers take us down a hallway in the Heaven department. We get to a huge room decorated in white and gold, where I see my father in the center, tied to a chair.

"Dad!" I yell, as I pull against the reaper holding me back. He looks up at me, and he looks horrible. One eye is swollen shut and there's blood everywhere. I would be even more concerned if I didn't know that reapers heal fast.

"Joyce," he says weakly, as if it hurts to talk. They tie Aiden and I to similar chairs and take a step back waiting for their next command. Aiden is still unconscious, which is making me more angsty by the second.

Director Young strolls in with her signature smile back on her face. "Glad you can have your family reunion, but let's get back to business." She stands by my father and looks at me. "I needed you here, Joyce, because your father is being difficult."

My father looks at her with a hopeless expression, "Jia, why are you doing this?"

She leans over to get closer to my father's face. She hisses, "Because I fucking deserve it."

"Deserve what, Jia?" my father asks in confusion.

"Eden. I deserve to rule over Eden. Eden is *mine*."

I sigh, annoyed with her antics. "You don't own Eden, *Jia*."

She straightens up and sneers at me, which, by the way, is not a good look on her. "That's where you're mistaken, Joyce. I *am* Eden. Eden is me. I am the God they need. I built this place up. I've been here since the beginning. All the original directors have retired, but I'm still here. You want to know why?"

I roll my eyes. "No, but I'm guessing you're going to tell us anyway."

Ignoring me, she continues, "I was created to be a God. Do you know I was royalty in my past life? I lived amongst the rulers of my land. I was not meant to be a mere director. I was meant to rule, and that's exactly what I'll do."

"What made you this way?" I ask, curious as to how long she has been delusional.

"Not what, *who*," she seethes. "All these good for nothing directors! They sit around content on keeping Eden average. We could be doing so much more. But *no*. All the directors have to agree in order for there to be any changes. Well, I'm sick of it. The karma system is fucking flawed. There's too many pathetic, evil humans going to Heaven and not enough to Hell. Then, they thought I was going to let *you* into Heaven? Not a chance." The list of people that have beef with me is getting longer. Mr. Reynolds, Joey, Mac and now this psycho—correction—this bitch.

What's the saying? If you ain't got haters, you ain't poppin.

I let out a deep sigh, eager to get on with the villain monologue. "Okay, all-mighty Queen. How exactly did you plan to pull this off?" Because no way could she get enough reapers on her side for a hostile takeover.

"Well, everything would've gone according to plan, if your dear old dad didn't go snooping around my apartment and find out what I've been up to." She looks at my dad and winks. "You were a good lay, but I didn't think you would go through my stuff. That was on me." She walks towards the desk in the room and sits on it, crossing one leg over the other.

I am stuck on the fact that she and my father slept together. I raise a brow at him in question of his choices and he just shakes his head in defeat.

Men.

She continues, "Hostile takeovers are what weak-minded men do. They think they deserve power due to the mere fact they are a man. But me? I deserve it because I know what's best for Eden. I know what—"

I cut her off, needing her to get to the point. I have never been a great listener. "Okay, we get it. *You deserve it.* But can you please just share what your plan is and where we go from here. These restraints are not comfortable."

She tilts her head at me. "I'll let that disrespect slide. But if you keep on with it, I'll ensure you learn a lesson."

I roll my eyes at her. Director Young raises an eyebrow, but finally gets on with it. "As I was saying before, hostile takeovers are for weak-minded men. My plan was simple—make it appear as though Eden is slowly falling apart. I create the problem, and I will be the solution. The problem? Eden needs one central leader. Obviously having many directors is not working. Solution? Me. But your father figured me out, and planned to expose me. So, I had to threaten him with something—or should I say someone—that would keep his mouth shut and that's where you come in."

I tilt my head and look at her with pity. "So what? You're going to threaten to hurt me? News flash...I can't die again. Congrats, that's the best villainous plan I've ever heard."

She chuckles. "No. Of course not. I'm going to give him a choice. Eden is all about free will."

She places her hand on my head, then roughly grabs my hair. First of all, does she understand how long I waited to get my hair done? She really is a villainous bitch. Second, when I finally work my way out of these binds, I am going to beat her to Hell and back. I am glad some of my evil foster brothers used to tie me up and throw me into a closet. I had to figure out fast how to undo those binds or else I would be stuck in the closet for hours. Maybe for days, depending on whether my foster parent was drinking or not.

Director Young continues to talk. This time, directly to my father. "I have something you hold precious. Your daughter. You have a choice. You either join my side, or I'll make sure you never see your daughter again."

I hear Aiden snicker and we all turn to look at him. Relief floods my body. *Thank God.* He is finally awake. Even though she said he would be fine, she could have been lying.

His voice hardens with determination. "Do you think there is a place in Eden or on Earth where you could hide her, and I wouldn't find her? I'll tear apart this entire fucking universe if I have to."

I stare at him, realizing that what he just said was

completely true. He wouldn't stop. *It's the wrong time to be turned on, Joyce.*

Her grip on my hair tightens further and I yelp out in pain. Aiden clenches his jaw.

I complain, "Can you loosen up on my hair a little, please? My braids did nothing to you."

She ignores me. "You're mistaken, Aiden. I'm not going to hide her. That'd be too easy. Too *kind* of a gesture for her father. No. I'm going to do worse. I'll destroy her soul."

Aiden and I look at each other confused, as my father gasps and says, "No, you couldn't have it. It's locked away. The only way to get it is with all the directors scanning in."

Then, it finally clicks why he looks so horrified. The only way she could destroy a soul is with a weapon that was banned and locked away—'The Obliterator'. The same weapon used on the worst of the worst souls. The same weapon that may be used to destroy me. *Shit.*

"That's where you're wrong." She moves her hair to the side to show us behind her ear. There is an infinity sign tattoo. "I spent years finding back doors to every department and programmed it into this tattoo. It works as its very own department, but leaves no trace when I use it. I have access to almost everything in Eden." That's when I realize, it's not an infinity sign—it's the number '8'. As in the eighth department that shouldn't exist.

I recall seeing Joey with the same tattoo. That's how he was able to easily frame Aiden and knew Taevian was my father. He was a part of her plan too. I can't believe I ever trusted him. Mac also has the tattoo. *Man*, she really is collecting reapers like Pokémon.

She finally lets go of my hair—I am nervous to see the

damage—and walks back to the table, picking up a gun. I'm assuming that's 'The Obliterator'. She walks back over to me and aims it at my head. From what I've read, I know there's no actual bullets in there. It's more like energy is released from it.

She presses it against my head. "Join me or she dies. Permanently. *Choose*."

"What's to stop me from telling everyone your plan once that weapon is not pointing at my daughter's head," my father asks. I am still working at my binds. I'm almost there.

She grins wickedly. "Because you don't know what reapers are on my side or not. If you run and tell anyone, I can assure you, someone, if not me, will destroy your daughter." That sick bitch. Didn't she just say earlier that she wasn't going to harm us. What a liar.

My father looks at me desperately and I aggressively shake my head. "Dad, you can't do this. Look at the lengths she went for power. Imagine what she would do to Eden."

"Taevian, just do what she wants," Aiden pleads.

I whip my head to Aiden, confused at his words. "Why the hell are you helping her?"

His face hardens. "I'm not helping her. I am trying to make sure nothing happens to you."

"What about Eden?" I push, knowing how much he cares about Eden. It is shocking that he is not conflicted right now.

"You think I'm concerned about Eden when there is a gun that can destroy your soul pointed at your head? This place can burn for all I care."

"*See.* Someone with common sense," Director Young remarks. I turn to my father to see him already staring at me.

He looks up to her. "Jia, you don't have to do this."

She sighs, then moves the gun to my chest, where my heart is. "Taevian, honey, *I do*. One last chance. Help me or she dies. *Choose*."

I wiggle the last piece of rope off my wrist. *Yes!* I finally got my binds undone. If I can get that gun away from her then we will have a fighting chance to get out of here. I can't let my father help that evil bitch hatch her plan. I've grown to love Eden and if she takes over, who knows what she will do.

Quicker than I've ever been, I grab her hand moving the gun away from my chest. She wrestles to get the gun pointed at me again. I swipe my legs out, making her fall on her back. The gun falls out of her hand, sliding across the floor. We both pause, then we race for it. I almost reach it when she disappears from beside me and appears right by the gun.

Crap.

I crash into her and down to the floor we go. She tries to point the gun at me again but I move on top of her, struggling to turn the gun on her. I know it won't kill her, but it may cause her to take some serious damage. I can hear Aiden and my father yelling my name.

I can't focus on them right now.

I almost have the gun on her when she knees me in the stomach. I let out a grunt and lose my grip on the gun. In an instant, she turns it on me, and a shot rings out. I let out a breath as a force slams into my chest.

Well, this can't be good.

I don't feel pain. Instead, I feel an extreme sense of peace washing over me, bathing me in tranquility from top to bottom. It is completely different from when I was shot in the courtroom. I was confused and a little scared then. Those emotions aren't present now.

Glancing down at my chest, I see it is glowing gold. I look back up to see Director Young scrambling backwards on her behind. I lean back, my hands pressed against my chest.

"Joyce!" I hear Aiden shout and I turn to look at him. His face is masked in complete horror. I already feel my skin beginning to hum. I look from Aiden to my hands to see them slowly turning into gold flecks and sprinkling away. After two seconds, my hands are no longer there. I don't have a lot of time to process what is happening.

Aiden struggles with his binds, trying to get to me, and yelling my name repeatedly. But it's too late. Pain rips through my chest, but not from the gun. It's from the thought that Aiden will be alone again.

With my last breath I look into his tear-filled eyes and whisper, "I love—" Before I can finish, the world goes black.

27
PLAN B
NOT THAT ONE

Aiden

"*No!*" I hear Director Taevian yell out. Pain is etched in that one word. Pain that only a father who has lost his daughter twice can feel. Once before she was born, and now again. But this time, there won't be a third.

For me, it is different. Every single emotion—rage, hurt, shock, pain—explodes inside of me. I couldn't do anything. I can't breathe. I can't move. I can't make a fucking sound.

The woman I adore, the woman I worship, the woman I fell in love with—

I just watched her die.

No.

This is beyond death. She didn't die. There's no Heaven or Hell for her. No reincarnation. Her soul was destroyed. I watched her get hit. Watched as she fell back. As she disappeared. I didn't do a single thing. I couldn't do anything. I couldn't protect her. I heard her that one night when she laid on my chest and told me that when she was with me, she felt safe. I let her down.

I haven't even reacted yet and I won't. There's nothing to react to. It's over for me. It was over the minute she disappeared. Destroying that bitch who took Joyce wouldn't be enough. This place can burn for all I care. It could crumble to a million pieces, and it wouldn't be enough.

I want to take the weapon and shoot myself with it, but it won't work on me. It only works on non-reaper souls. For me, it would just cause eternal soul-wrenching pain.

I can't even fucking follow after her.

My chest tightens, making every breath hurt worse than the last one. If I could die from suffocation, I would. I would accept it with a smile, too, because it would mean I wouldn't have to exist another second without my Joy.

Director Young looks at the gun in her hand, then to where Joyce just was, and yells, "No! Fucking hell! That bitch ruined my plan." She aggressively taps her head with the gun and starts to pace, mumbling to herself about what she's going to do.

I look towards Taevian and see his head bowed and shoulders shaking. His daughter, who he just got back, the daughter who he fought to be able to love, is gone.

Director Young stops pacing and looks at us. Her face set in determination. How is she so cold to the fact that she just destroyed someone? By taking away Joyce, she destroyed us as well.

"Well boys. Plan B." She walks over to Taevian and lifts his head up using his chin. "Since your daughter decided to ruin my plan, I'll probably have to delay my ascension for a couple of years. However, to ensure you are kept quiet, you will be taking the blame for all the disturbances at Eden. I will have my reapers plant all the evidence to show it was you. With all the evidence pointed against you, no one will believe a word you say." Taevian doesn't reply. His eyes are void of any emotions.

She walks over to me, running her hand through my hair. "I can make you forget about her," she whispers as she smiles wickedly at me.

I look up at her, my lips curling in disgust. "Get your fucking hands off of me." I yank my head away from her.

She snatches her hand away. "Fine. I already had other plans for you anyways." Mac walks into the room. That fucking traitor. *He* is part of the reason Joyce is gone.

She commands, "Take Aiden to Hell and lock him up. You'll be there, well, forever. My access enables me with the ability to tuck you away in a corner of Hell to never be found again. Can't have you running your mouth about my plans."

Mac walks up to him with sad eyes. "I'm sorry about Jo—"

"Don't you fucking say *her* name," I growl. "When I find a way out of Hell—and trust me, *I will*—I'm going to find you and make you wish reapers could die again. That's not a threat. It's a fucking *vow*."

"Aiden—"

"Stop talking to the prisoner and take him to Hell!" Director Young yells. He obeys her, cutting my binds, and grabs me from the chair. Mac guides me to a door to the Hell department I've never seen before, our journey here a blur. One of the reapers who works for the department lets us in. *Well, there goes another reaper who turned evil.*

They drag me through the door and keep their promise of throwing me in the corner of Hell.

My Hell?

Watching Joyce be obliterated over and over again, unable to do a single thing.

28

THE FLOOR IS LAVA

SHIT. That hurts.

I lift myself from the floor and look around. The room is now empty. *What the hell happened?* I remember being here with Aiden and my father. But then it's a blank. I stand up trying to stabilize myself. I feel an ache in my chest, so I rub it. A jolt of pain hits my head as my memories come back. *Aiden.*

Where the hell is Aiden? And aren't I supposed to be, like, gone? I look at my wrist and still see the scythe tattoo, but it's more faded than before and still fading. I wonder if this is what brought me back. I don't feel whole though, but I don't have time to contemplate my condition. I need to get to Aiden and my father. I don't know what happened to them, but it can't be good. That bitch probably did something to them.

Glancing around, I move quietly towards the door, only stopping at her desk when I notice the blue serum that the reapers used on us to prevent us from getting away. I also notice a long gold dagger. I grab both items, placing them in my back pockets. I continue to the door. Once I'm there, I open it slowly, peeking my head out. I do not know where anyone is, so I have to be careful. I see a reaper at the end of the white and silver hallway with his back to me. He is looking down at something.

Perfect.

I take a deep breath then teleport. Thank goodness the serum ran out. I pop up right behind him and before he can turn, I kick behind his knee. As he starts to fall, I wrap my arm around his neck and stab the serum in his arm. I let him go and he drops to the ground. The serum won't knock him out, but it will make him weak enough to where he can't use any reaper abilities. He looks at me in shock. I grin down at him as I pull out the knife. I would prefer to not have to use it, but I will, to find Aiden.

I hold the knife against his chest and ask, "So we meet again. Where is Aiden, Mac?"

Face set with determination, he replies, "Screw you." We could really save each other time and pain. But alas, he's being an idiot.

"Wrong answer." I cover his mouth and slice his chest. He lets out a scream, but it's muffled beneath my hand. I remove it from his mouth and give him a second chance.

I pat his chest. He winces from the pain. "Okay buddy, let me explain how this is going to go. Sooner or later, you are going to tell me. You can voluntarily tell me and save yourself pain. *Or*—and hear me out—I will slice and dice you until you tell me where Aiden is. What is it your boss said? *Oh yes.* Eden is all about free will."

A couple of seconds tick by. He says nothing. I roll my eyes. Alright, I guess we have to do this the hard way. I move the knife down to where his cherished jewels are and start to press the knife down into the fabric of his pants. Before I can do any real damage, he finally yells what I want to hear.

"Okay! Okay! I'll tell you! Please move the knife!"

I let out a breath. I'm glad he gave in. That was not going to be pretty.

He continues talking, "She had us take him to the Hell department. But deep in Hell. Next to tier three. I can get you in. But since you injected me with the serum, you'll have to find a way out."

I narrow my eyes on him. "You better. This serum doesn't run out for another hour. I'll hurt you if you trick me and I'll be going straight for the balls." He nods his head, fear in his eyes. I pull him up with my knife pressing against his side.

"Before we go, why can't Aiden just get himself out?" It would make this a whole lot easier.

"Because we put him in while he was under the influence of the serum. Usually reapers aren't affected by Hell, but since he entered under the influence, his mind got taken over. He is trapped in his own personal Hell and probably doesn't even realize it. He could technically leave at any point, but it will be near impossible to snap himself out of a Hell trance."

"How long has he been in there?"

"About thirty minutes." Shit. That's about six months in Hell time. I need to get to him quickly. I shove the reaper forward with a newfound urgency.

"Aiden helped you through something and you just...help throw him in Hell? You're a piece of shit."

"I would do anything for Director Young," he replies. If I hear her name one more time, I'll lose it.

"Oh, shut up and take me to Aiden," I demand. He walks us towards an elevator I never noticed before. It is tucked away in a corner. It's different from the main elevator I've used to get around Eden.

Once we are inside, he clicks level zero, and we zoom down. I stumble a little at the speed, but find my balance. A few seconds later, the elevator stops with a ding to announce our arrival and we walk out of the elevator with Mac in front of me. I trip over my feet a little from the sudden wave of dizziness that hits me. But just as quickly as it comes, it's gone again.

Glancing around our new surroundings, we are in a barely lit empty room. I look at my scythe tattoo again and see its fading even more. Time is running out. The more the tattoo disappears, the weaker I feel. It is probably the only thing that is keeping me here right now.

"Where are we?" I ask.

"This is a secret entrance into Hell. But it is only an entrance. Director Young had it built in secret to send souls she believes should be in Hell."

"And you don't think that's messed up? Who is she to make the determination of who should be in Heaven? That's why there is a non-bias system called Karma."

He shrugs. "Sometimes certain behaviors shouldn't be overlooked because humans decided to make a change."

"You were once a human too, you know. Probably not a notable one with the way you follow after people."

"Oh, and you were so amazing, huh?"

"No, but I sure didn't follow blindly after anyone." Well, that's not all the way true. But he doesn't need to know that.

I shove him forward towards the door. It requires him to scan his tattoo to unlock it. He scans his tattoo and the door opens. I can't see anything as I look inside.

"How do I find him?"

"This door takes you to tier three. You are already at the corner he is in, so you just have to walk through about two different people's Hell. But you have to be a reaper to walk through. Only reapers can see the door to leave in each Hell."

I look down at my tattoo, praying that this tattoo has enough juice to work.

"Don't worry about that."

"He will be on the other side. Just make sure the people in Hell don't notice you," he warns.

"What would happen if they did?"

"They will attack you. If they touch you, then you'll get stuck in their Hell until someone comes and gets you, which no one will." That would not be fun. I could barely tolerate my version of Hell. Imagine someone else's.

I let him go. "Thank you." Then, I roundhouse kick him in the head, causing him to collapse on the floor, knocking him out cold.

That's for taking my man to Hell.

I step through the door and right into a nightmare. Or maybe just a painful game. I glance around looking for the door until my eyes land on it. The problem? It's on the other side of a *goddamn* lava pit.

I do some stretches and crack my knuckles. I remember getting in trouble with one of my foster parents for throwing their pillows off the couch and pretending they were the rocks and the ground was lava. I've prepared for this my whole life.

Why is this someone's Hell? I hear a scream and whip my head in that direction, just in time to see a woman stuck on a rock in the middle of lava with no way of getting off. She must have had a very traumatic childhood for this to be her Hell.

But for me, I have a path to the door. It will take some hard leaps but if I'm anything, I am competitive. It is me versus the lava. I hear an imaginary bell ring, signaling the beginning of the game. I hop on the rock closest to me then jump to the next. I keep doing this until I reach halfway through. I pause to catch my breath. When I'm ready to continue, I prepare to jump. My actions are halted when I feel the ground begin to vibrate. I squat on the rock to help keep my balance. As the vibrations stop, a huge blast of lava right in front of me shoots into the air.

You got to be fucking kidding me.

What is this? Super Mario? This level just got harder, and I absolutely do not have time for this. I need to get to Aiden, then to my father.

I take a moment to study the lava bursts. There may be a pattern to it. I count how many rocks I have to leap onto to get to the other side. It's five. I wait patiently for another blast. A second later, lava shoots out right in front of me.

One.

Two.

Three.

Another bursts in front of the rock, then in front of the second rock. I continue counting and studying the blasts until it happens again in front of me.

There we go. I figured out the cycle. I leap onto the rock and continue doing this until I finally reach the last rock. As I land on it, my feet slip.

"Fuck!" I yell out as I lose my balance. I throw out my arms to help stabilize me.

Luckily, it works.

Without a second thought, I walk through the door and straight into the worst Hell I can imagine.

There are spiders everywhere.

And I mean *everywhere*. On the walls. On the floor. Even the damn ceiling, where a man is stuck in a spiderweb and screaming for help. There's a huge spider resting right next to him.

Sorry man, I can't help you.

You see, spiders are cool, if they respect my personal boundaries. I doubt that will happen here. I feel something on my feet, and I glance down to see a spider trying to make its way up my pants. I let out a scream, but cover my mouth. I flick the spider off and try not to throw up. My skin prickles. I look up to see if the spider or the man noticed me. They did not. *Whew.*

Honestly, does Aiden really need me? I can come back for him later.

"Yeah, I'm not staying. There is no way I am doing this. Nope," I whisper to myself.

I turn around to go back through the door, but it's gone. Damn. I really have no choice now. I look around at the spiders and send a prayer to no one in particular.

Taking a deep breath, I think about my plan. All I have to do is make it to the other side. I can see the door to get out of here. I should just make a run for it. But what if that disrupts the spiders too much? Slowly might be the best way. If one of them bites me though, I will lose my shit.

Lifting my left foot, I gently kick away the spiders, then begin my journey forward. I hold my breath as I walk through the trenches. When I am halfway through, I feel something on my shoulder. I turn my head to the side and see a giant hairy spider on me. I scream and hit the spider off, tripping over my feet in the process. I fall to the ground, causing my life to get ten times worse. Hundreds of spiders are racing to me. Crawling over me. I'm trying to hit them off, but it's not useful. I look up to see I've caught the attention of the giant spider. He is quickly climbing down the wall.

The giant spider leaps off the wall towards me. I pull out my knife, pointing it at the spider. With spiders crawling all over me and the giant beast in the air, I do the only thing that any desperate person would in this situation—I say a prayer hoping the universe will finally give me a fucking break.

Please God, the universe, whoever is listening, just help me this one time. I don't have any more tricks in my back pocket.

To my complete shock, everything freezes. The giant spider is in the air. The mini spiders stopped crawling all over me. Well, that will do it. Not wasting time or questioning what happened, I dust off all the creepy crawlers and race towards the door. I step on as many spiders as possible as payback for my misery.

When I reach the door, I grab the knob and twist it open and cautiously walk through. My previous experiences have taught me that anything is possible in Hell. I squint my eyes as it adjusts to the dimmer light in the room. I see Aiden in the middle of the room and I smile in relief. *Finally, I've made it to him.*

"Aiden!" I yell out. But he doesn't react. The bottom falls out of my stomach as I take in my surroundings. He is in the same position that I last saw him. Arms tied behind his back and in his chair. This is different though. I remember us all being in the conference room in the Heaven department, but his Hell is missing a lot of things.

In his version, there is just him tied up, and me on the ground holding my chest. Tears are running down his eyes and he is repeatedly calling out my name. I whisper, "I love —" then I disappear. The light in his eyes just vanishes. He drops in defeat, and then the scene restarts again. I pop back up already wounded and holding my chest. *My god.* This is absolute torture. Watching someone you love die over and over again.

Pained by what I am seeing, I run up to him. I drop to my knees next to him and grab his face to look at me. He forces it out of my grip, turning it to face the version of me that is dying over and over again.

"Aiden! It's me. I'm okay," I beg, but it's like he doesn't see me. I shuffle to get behind him. I untie the restraints and throw the rope across the room.

I move back in front of him, crawl on top of his lap and grab his face again, forcing him to look at me. "Aiden! You need to snap out of this!" I yell. I'm getting frustrated with every second that passes. I thought my presence enough would've snapped him out of it.

I shove my hands through his hair, yank his head forward and slam my mouth onto his. He doesn't react at first. His mouth is stiff and unreactive. Then, I'm roughly pushed away. I land on my ass with a grunt in pain. Before I can react, I'm yanked forward and pressed into a soft, warm chest. Aiden's arms wrap around me, and he shoves his face against my throat.

"Are you real?" he whispers into my neck. I let out a

breath of relief. If kissing him didn't work, we would've been stuck in Hell forever.

"Yeah. My ass hurts from you just shoving me," I reply jokingly.

He leans back and examines me. His hand lands on my chest where it should've been glowing gold. He looks up to me.

"How?" he asks, his grip on me tightening. I lift my arm to show him the scythe tattoo that is still there. It is almost gone.

"You protected me, Aiden," I inform him. If it wasn't for this tattoo, I would not be here.

His eyes are tormented as he admits, "I failed you. I should've never taken my eyes off you. I should've known they would find us." I roughly yank his ear.

"Ow! What the fuck was that for." He glares at me.

"Could've, should've, would've!" I yell, losing patience with him blaming himself for my choices. "You did your best. You were trying to get us food, for goodness sake. It was the only moment we were separated. The only place I may have possibly been safer was up your ass at that point."

His mouth twitches. "Okay, I get it."

I nod. "Good. Now, let's save Taevian." I move to get off his lap, but he stops me.

"I love you, my Joy," he whispers. My heart squeezes every time he says, 'my Joy'.

I place my forehead against his and close my eyes. "I would walk through Hell for the rest of eternity if it led to you. I love you too."

He gently wraps a hand around my nape and brings my lips to his to kiss me. He deepens our kiss, his tongue swirling against mine. I shove my hands through his hair as he devours my mouth, his hold on me tightening as if he is afraid I will disappear again.

A sudden pain pinches my chest. I rip my mouth away and look away, squeezing my eyes shut. The pain passes as quickly as it came. I open my eyes and look at Aiden.

"Hey, are you okay?" he asks, his brows furrow with concern.

"Yeah, I'm fine," I reassure him.

He narrows his eyes. "You didn't seem fine."

"It's probably a side effect from getting shot," I inform him. It isn't a lie. It just isn't the whole truth. Now is not the time to worry him. I look at my wrist, internally sighing. "We need to go."

Aiden stands and helps me up. "We do. Director Young plans to frame your dad and show that he caused all the chaos at Eden."

I grab his hand. "Teleport us out of here."

29
KICK THE DAMN DOOR IN

In a blink, we are in our office. I let go of his hand and walk over to my computer with Aiden in tow.

"How exactly are we going to stop her? She has all the evidence, and we don't know how many reapers are supporting her," he says. I pull out something from my bra and show him. It wasn't the best place to hide it, but it was the only place the reapers didn't pat me down. Thank goodness for that. At least they weren't perverts.

I started to keep a recorder on me when things at Eden began to get weird. You learn the importance of evidence as a lawyer.

I connect the device to my laptop and upload the file. Then, I email it to Valerie with a message.

To: *Valerie Pierre*
From: *Joyce Parker*
Subject: *Villainous Bitch Confession*
Attachments: *audio.mp3*

Val,

The Reaper's Resources department has access to the PA System in Eden. I need you to play the attachment out loud in five minutes. Consider it payment for the free phone porn.

Thx,

JP, Esq.

Once I am sure the email is sent, I explain my plan to Aiden. "I recorded her whole confession before she shot me. Now, all we have to do is confront her and let it play. Then, it's game over for her."

Aiden tilts her head. "Why don't you just play it now?"

I clasp my hands together, an evil smile spreading across my face. "The excitement in fucking someone over is seeing their face as they realize they are fucked."

Aiden gives me a sexy smile. "I love when you are vindictive."

I wink at him and hold out my hand. He grabs it, lifting it up to his lips and placing a gentle kiss on it. We walk out of the office toward the director's conference room. When we arrive, I look at Aiden.

"Kick it in," I demand, needing to show them that we mean business.

Aiden gives me a look. "I'm pretty sure it's unlocked." Everything would go a lot smoother if Aiden wasn't so stubborn.

I let go of him and place my hands on my hips. "We need a dramatic entrance."

"Let's compromise. How about I slam the door open rather than kicking it?" he suggests.

I contemplate it for a second then nod. "I agree to your terms."

He rolls his eyes then places his hand on the doorknob. We burst into the directors' conference room, the door slamming against the wall, and everyone turns to look at us. At the front of the room stands Director Young with my father in cuffs next to her and looking at the ground. When she sees us, Director Young freezes and her jaw goes slack. She quickly corrects her face. My father's head snaps up, his eyes filling with tears as he examines me from top to bottom. I wink at him, then turn my attention to the directors.

"What is the meaning of this?" Director Onai demands.

I stroll across the room until I am at the opposite end of the table from Director Young. I turn to locate Aiden and see he is leaning against the wall. He nods his head once as an encouragement to continue. Director Young steps forwards, clearing her throat to ensure everyone can clearly hear whatever horseshit is about to leave her mouth.

"Directors, here is Joyce Parker, the proof of Director Jackson's disregard for Eden. If he would manipulate the system for his daughter, imagine what else he is capable of."

Everyone nods their heads in agreement...except Director Onai, the director of Hell. I look at her with an arched eyebrow.

She shrugs, twisting the gold ring on her finger. "Director Jackson mentioned to me ten years ago about having a daughter. He let it slip that her name was Joyce." She pauses and gives me a look. "I doubt it was a coincidence that your name is also Joyce. What happened in court was just confirmation of what I already knew."

"Why didn't you say anything?" I ask.

"Director Taevian is the kindest and most caring man I've ever met. He deserved some happiness." She points to Director Young. "Plus, I don't believe a word coming out of her mouth."

Director Young glares at Director Onai. "As a director, you should not let personal feelings blind you from the truth." She pauses, making it a point to look at each director. "I have served as a director for the longest. As you all can see, I care deeply about Eden. For Eden to continue in its glory, we need a centralized power. Look what happens when one director uses his role for personal reasons."

I say, "You're forgetting one thing—you're the person who actually did all the things you are accusing my father of."

"How could you make accusations against Director Young, Ms. Parker? It is clear Director Taevian has a pattern for blatantly disregarding the Reaper's Code of Conduct," Director Woody of the Reaper's Resources department admonishes. I roll my eyes at him.

"Please, do tell. What reason would he have to take over Eden?"

Director Woody shakes his head. "That's for him to answer during his trial."

Mac bursts into the room looking disheveled and rushes to Director Young's side. Before he can speak, Valerie's voice sounds over the intercom. Ah, it's time for the show. I wish I had some popcorn.

"Reapers of Eden, Attorney Joyce Parker has made a special request."

We hear her shuffle for a moment, then Director Young's and my voice begins to play over the intercom.

"As I was saying before, hostile takeovers are for weak minded men. My plan was simple—make it as though Eden is slowly falling apart. I provide the problem, and I will also be the solution. The problem? Eden needs one central leader. Obviously having directors is not working. Solution? Me. But your father figured me out and planned to expose me. So, I had to threaten him with something— or should I say someone—that would keep his mouth shut, you."

Everyone in the room gasps, their stares directed at Director Young. The recording keeps going.

"So what? You're going to threaten to hurt me? News flash. I can't die again. Congrats, that's the best villainous plan I've ever heard."

Director Young lets out an evil laugh over the intercom, a sound most have not heard before.

"No. Of course not. I'm going to give him a choice because Eden is all about free will."

"I have something you hold precious. Your daughter. So,

you have a choice. You either join my side or I'll make sure
you never see your daughter again."

I begin clapping, Aiden watching me with a smile on his face. Everyone switches their attention to my father at the sound of him speaking.

"Then, she proceeded to shoot my daughter with 'The Obliterator'," my father says, "right in front of me. I thought she was gone forever."

"How are you standing before us? Never has a soul survived that," Director Davis asks, shock emanating from him as he looks at me.

I lift my wrist to show them the scythe tattoo. "When we were on the run from the reapers working under Director Young, Aiden took one of the mini tattoo machines from the armory. He knew it was one of the ways to protect me. If it wasn't for him, I wouldn't have been able to get him out of Hell—where she placed him—and come here to reveal her plans."

Director Young begins, "Another blatant disrespect for rule and procedure—"

I groan in annoyance. "Please, for the love of everything, *shut up.*"

Director Onai smirks. "Director Young. I always knew you were too nice. Nobody is that nice."

"That's what I said!" I exclaim, giving her an air high five which she returns.

A reaper walks up to my father and removes the cuffs. He rubs his wrist, then points to Director Young. "Cuff her and Mac, then take them to the containment cells where they will await their trial."

Before the guard can restrain Director Young, she teleports next to me, pulling out 'The Obliterator' from her waistband, and pointing it at my head.

This again?

She laughs humorlessly. "I wonder...if I shoot her twice, will she be able to come back?"

Similar to when Mr. Reynold's held me at gunpoint, everyone in the room freezes. How many times am I going to get shot for goodness sake? But, I don't say anything, not wanting to trigger her.

My father pleads, "Jia, let's talk about this." She turns her head to look at him. Aiden uses that opportunity to teleport next to her, yank the gun from my face and shove her roughly into the wall. With the gun in one hand and her throat in his other, he throws her on the ground by the guard.

Menacingly, Aiden says, "I'm not *talking* about shit. Get her the fuck out of here and away from Joyce." The guard quickly grabs her and leaves the room. Aiden raises the gun to point at his other friend who betrayed him. Mac raises his hands, panic filling his face.

"Aiden! What are you doing?" I exclaim. He's just full of surprises today.

Ignoring me, he asks Mac, "What did I promise you?" Mac doesn't reply, so Aiden answers for him. "I promised you that I would get out of Hell and find you. *Didn't I?*" Mac opens his mouth to speak, but Aiden shoots him in the chest.

Goddamn it. Back to court we go. Mac grasps his chest and cries out in pain. At least his soul won't be destroyed. He will just feel pain for...well, forever.

All the directors gasp except Director Onai. She chuckles and nods her head as if she agrees with Aiden's actions. She is probably one of my favorite directors at this point, besides my dad, of course.

Director Woody sputters, "You cannot do that, Aiden!"

Aiden turns to glare at him. "I can *and* I will to anyone who hurts Joyce. Would you like to be next?" Goodness. He is so sexy when he's mad.

Director Woody points at him. "What do you mean by that?"

Aiden smirks. "What words are giving you trouble?" Trying to stifle my laugh, I cough into my fist.

"You will face justice in Reaper's Court!"

"He will do no such thing. Look around, Woody. No one cares but you," my father says. Director Woody looks around with angry eyes. When he doesn't see the reactions he wants, he lets out a huff but keeps his mouth shut. Smart.

My father walks over to me and brings me into his embrace. "I don't know how we can ever thank you," he pauses, "how *I* can ever thank you."

I smile shyly. "I'm a lawyer. It's what I do. Fight for the people I love." I lean back from him to look into his eyes. There is only unconditional love in them. A lump forms in my throat as I say, "and I love you."

His eyes fill with tears. "I love you too, my daughter." His voice is thick with emotion. He pulls me back into a hug. Aiden lets out a fake cough. We pull apart and look at him. I smile at him awkwardly standing there.

My father smiles at Aiden. "I see you both worked things out."

I chuckle. "Yes, we—" I let out a gasp. My legs give out from under me as pain erupts in my chest. My father catches me before I fall and holds me in his arms, gently lowering us to the ground.

"Joyce, what's wrong?" he asks, panic laced in his voice. Too excited about taking down Director Jia Young, I forgot about the tattoo. Aiden pulls me from Taevian's arms and against his chest.

Aiden looks at me, his eyebrows furrowed. "Joy?" he says gently. A stabbing pain hits me again. I can't believe I forgot that I'm running out of time. At least, I was given enough time to protect my family.

"As the tattoo fades...so do I," I confess.

30
CHOICES? NEVER HEARD OF HER

"No," Aiden calmly says.

My father falls onto his butt and stares at me with lost eyes. The directors gather around us, sympathy filling their eyes.

"Aiden—" I gently begin, trying to calm him down before he explodes.

"*No!*" he yells this time. *Yep.* I was right.

Aiden swivels his head around at everyone. "*I swear to God somebody better do something right now!*" he yells, the sound ricocheting off the walls.

Nobody moves. They all know there is nothing that can be done. With every second that passes, I am slowly disappearing. Soon, I'll be somewhere beyond Eden. My only regret is the pain him and my father will go through once I'm gone.

Aiden showed me that I never needed to earn love. I never needed a reason to love. Existing is enough reason to love and be loved. My dad showed me that there is always a little love lingering somewhere, sometimes it's just beyond your grasp. But it's there.

I put my hand on Aiden's face, swiping at the wetness on his cheeks. I whisper, "It's okay. It's going to be okay. I'm okay because you're here. I love you, Aiden."

He uses the back of his hand to swipe at his face aggressively. He clenches his jaw, tightening his grip on me as he fiercely says, "Don't tell me you love me. This is not goodbye Joyce."

"It's not goodbye Aiden...it's a till we meet again." *I know.* I know this is it. That there's nothing after this. But I can't help but hope that some way, somehow, we will meet again.

He hugs me tighter. "*No.* It's not fair. It's not fucking fair. You cannot leave me. Please. Baby." God, this sucks. I wish I could go back in time and figure out a different way to stop Director Young. A way that wouldn't be causing Aiden and Taevian so much pain.

"Please, tell me you love me," I beg him, not wanting him to regret not saying those words once I am gone.

"Fuck that. *No.* Someone tell me what to do!" He looks around desperately for someone to help, for someone to tell him that this isn't it. That this can be fixed. But as he looks around, everyone looks at him with painful, hopeless expressions. No one says a word.

Aiden lets go of me, leaving me to lay on the floor. I look at him to see him looking at his hands. When he looks at me, I see something I have never seen before.

I see defeat. I realize that I am disappearing too fast for him to have a solid grip on me.

"I can't even hold you anymore," he whispers. He takes a shaky deep breath and finally says the words I wanted. The words that make my chest tighten and the wetness in my eyes to finally run down my cheeks.

"I love you, my Joy," Aiden whispers.

My father is sitting beside Aiden, his hand is where mine should be. He has been quiet this whole time. At least we get to say a proper goodbye this time.

He lets out a gasp and looks at us with hopeful eyes. "There's something you can do. But it's risky."

Aiden desperately looks to him. I feel myself slipping even more.

"I don't give a fuck if it's risky. Tell me right goddamn now," Aiden snaps.

"If you tie your soul with hers, you may be able to stop it..." my father pauses then warns, "or it may destroy your soul along with hers."

Aiden shakes his head. "I don't care. There's no me without her. Let's do it." This sounds like an all-around bad plan. I refuse to let Aiden risk himself for me.

"No, Aiden. It's too risky."

He glares down at me and snaps, "What about this situation makes you think you have a choice?" I chuckle at his words, thinking back to the first time he said them. We really have come a long way.

Looking into his eyes, I see how much pain he is in. How could I say no? Screw it. One more reckless decision for the road.

I turn to my father. "Okay, how do we do it?"

My father hurriedly replies, "It's actually very simple. First, you need to place your hands on each other's chest, where the heart is."

We do as he says. However, Aiden's hand is not actually

pressing against me due to my fading condition. I smirk at Aiden and say, "You always got to cop a feel, huh."

Aiden sighs. "Can we joke when you are not moments away from disappearing forever?" He looks at my dad. "Please continue."

This is it. This is the final thing that the universe can take away or give to me. I can die with the man I love, or I can spend eternity with him. Either way, I'll be with him.

My father continues, "Now, all you have to do is think of an invisible string coming from you and another coming from the other person. Once you do that, envision it tying together." He pauses, giving us a second to do it. "Now say the words *'Semper et Perpetuo'*."

At the same time, we both say the words, never taking our eyes off each other. *"Semper et Perpetuo."*

A jolt runs through my body and we both gasp. I feel an overwhelming pain in my chest as if it's going to burst. Just as quickly as it came, it goes away. I look down at my hands, seeing that I am once again solid. *Holy shit.* It worked. Not that I doubted it.

No. Actually, I did. With my luck, we should be floating off into oblivion.

Aiden's eyes wildly run over me as he pulls me against his chest. He shoves his face in my neck. His head is kind of weighing down on my hair causing some of my braids to pull. I let him be, ignoring the pain. I can hear him breathe me in as I rub his back to soothe him.

I can feel his emotions in the back of my mind now. It isn't too overpowering. There's a pull to him now as if my soul is reaching out to him. It feels strange.

"You're okay. I got you," he breathes out. I don't know if

he's trying to convince me or himself. My father helps us up and tries to hug me, but Aiden won't let go.

I lean slightly back from Aiden's grasp to place my hands on either side of his face and kiss him. When we part, I start to smile at him, but freeze at the sight of something on my hand.

His eyebrows furrow. "Joy, are you okay?" I ignore him and bring my left hand closer. I grab Aiden's hand and see the same thing. We both have red tattoos wrapped around our ring finger. They have little intricate designs that are just gorgeous.

I am admiring the rings when Yirah bursts into the room with tears in her eyes. "Oh, thank God! I'm not too late." She runs next to us and tries to pull me out of his grasp, but he still refuses to let go. Yirah gives up and settles for grabbing my hand.

My father informs her, "She's okay. Aiden and her tied souls. She's now a reaper."

"Wait, what?" She looks at me with wide eyes, then grins. "That means you don't have to leave!" She claps her hands in excitement and I can't help but laugh.

"How can you all be excited right now? She was seconds away from permanently dying," Aiden admonishes. Before anyone can reply, Aiden tightens his hold on me and teleports us away to his home—our home.

Without letting me go, he walks into the bathroom, gently places me on my feet by the shower and reaches over to turn it on. He hasn't said a word since he teleported us away. We have a lot to talk about. Including our new future together now that we are bound to one another for—well—eternity.

"Aiden—"

He shakes his head. "Not right now." I can feel his anger and worry swirling in him. He doesn't know how to react. Instead of talking, he slowly strips me naked then himself. He grabs a hair tie from the counter and motions for me to turn around. When I try to help him with my hair, he gently pushes my hand away. His hands move through my scalp massaging it. He lifts my braids and twirls them into a bun on top of my head, securing it with the hair tie. Once he's done, he moves us into the warm shower. We remain silent as he washes every inch of me.

When he finishes, he turns off the shower, wraps us in towels and lifts me into his arms. He brings us into the bedroom and places me on the ground again. He dries us with the towels, then drops them on the floor by the bed.

Still standing, he grabs the lotion and gently moisturizes every inch of my body. He caresses my thighs, massages my shoulders, and places kisses up my arms. Throwing the lotion bottle to the side, he commands, "On the bed."

I open my mouth, but close it at his arched brow. I know him well enough to know that it is a dare for me to talk. I can still feel his emotions in turmoil, so I decide to keep my mouth shut for now. Slowly, I back up until the back of my legs hit the bed. I sit, then slowly climb backwards with him watching me the whole time.

"Open," he gently says. I make a soft sound and spread my legs wide, welcoming him. He takes a deep inhale and closes his eyes. He wraps a hand around himself and strokes himself, making me watch. I begin to pant as I watch him pleasure himself with slow strokes.

"Aiden," I whisper. "I want you."

Releasing himself, he climbs into bed and right between

my legs. My whole-body jerks as he parts my folds and blows on me.

"You're already so wet and I've barely touched you. At least your body listens, unlike you," he murmurs.

He dips a finger into my wetness and smears it on my clit as he begins to toy with me, switching between sucking and flicking it with his tongue. I moan when I feel him groan against me. I put my hands through his hair, but he roughly grabs them with one of his hands. I feel myself close to the edge and just as I was about to find my release, he stops and chuckles. He waits till the tension in my body relaxes, then starts again. This goes on for five more minutes.

"*Please,*" I sob, tears running down my face in frustration, wanting him to let me find my release. This is torture. He is torturing me, and I can't fathom why. I don't have enough brain cells functioning to even think beyond wanting him to push me over the edge. His mouth stops and I look down to see him looking at me.

"My Joy, I want you to feel how frustrated I get with you." He moves up my body, nestling himself between my legs. "Tell me what you want."

"*You.*"

"Me?"

"*Aiden.*"

"What do you want me to do?" He *oh so* slowly pushes in, inch by inch. We both groan in unison once he's fully inside. He slowly slides in and out of me. He leans down and licks one of the tears from my cheeks.

"Make me come!" I yell, frustrated with the games he is playing.

"You think you can demand anything right now?" His

eyes narrow dangerously. "After you went to collect souls, I told you to stop doing stupid shit."

"But I—"

He slams into me, ripping a scream from my throat as I tighten around him. He stays buried in me, watching me catch my breath.

"That's not how this is going to go. I'm going to do whatever I want with you and you're going to take it. *Okay?*"

"You fucking asshole," I hiss.

He grins wickedly. "What did you say? You want me to fuck your ass?"

"Don't you dare—"

"For a lawyer, you don't have good listening skills. I just told you I'm going to do whatever I want with you. Got it?"

I glare at him. He shifts his hips, hitting that sweet spot inside of me.

"Okay," I mutter.

"Now, say you'll *never* do something like that again." A hard edge to his voice. "Fucking say it." I get it now. He's worried.

I place a hand on his cheek. "I won't ever do something like that again," I promise.

He holds my gaze and searches my eyes. When he finds what he is looking for, he nods. I move my hand up his cheek and into his hair. I yank his head close to me so his ear is almost touching my mouth. I suck on his earlobe. "Now, fuck me like I'm yours. Unless, I'm not?" I taunt, knowing exactly how he will react.

"You are mine," he growls, then pulls all the way out and drives into me. I cry out in pain when I feel how deep he is. But his pace doesn't falter once. It's brutal. *Territorial.* I rake my nails down his back as I cry out his name. The only sound in the room is of our skin slapping loudly, my moans, and his grunts in my ear.

"Who owns this?" he demands, as he lifts my hips up causing him to hit a deeper spot.

"You do," I pant.

"And you own me too, baby." The chain he always wears brushes against my face. My back arches when he presses down on my clit. I violently find my release and my body goes limp. However, Aiden's not done. He continues to own my body. I whimper with every thrust.

"Aiden. I can't. *Please.*" My exhausted legs quiver as he continues to drive into me without mercy.

"You can and you will." He places his hands behind my knees and lifts my legs over his shoulder. This angle allows him to hit that sweet spot. A sob catches in my throat. I feel as he pounds unforgivingly into me. Taking me. Owning me. *Showing me* where he belongs.

"*Aiden.*"

"Not yet, Joy."

"*Aiden.*"

"Not fucking yet," he orders, his voice guttural. I let out a cry of frustration and hold on. I grab the sheets and bite my lips. I squeeze my eyes shut tightly.

"My sweet, *sweet* Joy. Such a good girl," he praises. I whimper in response, trying to hold on just a little longer.

"Eyes on me," he commands. I try to keep them open but closing them helps me from coming. He stops moving and pulls completely out of me. He flips me onto my stomach, drags my hips back and slams into me. He pushes into the arch in my back, causing him to hit my clit with every brutal thrust.

Finally, the hand at my throat tightens and he growls, "Fucking come."

White-hot pleasure like I've never felt before slams into me. I let out the loudest scream I've ever made. My body is shaking as he milks every drop of pleasure from me. I feel him thrust deep into me, emptying himself inside, with a loud groan. With no energy left in me—I pass out.

I gently run my hand through his hair. "Are you feeling better now?" After an hour, I woke up with my back to Aiden's front, him still inside of me, and his hand on my breast. When I realized he was awake, I turned to face him.

He sighs. "I was furious."

"At me?"

"No. At the fact that I almost lost you again. I didn't even think of the soul ties. If it wasn't for your father, you would've disappeared again. Joy, I wouldn't have been able to make it a second time." He shakes his head. "Don't ever risk yourself like that again."

"I'm here now. I'm not going anywhere." I peck his lips. "Haven't you heard? I'm no longer just the Grim Reaper's lawyer. I'm a reaper myself," I joke.

"You're the sexiest reaper I've seen," he teases, rubbing his hand up and down my back.

I scoff. "Not if Beyoncé becomes one."

"You've never spoken truer words."

I pinch him hard on his arm.

"*Ow!* It's Beyoncé! What do you expect?"

I purse my lips then smile. "You're right." Who can top the queen? Certainly, not me.

I can't believe we really tied our souls together. This is not something I ever imagined doing when I first heard of the concept. But here we are. Together. Forever. But I'm worried about whether he feels the same. I'm also concerned about—

"I can feel your worry through the bond. What's wrong?" he questions.

I bite my lip. "The last couple that tied their souls ended up reincarnating. Then, they went to Heaven when they died again. What if they hate each other? What if we grow to hate each other. What if we decide to break up? Can we even do that? We can feel each other through the bonds. I'll feel if you have sex with someone else. You'll feel if I—"

"You're done talking. We are not having sex with other people. You are mine, Joyce Parker, and I am yours."

"We haven't even known each other that long and now it's me and you. Forever. What if we choose to reincarnate?"

"Time is irrelevant. There's no time frame for falling in love. It can be at first sight or fifty years from now. The beautiful thing about love is how it transcends time. People find each other over and over again in different lifetimes. I wouldn't be surprised if I knew you in my previous life before I became Aiden." He places a hand on my cheek. "My point is —I love you. You love me. Nothing else should matter."

"You always have a way of calming me down," I admit. He always says the right thing, despite it being harsh sometimes. But tough love is needed at times.

He nods. "Someone has to be the reasonable one in this relationship."

I gasp, knowing very well I am not the most reasonable person. "I'm very reasonable. I'm a lawyer."

I think I lost all reasonable behavior in law school. You would think I would have left law school with more sense. However, I left with fewer brain cells.

He gives me a look. "Keep telling yourself that."

"You're annoying."

He rolls on top of me and leans down until his lips are almost touching mine. "Well baby, you're stuck with me."

I smile. "There is no place I would rather be stuck."

"Aren't you glad I sent you to Hell?"

I narrow my eyes. "I've gone to Hell two times now because of you." That was two times more than I ever thought I would be in Hell.

He chuckles lightly. "Hopefully, there won't be a third."

I laugh. "Buddy, if there is, you are on your own," I lie, knowing I'll go wherever he is.

His face turns serious as he stares deeply into my eyes. "Thank you."

I scrunch my brows. "For what?"

"Existing."

31
MY ANSWER IS STILL NO

A Week Later

As I am finishing the last touches on my make-up, Aiden walks into the bathroom and positions himself behind me.

He kisses my neck, then looks at me in the mirror. "By the time you finish, they'll have started and finished the meeting without us."

I give him a look. "*They* invited *me* to the meeting. I doubt it."

"Are you sure it's okay if I come? I don't know if the directors intended for me to be there," he murmurs.

"I'm anxious and you keep me calm. Plus, you have to come, or I might say something stupid," I insist. I really do mean that too. I don't want to mess this up. I know my father will be there, but I want Aiden there, too.

He chuckles. "You already know what they might ask you. Just retort with your counterclaim. We both know how you like to push for alternative options." I elbow him gently in his stomach.

I finish my make-up by applying my lipstick. Aiden—knowing that is the last step in my routine—turns me around to face him, placing a hand on either side of me on the counter.

He gazes into my eyes, pride emanating from his own. "Baby, you are Joyce Ann Parker. You not only protected me, but you protected Eden, almost getting your soul obliterated in the process. You've earned what you are asking for. Do not accept less." I lean up and press my lips against his. Before we can deepen our kiss, my phone rings in my pocket. I lean slightly away from Aiden and take it out. I roll my eyes at the name that pops up on the screen.

"Hello, father," I say drily when I answer the call and place it on speaker. I wasn't surprised to find out that he had served in the military during his life. He has a thing about being early.

"You're late," he states. Aiden quietly chuckles as he plays with my hair.

"We still have five minutes," I inform him.

"On time is late."

"We are on our way, Commander Jackson," I reply sarcastically.

"Roger that. I'll see you when you get here," he says, then clicks off.

I lean up and peck Aiden on the lips. "Let's be on our way. Apparently, we are awfully late."

He raises a brow. "I told you. I know your father pretty well. On time is late and—"

I wave him off. "Yeah, yeah. You're the perfect son-in-law. I get it. Let's go."

"Do you want to practice teleporting?"

"We don't have time today. We might end up in Mexico again."

"I told you. You have to think of the place you want to go to. You can't let other thoughts distract you." All I do is let other thoughts distract me.

I wave dismissively. "We will resume lessons later." I grab his hand then pull him into the bedroom and grab my purse from the bed. "I'm ready." He nods then teleports us in front of the director's conference room. In contrast to the last time we were in here, we calmly walk into the room. We greet everyone as we pass them on the way to our seats.

Once we have taken our seats, my father speaks. "Now that we are all here, let us begin."

Originally, Director Young led the meetings. But due to her imprisonment in Hell, my father took over the role. Everyone respects him, so naturally, they looked to him to lead.

"All of the directors met, and we came up with an offer for you Joyce," my father says with a wide smile, excitement glowing in his eyes.

I look at all the directors, then back to my dad and laugh. "Last time someone presented an offer to me, I ended up in Hell." I pointedly look at Aiden.

Aiden sighs. "You really got to let that go. I've apologized a million times. How long are you going to hold it against me?"

I tilt my head in thought. "Hm. How about fifty years?" I smile at him. He rolls his eyes and grabs my hand. Aiden and I are sitting next to each other in the conference room. All the directors are sitting at the table in their different color suits. The new director looks nervous, but does a decent job trying to hide it.

My dad coughs and we both look towards him. "Like I was saying. We have an offer." He smiles. "We would like to open a sort of public defender's office in the Reaper's Court department and would like you to run it and train new hires. Every reaper deserves representation and so far—you are the only one. You would be reporting to Director Barrett. What do you think?"

I open my mouth then close it. Aiden squeezes my hand. I take a deep breath. "No."

Everyone looks at me in shock. The only person not surprised is Aiden. He chuckled at my dad's offer knowing very well what my response was going to be. They all expected me to agree. But I have other plans.

My dad stutters a bit as he says, "E-excuse me?"

I smile. "I have my own offer for you all." Aiden's grip on my hand tightens in support. I've been talking to him about this for a while now.

"I don't want to work under anyone." I look at the director of Reaper's Court and say, "No offense."

Director Barrett shrugs. "None taken."

"I much rather run my own show. A law firm of sorts where I'll represent reapers but also provide mediation services to reapers. I'll not only handle cases where reapers violated the rules, but I'll also handle issues between reapers. A criminal and civil reaper firm of sorts. If I work at the department like you want, I would be only handling cases involving the RCC."

I finish and take a deep breath. I really like my idea and

what I can do with the new firm. My passion for being a lawyer slowly came back through my time here. I've healed my past trauma. While I have Aiden to thank for pushing towards healing, it's really me who did it. I wouldn't have been able to do it if I didn't take the time to forgive myself for holding on to guilt that was never mine. This firm can be a new beginning for me, which is ironic considering I'm in the afterlife.

Director Onai laughs. "She sure is your daughter. Straight to the point."

"She sure is," my dad says proudly. He contemplates my proposal for a moment then clasps his hands. "How about instead of a 'firm of sorts', we just make it a separate department?" I gasp and squeeze Aiden's hand tightly. He squeezes back in support.

"A whole department?" I whisper, my eyes still wide with shock.

"Well, we aren't going to give you half." He chuckles. "Shall we all vote?" The directors nod their heads in unison.

"All in favor of Joyce having her own department raise your hand," my father announces. I stop breathing as every Director raises their hand. He looks around the room then to me.

"Congratulations, my daughter. You are now Director Joyce Parker."

32
SO HELP ME...GOD?

IT'S BEEN a year since everything went down at Eden. Joey and Director Young went through trial and were sentenced to two-hundred years in Hell, then reincarnation. Gratefully, they will never become a reaper again, nor will they have any memories of being one.

New safety measures were put in place to avoid that situation from happening ever again, including restrictions on the use of department tattoos. Now that I have my own department, I have my own number—seven. Originally, the IT department had that number, but they merged with the Reaper's Resources department when the director retired.

Aiden and I still share an office. I love looking up from my desk and being able to see him. The office sex doesn't hurt either. Ever since we tied our souls, we can feel each other's emotions and pain. We also know each other's exact location. The location thing is super cool because now that I'm a reaper, I can teleport. So, I can randomly pop up to wherever Aiden is.

Teleporting took some time to get used to. But I can

finally pick up my own bottles of champagne without needing a ride. That does not mean I won't steal them from the lounge from time to time though. I like the rush.

Another thing the bond gave us is the ability to feel each other's emotions. It can get annoying, especially when he's hungry because I can feel his agitation. But I've loved every second of being soulmates. There aren't many reapers who have tied their souls, which I understand. It's a *huge* commitment. You are literally stuck with this person for the rest of eternity. So, even if they leave all the cabinets open after you told them a million times to freaking close it, you're stuck.

I glance down at my ring finger to see the permanent red design wrapped around where a ring would go. Aiden has the same design on his ring finger too. Every couple who ties their soul has their own special design. I can't help but wish it was gold. Red doesn't really match with my aesthetics.

Currently, I have on a dark purple suit with white sneakers. My feet need a break from heels. Now, I wear purple suits all the time. I chose it as my department color. The directors would not budge on the idea of letting me wear whatever suit color I wanted at any time. You win some, you lose some.

My curls look fantastic, courtesy of a great twist-out. Last thing I needed was my twist-out to not come out right. Why? Because Aiden would have to watch me have a complete meltdown. But that didn't happen. At least not this time.

In conclusion, I look fantastic. Since I'm a director, I make sure to look good all the time. I'm the boss. The big kahuna. I always knew this day would come.

My thoughts are interrupted when my father snaps his fingers in front of my face. I look at him in confusion.

"Director Parker, are you paying attention?" he asks. I

look around the table to see the other directors looking at me with humor on their faces.

"Yes, of course," I reply, knowing damn well I have no idea where we're at on the agenda.

"What did I just say?" he pushes. I narrow my eyes on my father. He and I both know I was not listening.

I sigh in defeat. "Now, why do you have to embarrass me like this? I was just thinking of some lawyer stuff."

He raises a brow. "Some lawyer stuff? Like what?" He is so stubborn. Thank goodness I am nothing like him.

I concede. "Okay, okay. I get it. I'm listening now."

He smiles at me and starts to speak again, "As I was saying—"

The door bursts open and Valerie stumbles in with an arm around Yirah, trying to keep her upright. Yirah is holding her chest with her face twisted in pain. When they reach me, they both collapse next to my chair. All the other directors stand, confusion echoing on their faces.

Dropping to the floor, I lift Yirah into my arms and desperately ask Valerie, "What the hell is happening to her?" I am panicking so much that I begin to shake. I lift one of my hands holding Yirah and see it covered in blood.

"I don't know. I found her like this in a hallway. I didn't know what to do so I brought her to you," Valerie says, her voice slightly shaking. I have never seen Valerie anything but fierce. But in this moment, she is terrified.

Yirah looks into my eyes, her own golden brown irises brighter than usual. She whispers one word as her chest bursts open.

"*God.*"

A burst of energy blasts out of her, throwing everyone

violently. My back hits the wall with a loud crack and I fall to the ground, my face smacking the floor. Feeling blood drip down my nose, I pinch it in an attempt to stop the bleeding.

Groaning in pain, I try to sit up when Aiden appears next to me, probably feeling my pain through our bond. He gently lifts me to my feet.

"What the hell happened?" Aiden asks as he checks for injuries all over my body. He grasps my face, wiping away the blood from my nose. Looking down at everyone, I let out a string of curses when I realize everyone but me is unconscious.

I turn and point to Yirah who's unmoving on the ground. "I don't know. Yirah said 'God' then a burst of energy came out of her, and we all went flying," I reply.

He squints his eyes in confusion. "Why did she say 'God?'"

Sometimes I have to keep my attitude in check. I want to tell him that if I knew, wouldn't I have said it? Luckily for him, now is not the time nor the place.

So instead, I start to say, "I don't know—"

"That would be me," an unrecognizable voice replies to the question that was not directed at them.

We turn towards the voice and standing there is a man— as naked as Adam and Eve before they ate the apple— leaning against the wall with his arms crossed. I slap away Aiden's hand that is attempting to cover my eyes.

Holy shit.

He is breathtaking in every way—creamy, rich dark skin, damn near seven feet tall, and a full beard. But it is his eyes that have me holding my breath. They aren't dark brown. They are pitch black and they are terrifying to look into. But I can't look away. However, that fear does not stop me from opening my mouth.

"First, why the hell are you naked?" I mean I don't mind the show, especially since it's free.

He looks down then back to me with a smirk. "I haven't been in my physical form for what feels like a thousand years. But that could be off."

"And that brings me to my second question. Who the fuck are you?" I demand, angry that he may not only be the reason my best friend is knocked out cold on the ground, but also the reason my suit is ruined.

"Well, *darling*," his grin widens, showing his perfect white teeth, "I'm God."

Well, shit.

THE STORY CONTINUES IN 2023 WITH
"THE MISSING GOD'S LAWYER"

ACKNOWLEDGMENTS

I want to thank everyone who has followed me on this journey. Thank you for your constant support on the release of this book. You all pushed me—gently—to make sure it was released on time. I hope I have met your expectations. I look forward to continuing this journey with you for the rest of this series and for the future ones to come. Leave a review of the book on Goodreads and Amazon! Your thoughts matter.

Thank you to my parents for your constant support and love throughout my life. When you learned of my passion to be an author, you were nothing but supportive.

Thank you to my wonderful sisters, Kayla and Haleigh, for looking at me as if I placed the sun in the sky and for also consistently roasting me to keep me humble. I'm a little iffy on whether or not y'all should read this book. But y'all grown.

Thank you to my bestfriends—Destiny, Sabine, Aubrey, and Tray—for listening to me rant about this story a million times. Special thank you to my childhood bestie and soulmate—Destiny. She knows it's been a dream of mine to publish, and she has only ever supported me.

A shout-out to my uncle Bradley. Thank you for listening to this idea. But please, for the sake of my sanity and yours—I hope you never read this book. Thank you to my cousin,

Myia, for also listening to me rant about this book and throwing ideas for the next two books.

Lots of love and hugs to my cover designer, Jiyen Chen. You took my ideas and ran with it! You were just as passionate about this book as me. I thank you for that and I *absolutely* adore you.

A special thank you to my beta readers: Lola Crosby, Londra Snells, and Destiny Newman. My appreciation for you all runs so deep. I am grateful that you fought through all my plot holes and grammar issues.

Thank you to my editor, Alli Ferguson. She was absolutely amazing to work with and put in maximum effort into editing this book. You are the greatest! I hope your pillow is cold on both sides at night.

A huge thank you to Kirsha Fox (an author) for completing the first rounds of editing on the very, *very* rough draft. I wish you nothing but good fortune on your own book journey!

Thank you to my middle school teacher, Ms. Smith, for showing your passion for literature. Destiny and I definitely "borrowed" books from your classroom. If you have read this book...well, we're adults right? Yikes.

Lastly, thank you to the man who inspired Mr. Aiden Kim. Till 2025.

AUTHOR'S NOTE

Writing this book was hard at first. I didn't know where to start but I knew how I wanted it to end—with a finished book in my hand. I know that if I even sell one book, that I've accomplished my dream. So thank you so much for trusting me enough to pick this book up.

I learned three valuable lessons through my journey of writing my first book that I would like to share with you.

My first piece of wisdom for you all is—*done is better than perfect*. Because, my loves, perfectionism is a breeding ground for failure.

My second piece of wisdom is—*do it scared*. Do it on the verge of tears. Do it when the imposter syndrome is banging on your door telling you that you do not belong. Do it even though you may fail. Do it even if you *have* failed before. And if no one believes in you, know that I do.

My last piece of wisdom is—*don't ever tell yourself 'no'*. If you see an opportunity and you do not believe you are qualified, go for it anyways. Not trying is a 100% guarantee of *never* getting it.

My loves, be like Joyce by the end of the book. **Refuse anything you know is not for you and demand everything that's already yours.**

See you all in the next book :)

ABOUT THE AUTHOR

By day, Mea is a soon to be civil rights attorney. But by night, she is an avid reader and writer. She grew up in South Florida, but her family is from the Caribbean. She fell in love with reading one summer when she was ten-years old. It was the Magic Treehouse series that began her obsession. She remembers binge reading the series and being taken to a different world. This sparked her creativity and began her journey to write her own book. Follow her to see her reviews on other books, to get updates on her upcoming books, and to laugh at her funny posts. Subscribe to her newsletter on her website to get notified of book events, giveaways, ARC and Beta Reader registrations, and future books.

Tik Tok: @authormeamonique
IG: @authormeamonique
Website: meamonique.com

Printed by Amazon Italia Logistica S.r.l.
Torrazza Piemonte (TO), Italy

50148889R00202